the ISLANDERS

VOL. 4:

LUCAS GETS HURT *and* AISHA GOES WILD

KATHERINE APPLEGATE *and* MICHAEL GRANT

PREVIOUSLY PUBLISHED AS THE **MAKING OUT** SERIES

HARPER TEEN

An Imprint of HarperCollinsPublishers

HarperTeen is an imprint of HarperCollins Publishers.

Grateful acknowledgment is made for the use of lyrics from "Sometimes I Slip," by Clarence "Gatemouth" Brown, copyright © Real Records, Inc.
Excerpts from "Post Captain" by Patrick O'Brien are reprinted with the permission of W.W. Norton & Company, Inc. Copyright © 1972 by Patrick O'Brien. All rights reserved.

Originally published by HarperPaperbacks as *Boyfriends Girlfriends*

www.epicreads.com

ISBN 978-0-06-234082-5

Typography by Ellice M. Lee
❖
15 16 17 18 19   PC/RRDH   10 9 8 7 6 5 4 3 2 1
First Edition

the ISLANDERS

VOL. 4:

LUCAS GETS HURT *and* AISHA GOES WILD

LUCAS GETS HURT

PART ONE

"Sometimes things change so much you feel like you've come full circle and back to a place you've been before," Lucas said.

So. That's what this was about. Claire was a little surprised. Even a little disappointed in Lucas. "Full circle back to a beach a long time ago?" Claire asked, knowing the answer.

He nodded. "Our first kiss."

She should put an end to this. She really should. But the memories were strong for her, too. There had been a time when she would have done anything for Lucas Cabral. And it would be a down payment on paying Jake back. "Are you going to ask me as politely as you did then, Lucas, with your voice all squeaky and trembling?" she said, half-mocking, half-trembling with anticipation.

Lucas slid across the car seat toward her, closer, close enough that the slightest movement would bring them together. "Do I have to ask?"

"No," Claire said. "You don't."

✦　　✦　　✦

"Look man, look man, no, look, don't man. Don't shoot me, man."

He was begging. Praying to Christopher like he was some kind of a god. And with his gun, with his finger on the trigger, with the slightest pressure now the difference between life and death, wasn't he like a god?

From far away the sound of a siren floated through the trees. The dog had started barking, jerking frantically at its chain. The skinhead had sunk to his knees, crying.

And the gun felt so powerful in Christopher's hand.

Zoey saw her mother's eyes were full of tears. She realized her own were, too. This was it—the destruction of her family. The end. Even worse, the destruction of her parents, all their tawdry, humiliating secrets now laid out to sicken their children. Zoey wished she could just disappear. If she'd still had even an ounce of energy or will, she might have grabbed Benjamin's hand and run. But all she could do was watch and listen, helpless to change anything.

"You might as well tell them the rest," Zoey's mother said flatly.

Mr. Passmore nodded. "Yes. The rest. It seems while I was with this woman in Europe, well, it seems she became pregnant."

Zoey felt the world spinning around her.

"See, you both, Zoey, Benjamin, you have . . . a sister."

Zoey Passmore

If I believed in astrology, I would have guessed that some terrible alignment of the planets occurred on that Thursday when so many futures stood teetering between happiness and destruction. Sometimes I wish I did believe in something supernatural, because then you'd have a way of making sense out of things, you know? Blame it on the stars or whatever, rather than having to blame people. Or yourself. But I was left feeling that life was just unpredictable, that it might suddenly, without warning, blow up in your face. Which isn't a very reassuring thing to believe, even though it may be true.

For me that Thursday meant the end of my family as I had known it. In the blink of an eye my parents, who I had been sure loved each other absolutely, became enemies.

And each of them, my father and mother, came away seeming smaller, more petty, weaker than I had believed. Not that I had ever thought of either of them as perfect parents, but I guess I'd always thought of them as very good people doing their best to be perfect parents, and that was more than enough for me. No longer.

It was like someone had declared the end of illusions. Illusions about my boyfriend, Lucas, and about Jake, my previous boyfriend. And now my parents. It made me wonder what other people I had misjudged. Nina had been my best friend for years, but if I could be so wrong about my parents, was I wrong about her, too? And Aisha? And even Benjamin, my brother, the one person I told myself was absolutely real?

And myself? Was I just a lie, too?

I sat in that room while my father told me the depressing truth and I had the strangest feeling. We were all still alive, my parents and my brother and me, tired, sad, but alive. And yet something had died.

Just an idea, really. The idea of a family. An abstraction. And it really shouldn't hurt when an idea dies, should it?

ONE

SISTER. THE WORD HUNG IN the air between them. Zoey's mother looked away, her mouth twisted in a bitter line. Her father hung his head, ashamed.

"Where does this sister live?" Benjamin asked.

"I don't know," Mr. Passmore said. "Her mother and . . . and the man she thinks of as her father live in Kittery. I was never supposed to have anything to do with my—with the young lady."

"How *Jerry Springer,*" Benjamin muttered. "Or would this be more of a *Maury?*"

"I guess Lara—that's her name, Lara McAvoy—does know she has a biological father out there somewhere, but who, or where . . . I don't think she knows."

"This is not really what's important right now," Zoey's mother snapped in a brittle voice. Then, with an effort, she softened her tone. "The important thing is that you kids realize that both of us still love you and care for you. We don't want any of this to have to affect you."

Zoey laughed derisively. "Too late."

"Yeah, I think we kind of got affected," Benjamin said dryly.

"I'm just tired," Zoey said, shaking her head. "In a way I'm glad it's all out in the open."

Her mother leaned forward, trying to meet Zoey's evasive gaze. "What I said to you the other day, Zoey. About this being your fault. That was totally wrong. We're to blame. Your father and I, we're the only ones to blame."

Zoey stood up, wobbly with spent emotion and exhaustion. Outside, the night had fallen. Inside the room, no one had turned on more than a single dim lamp. Her parents' faces were in shadow, unknowable, almost unrecognizable in their masks of grief and shame and poorly concealed anger.

"Yes," Zoey agreed. "You are the ones to blame. But if you're waiting for forgiveness from me, Mother, you can forget it."

"People make mistakes," Benjamin said, so quietly Zoey wasn't sure she'd heard him.

"People make mistakes," Zoey agreed. "But they don't end up sleeping with men they're not married to on a tiny little island where everyone knows everyone else's business."

She was gratified to see her mother swallow hard. The barb had hit home. Good. They could say all they wanted that it was both their faults, but it had been her mother she'd walked in on. Her mother with Jake's father.

Zoey walked away. She heard Benjamin rise too and follow her from the room. Zoey began climbing the stairs, almost too exhausted to move her legs.

"Zoey?" Benjamin called out softly from the hallway.

She halted, waiting silently.

"People do make mistakes," Benjamin said.

The car swerved sharply around a cyclist, nearly invisible in the darkness, and fishtailed into a turn. In the backseat Aisha Gray was thrown against the door, bruising her narrow shoulder. But she didn't ask the driver to slow down. The speed of the car, now flying down the dark road, siren wailing, was Aisha's only hope.

"How do you know where we're going?" Aisha yelled at the detective on the passenger side, the older of the two men. Sergeant Winokur.

He half-turned, and Aisha could see that his eyes were wide from the adrenaline rush. They glittered with reflected green dashboard light. His voice, though professionally measured, showed the raggedness of excitement, maybe even fear. "We *don't* know," he said. "But there are three possibilities. I put units on the others, too, as soon as you told me what was happening."

Aisha was confused. "Wait a minute; you *know* who these guys are?"

Sergeant Winokur nodded. "We've known from the start. We have a pretty good idea who's in these skinhead gangs." He made an annoyed face. "Actually, we were hoping these particular lowlifes would lead us to bigger fish."

"Just ahead, Sarge," his partner said, killing the siren.

"Yeah. Look, miss, you stay in the car and keep down. Do you understand? Head below the back of this seat."

Aisha nodded. Her throat was tight. Her chest was a vise around a pounding, fearful heart. "Don't hurt him," she pleaded. "Just don't hurt him, please."

The sergeant gave no response. He tried unsuccessfully to hide the fact that he had drawn an automatic pistol from the holster beneath his sport coat. The gun was low by his side.

The car skidded to a stop, headlights illuminating a crazed, fleeting montage of dark tree trunks, a tilted mailbox, a gravel driveway, an old car, before coming to rest. Just up the street Aisha could see the van that Christopher had taken from the school's athletics department. She squeezed her hands together and prayed with all her might. Prayed like she had not done since she was a little girl.

"There he is."

"Yep."

Doors opened. Aisha looked up. Christopher walked blindly, head bowed, a stark figure in the blue-white glare of headlights. The gun hung loose in his hand. He seemed to be stunned, immobilized. He looked down at the gun, then up, straight into the headlights.

"Drop it." The sergeant rapped out the words. He stood behind the shelter of the open door, one foot still in the car, gun leveled at Christopher.

"Drop the damn gun!" the driver ordered.

Christopher still seemed confused, surprised, lost.

"I said lose the gun! Lose it right now or I'll shoot!"

Lucas's first kiss was tentative. Claire half-thought he might back away at the last minute. She half-thought *she* might back away, too. But neither did. And Lucas's lips met hers.

The betrayal was sealed. With that first kiss Claire had begun to pay Jake back for sleeping with Louise, for still secretly loving Zoey, and for the worst crime of all—for not really loving Claire.

But it wouldn't stop with one kiss. On the next kiss Lucas was bolder, taking her in his arms and holding her close. The feel of him was different. Not like Jake, not the wall of hard muscle, the bristly chin, the sense of physical power barely restrained.

Nor was this Lucas like the Lucas that Claire remembered from a long time ago, when his kisses had been sweet, his touch so gentle. This Lucas was more urgent, almost harsh.

And yet Claire felt her body responding swiftly to his touch. Her lips, her throat as he trailed kisses down to her collarbone, her heart as it pounded frantically. It was as if her body was somehow a separate creature from her mind. She felt a warm, spreading, intoxicating pleasure, but at a distance, not real.

He drew back just a little, catching his breath. His face was too near for her to see his features distinctly in the dim light from the dashboard. He was a blur with warm breath and dark eyes. He came closer still, and this time she opened her lips to him, and felt an answering increase in his own excitement.

It was strange. Such a combustible feeling, as if the two of them brought together would inevitably cause an explosion. And yet it was a cold fire whose warmth reached just the surface of her skin, tingling just the nerve endings while somehow leaving her mind unaffected.

Was she the only one feeling this strange disconnection?

Was it some consequence of guilt? Was it concern for Zoey, for Jake? Did Lucas feel it, too? Was that the reason for his urgency? Was he racing to stay ahead of feelings of guilt?

She fumbled for and found the control button that lowered the plush leather seat into full recline with a mechanical whir. Her luxuriant black hair fanned out across the tan leather. Guilt, maybe, but sheer pleasure, too. Lucas was over her now, his weight pressing down on her, kissing her deeply, the two of them panting, groping, unrestrained.

His hands touched her, eliciting shudders of sensual response. His movements were so barely controlled, his fingers trembling, his breathing ragged.

Why not? Claire wondered. It was very clear what he wanted to happen next. *Why not?* It was a wild, passionate, insane moment. How often did anything like passion infiltrate even the corners of her dispassionate mind?

And if Jake could do it with Louise . . .

Lucas was undressing her with hurried fingers, driven by desire . . . no, by two desires.

The second of which was to hurt Zoey.

"Sister?" Zoey repeated the word into the mirror over her dresser. "Half-sister," she corrected, but that formulation made her uneasy. She'd always felt there was something ungenerous about phrases like half-sister, half-brother. Like you were making an issue out of it. Like you didn't quite want to accept a person.

"I *don't* want to accept *any* of this." Her eyes showed the signs of sleeplessness and tears, the blue surrounded and invaded by redness, lids puffed, expression dull and lifeless. Her blond hair hung lank and straight to her shoulders. She glanced at her clock. Ridiculously early to get in bed. And yet when had she last had a real night's sleep?

She began to undress, letting clothing fall on the floor, feeling a deep physical craving for her bed. In a strange way she was almost relieved. Things became simpler when you were too exhausted to think. She could feel her mind finally shutting down, her awareness like a diminishing circle of spotlight, smaller, smaller, releasing more and more into dark indifference.

She found her Boston Bruins jersey and slipped it on, reassured by its familiarity. At least some things didn't change. Her sheets were cool, her pillows soft. She stretched her legs out, feeling the tension in her every muscle. Her toes invaded the cold corners of her bed.

Her parents were breaking up. It was impossible to imagine that anything could stop the disintegration now.

And she had a sister, somewhere, maybe not far away, with no face as yet. An abstraction, but full of possibilities and problems that Zoey was simply too tired to contemplate.

Tomorrow she would have to begin confronting all the stories, the details, the trauma of this terrible day. But first . . .

. . . sleep.

TWO

"DROP THE DAMNED GUN!"

Christopher stood paralyzed. The bright light had come up from nowhere, and now voices were shouting. He looked down at the gun in his hand. It looked alien and alive. He opened his hand slowly and the creature slipped from his grip.

It was a shocking sensation, the emptiness of his hand, just fingers again. He shook his head, feeling like he'd been sleep-walking.

Strong hands grabbed him, a leg swept his feet from under him, and he was facedown in the gravel. Sharp rocks cutting into his cheek. Dirt in his mouth. His arms were twisted roughly behind his back. He didn't resist. He stared at the gun lying a few feet away, still more than just another artifact. Still like something living that had become a part of him.

Or was it the other way around? Was it he who had become a part of the gun?

He was jerked to his feet and pushed, staggering back against the hood of the car, blinking again in the lights.

"Christopher!"

Aisha. Her arms around him, her wet cheek pressed against his. Was she crying? Was he?

"I'm making the weapon safe," a far-off voice said.

Sirens and wildly swinging blue lights were coming down the road at breakneck speed. One by one they skidded to a halt in a shower of gravel.

"This weapon has not been fired," the first voice said.

"Oh, thank God," Aisha said. "Oh, thank you, God."

"I couldn't do it," Christopher admitted, feeling embarrassed and defeated.

"Check around the back of the house," a second voice ordered. "I . . . Look, if the kid back there is in one piece, I don't need any formal statements from him at this time. You understand me?"

"Your call, Dave," the first man said, sounding doubtful.

"I couldn't do it," Christopher told Aisha.

"I know. I prayed so hard . . . I knew you wouldn't."

"I had him. I mean, he was scared, he was crawling and begging and all I had to do was pull the trigger—"

"But you didn't."

"I couldn't, Eesh."

Uniformed policemen were everywhere now. At least a

half-dozen cars were spread out across and on both sides of the road.

The first cop was back. He jerked a thumb over his shoulder toward the dark backyard, back to the sound of a frantically barking dog and a high-pitched, almost hysterical voice crying for revenge, screaming obscene threats now that the danger was past. "He'll live. Just shaken up pretty badly."

"Any evidence of shots fired?" Sergeant Winokur asked.

"No shots. No witnesses aside from the victim and this clown." He indicated Christopher.

"All right, Curt, see if you can't break up this party while I have a little talk with the tough guy here. All right, tough guy, come with me," the sergeant said to Christopher. He hauled Christopher by his pinioned arm, pulling him, stumbling, down the dark road, away from the barking and the flash of blue lights and the wailing threats.

"Where are you taking him?" Aisha cried.

"See this?" the cop demanded angrily. "Do you see what you've done to this girl who cares about you? She has to call us and come racing over here scared half to death?"

Christopher shook his head in confusion. It was all happening in a blur. They were in darkness now, walking across dead leaves and fallen pine needles. A branch scratched his cheek. A sound was growing louder. Water. The river.

"Sergeant, what are you doing?" Aisha cried again, still keeping pace, clutching at Christopher's other arm.

They stopped beside the river, an almost unseen but definite presence, running fast and loud, swollen with new rain and too-early snowfalls melting off the mountains.

Christopher was turned around. There was a metallic click and suddenly his arms were free of the handcuffs. He was aware of the police sergeant standing no more than a foot away. He could feel Aisha wrapped around his right arm.

"That punk back there is named Jesse Simms. He was the third individual involved in the attack on you. Within about twelve hours of the incident, we'd rolled this kid over on his buddies. We've been trying to use the other two to identify additional members of this particular skinhead organization."

"You knew?" Christopher asked.

"Yeah. Oddly enough, that's our job." The cop's tone was coldly sarcastic. "Sometimes we actually succeed. What was *your* job? What the hell were *you* doing here tonight with a gun?"

Christopher shrugged. "I . . . Look, they put me in the hospital, man."

"And the penalty for assault and battery is death now? Someone beats you up, you kill them? I'm curious, you know, since you're making all the laws now."

Christopher shrugged again. The sergeant was clearly angry

and growing more so. Christopher felt too drained to say much in his own defense.

"So you were going to kill him," the policeman accused.

"He didn't, though," Aisha said fiercely.

"No. What he did was commit assault with a deadly weapon. We could probably also call it kidnapping since he held the poor bastard with a gun to his head. But I don't think Mr. Simms will be wanting to press charges, because I'm going to tell him not to."

Christopher exhaled and for the first time realized he had been holding his breath.

"So. Tough guy. Why didn't you shoot him?" the policeman asked more gently.

"I don't know."

"It would have been easy. You had the gun. He was helpless."

Christopher felt a wave of nausea at the memory. Yes, he'd been helpless, crying, begging. "It made me sick."

"What made you sick? That he was scared? That he was begging for his life?" the sergeant bored in relentlessly.

"No," Christopher said sharply. "It made me sick that I made him beg."

"You enjoyed it. The rush of all that power from that little gun."

"No. Yeah, at first," Christopher admitted. "And then . . . Look, he deserved it. He's a racist piece of crap."

Surprisingly, the policeman laughed. "You know what? Lots of people deserve lots of things, kid. Sometimes they even get what's coming to them. Not all the time, but sometimes."

"And now what? Him and his friends will maybe spend ninety days in jail? Then it's right back out on the streets."

"That's about right."

"Maybe I should have killed him," Christopher said, but without conviction.

"And now you're ashamed because you didn't? You think you'd be proud if you had? You think you'd be standing here feeling like a big man because you took a life?"

"No," Christopher admitted.

"No. And you didn't get off on scaring that little punk. You know why? Because it takes a weak individual to enjoy causing fear. It takes a very small man to get pleasure out of another individual's pain. Maybe you just aren't a small enough man."

Christopher realized he was trembling, barely understanding what the cop was saying. All he knew was that a wave of relief so powerful it rattled him to his bones was sweeping over him. He had been so close to pulling that trigger.

Something was in his hand again. The gun. Emptied of shells, harmless, and yet so seductive.

"We checked you out after you first filed the complaint," Sergeant Winokur said in a quieter voice. "You work hard, kid. You have plans and you have a girlfriend here who is probably too damned good for you. And there was some provocation. So you're going to walk away from this one."

"Thank you," Christopher said in a whisper.

"Don't thank me," Sergeant Winokur said sarcastically. "I want a nice, clean case when we bust the rest of these punks. I don't want the jury having to deal with you playing vigilante. Now if you'd been found with a firearm, I wouldn't have much choice but to bust you and pretty much flush your life down the toilet. Do you follow me?"

"No . . . I . . ."

"What I'm saying is, that river is surprisingly deep way out in the middle."

Christopher nodded, comprehension penetrating his confusion. The sergeant gave him a long, thoughtful look. Then he turned his back deliberately and began to walk back toward the flashing blue lights.

"Thanks," Christopher called out after him. "I won't . . . you know."

There was no response. Christopher realized Aisha was still there, almost holding him up while his legs felt watery, his knees threatened to buckle. He felt weak as a newborn.

Aisha stepped away, waiting.

Christopher drew back his arm and found that he still possessed a reservoir of strength. The gun flew invisibly through the night. Seconds later there was a splash far out in the river.

"Let's go home," Aisha said.

"We can't do this, Lucas," Claire said a little breathlessly. "Not that I don't want to, but I think maybe it's a little far to take payback."

Lucas stopped his hand where it was but didn't pull it away. For a fleeting moment Claire wondered if he *would* stop. She had let things go way too far.

His voice was challenging. "That's all this is to you? Payback?"

"Oh, come on, Lucas, what is it to you?"

"It's . . . " He began cursing. He snatched his hand away, breaking contact.

Claire laughed. She used the button to raise her seat and began refastening everything Lucas had done such a good job of unfastening.

"You're cold, you know that?" Lucas demanded, sliding back across the seat.

"Uh-huh. I'm cold, but you've suddenly fallen madly in love with me, right? It isn't just that you're horny and you're mad at Zoey for refusing you. Or that you're worried about that long, very long hug between her and Jake? It isn't that you're thinking, 'well, I get laid, plus I get to pay Zoey back'?"

A semblance of humor returned to Lucas's features. "As revenge goes, it *would* be pretty effective."

"You and me. Could either of us have come up with a better way to piss off Jake and Zoey?"

Lucas laughed unwillingly, unable to resist the truth. "Still," he said ruefully, "it's not like I was just faking it."

"No, me neither," Claire admitted.

"You haven't exactly turned into a gorgon."

"We could definitely be dangerous together," Claire admitted. "But you're still in love with Zoey."

He shrugged and looked away.

"I think Jake is, too, at least partly."

Great, now she was feeling sorry for herself. Well, why not? Benjamin had obviously gotten over her a lot more completely than she'd ever expected. The level of affection between him and Nina was nauseating. And Lucas, and maybe even Jake, carried torches for Little Zoey Pureheart.

What did Jake feel for Zoey? What, if anything, did he feel for Claire? What, if anything, did anyone ever really feel for Claire?

Claire stole a glance at Lucas. Already the look of charged

excitement was fading, replaced by a sober, worried expression. That worry was sure to grow. In a few minutes it would begin to occur to him that Claire now held his relationship with Zoey in the palm of her hand.

Claire turned the key in the ignition.

Claire

We all live on Chatham Island. Not a large island; in fact, it's small even by Maine island standards. Some maps don't even show it. It only has three hundred or so year-round residents. We get a lot more people in the summer, but the real, hardcore island population is just three hundred. North Harbor, which we jokingly refer to as our town, is really only a town when the tourists are in. Once September rolls around it starts to empty out, and by late October it's reduced to a few active businesses, a small grocery store that's only open a few hours a day, one year-round restaurant and bar, Passmores', which belongs to Zoey and Benjamin's parents, a hardware store, and an automatic teller machine.

All of which is swell. Weymouth, which is a nice little full-service city, is just a half-hour ferry ride away, and from there we can always drive down to Portland or even Boston. But on a day-in, day-out basis I live on the island. And this can be a problem, because there is no natural camouflage in a community this small. There's none of that automatic invisibility you get in a real city, where no one knows anyone else and people on the street avoid making eye contact with each other. In a real city you can do what you want and be what you want, and if you don't like what you were last week, you can just change to something new.

You can't do that on an island where everyone knows you and your family and where you live and probably what you had for breakfast. It places some limitations on you. Because, see, if you start trouble with another islander, it never entirely goes away. And likewise, if you fall in love with another islander, that never entirely goes away, either.

I live on an island where I have gone out with three of the four guys my age. Anywhere else it would be no big deal. But imagine you have one boyfriend now, and two ex-boyfriends, and every morning and again every afternoon, you find yourself on a ferry with them. And one of the ex-boyfriends is now going out with your sister, and another is now going out with one of your friends, and that friend used to go out with the guy you are now seeing. You can't develop a healthy hatred for your ex and just put him out of your life, because you're going to be seeing him every single day. So relationships never seem to completely die.

It tends to make you cautious in some ways.

THREE

CLAIRE AND LUCAS CAUGHT THE nine o'clock, the last ferry back to the island, steaming away from the still-bright neon glow of Weymouth's restaurants and bars toward the darkened island, visible only as a few distant pinpricks of light.

Claire was surprised and a little disturbed to see Aisha and Christopher sharing the nearly empty deck. They were sitting toward the front, holding each other in a way that reminded Claire of the TV pictures of refugees. Something had gone wrong with those two on the mainland tonight, but whatever it was, Claire was pretty certain she didn't want to hear about it just now. At the moment she felt annoyed with herself, unsettled, and perilously emotional.

"Should we go back downstairs?" Lucas wondered in a whisper.

"Aisha saw us," Claire said. "It would look even more suspicious if we went below, or if we split up and sat on opposite sides of the boat. I mean, maybe we just both happened to be on the mainland for perfectly innocent reasons. That's how we should act, anyway."

"Cool. Besides, it's not like what we did was that big a deal," Lucas said.

"Yeah, you're right, Lucas. No big deal at all. You have half my clothes off and your tongue down my throat. No big deal." *Jerk.* She'd been planning to reassure him, but he was grinding on her nerves now. At least, something was grinding on her nerves. Probably just the after-effects of a strange week and a stranger evening.

Lucas looked around as if he was worried someone might have overheard. "Okay," he said in a low, urgent voice. "It was a big deal."

Claire rolled her eyes. "You know, your half of the human race is so pathetic sometimes."

"My half?"

"The male half. An hour ago you were all over me; now you're scared silly that Zoey will find out. You wanted to get laid so you could walk around all smug thinking, 'well, I guess I showed Zoey.' Except that one way or the other you don't want Zoey to really find out. Your hormones and your heart seem like maybe they're a little out of sync."

"You were in that car, too," Lucas pointed out. "You know, I'm not stupid, Claire. You enjoyed our little drive in the country as much as I did."

Claire shrugged in a show of nonchalance. "I enjoyed kissing you."

"Thanks, I guess."

"But it's like saying I enjoy ice cream or a nice hot bath. Physical pleasure is kind of thin and insubstantial and temporary, isn't it?"

Lucas looked thoughtful. "Yeah. I guess it's a bad idea to have a relationship that's purely physical. I mean, I guess."

"I don't know if it's good or bad," Claire said impatiently. "But it's not going to happen. Not with me."

Lucas grinned. "What are you, Claire, some kind of secret romantic? You're holding out for true love and Mr. Perfect? Somehow I can't picture you that way. I always thought you were too . . . you know, too tough. I sort of pictured that when you decided to have sex, you'd just point at some good-looking guy and say 'Hey, you, come here.' "

"That's what you think?" Claire asked. "Is that really what you think about me?"

"Don't get bent, Claire, I was mostly kidding."

"Yeah, well, grow up," Claire said disparagingly. Of course it was what Lucas thought. It was what everyone thought. Claire could always take care of herself. Claire didn't need anyone. It's what Jake thought, too.

"I'm trying to grow up," Lucas muttered.

Claire resisted the urge to say more. The last thing she should do was open her heart to Lucas, of all people. But his neat caricature of her burned. Possibly because there was an element of truth to it. "You know what I think, Lucas? I think sex is easy. Any monkey, any cow, any pair of insects can have sex. Love is what's difficult."

"Sex doesn't seem to be all that easy for me," Lucas said wryly. "At least, not with Zoey. And even the love part . . . I mean, you're right, I do love her. But I feel like that's never enough for her."

"Zoey's an idealist," Claire said. "Zoey doesn't just believe in love, she believes it has to be perfect love. It has to be cosmic and flawless and unquestioning. See, people have always loved Zoey. Everyone loves Zoey. It's easy for her, so she's not interested in anything flawed or uncertain, where one person maybe cares about someone and yet that person doesn't always show it the way she should. Zoey would never understand what it's like to be afraid that—" She stopped herself cold. She had been twisting her fingers together in agitation. She had been on the edge of saying far too much.

Lucas waited. Then, in a newly gentle voice, he asked,

"What doesn't she understand, Claire?"

What it's like to be afraid that no one will ever love her, Claire answered the question silently. But aloud she said, "Forget it, Lucas. Forget it, and forget this night ever happened. You can relax. I won't tell Zoey anything."

Lucas said good night to Claire at the ferry landing. She ignored him. She had raised her invisible shield and dismissed him as no longer being of any interest.

He wondered what it was that Claire had been looking for tonight.

He knew what he had been looking for, and now that the warm glow had worn off, that feeling was being replaced by a certain amount of disgust with himself. He had not been handling things well lately. First flying off the handle when Zoey had said no to . . . to moving their relātionship to a new level. Then somehow (he wasn't sure exactly how) failing to make up with her, then *probably* overreacting to what was *probably* an innocent hug between Zoey and Jake, and now this exciting but definitely unacceptable make-out session with Claire.

God, it had been hot.

But wrong. Very wrong. Definitely wrong, and he was a pig.

Besides, it hadn't helped in the end. He didn't love Claire, he loved Zoey. He was trapped, unable to escape. He loved Zoey. If he lost her, he wouldn't know what to do with himself. And yet at the same time, they had reached an impasse. He wanted to move their physical relationship forward, she didn't. Neither was prepared to give in. At least, he wasn't for long. And neither wanted the relationship to end. At least, he didn't.

He walked from the ferry through the silent streets alone. He had to pass Zoey's house on the way to his. He ought to stop by; it was only nine thirty and she wouldn't be in bed yet. Unless she would somehow guess what he'd been up to. Had Claire been wearing perfume that Zoey might recognize? What a disaster that would be.

So maybe it would be stupid to stop by Zoey's house. Besides, why should *he* crawl to *her*? She was the one who gave him that "I don't know" response when he'd asked her if she still loved him. She was the one who'd been treating him like crap lately.

Lately, as in ever since he'd told Zoey it was do what he wanted or forget it. Ever since he'd trotted out that pathetic "Hey, look, if you won't, then there are lots of girls who will" line, sounding like some old, gold-chain-wearing, hey-baby-what's-your-sign bar lizard. He winced at the memory. Yeah, ever since *he'd* been a stupid, hormone-deranged jerk, *she'd* treated him like crap. And now he'd added to the mess by going behind her back and trying to get Claire to sleep with him. So now he could feel ten times as guilty, plus, he'd managed to get Claire pissed, too. Wonderful. He was certainly handling his love life well. Yes, he was a regular genius when it came to romance. Another week or two and he'd be about ready to join a monastery.

Maybe if he just went to Zoey, threw himself at her feet, and said "I confess, I'm scum, please forgive me and take me back." Maybe that would work.

Because, despite everything, he couldn't conceive of life without Zoey.

So he would crawl. He wouldn't confess everything; that would just be stupid, but he would crawl, beg, whine, plead, and if all else failed, squeeze out a few tears.

He turned the corner onto Camden and walked with renewed determination toward her house. "Zoey, I'm a jerk but I love you so please forgive me and take me back and tell me you love me too because otherwise—"

He came to a stop on the dark street. *Otherwise what?* he asked himself. Could she have really meant it when she said she didn't know if she still loved him? The pain of that thought pierced his heart.

No, of course she still loved him. She'd just been teaching him a lesson. Like he'd been trying to teach her a lesson with Claire tonight. But underneath it all, even if *she* was being bitchy and *he* was a jerk, there was still love. Wasn't there?

He had to find out. He started walking again, faster, determined. He had to find out because if the answer was no, then . . . well, what was he going to do then?

He looked up and saw her house, dark windows within darkness. His heart sank. Nine thirty and the whole place was dark? Since when did Zoey go to sleep this early?

Well, it wasn't like he could knock on the door and wake everyone up.

No.

But almost no one on Chatham Island bothered to lock their doors. And he knew about the squeaky stair. Third from the top, he was pretty sure.

He stood on the Passmores' front steps. He opened the door with painful care. Inside all was as dark as it had seemed. No TV, no stereo from Benjamin's room, just a deep silence.

Nine thirty and they were all asleep. What was that all about?

It was possible that going up to her room would just be another stupid move after a series of stupid moves. Very possible. But his mind was churning with a potent mixture of guilt and anxiety and still more guilt. He needed to talk to Zoey and find some reassurance.

He climbed the stairs like a burglar, stepping over the third step from the top, the one that squeaked. Barely breathing, he opened Zoey's bedroom door. Fortunately, he knew, she didn't sleep naked or anything.

What's fortunate about that? he asked himself wryly.

What's fortunate, he answered his own question, *is that when she jumps out of bed screaming hysterically, she'll get over it much faster if it turns out she's wearing clothes.*

He closed the door behind him. "Zoey?" A voiceless whisper. No response.

He went to her bed and knelt beside it. She was breathing in fits and starts, restless, as if she was having a dream. If she woke up screaming, he was going to have a very interesting time explaining this to Mr. Passmore. *Well, see, Mr. P., I was feeling guilty after making out with Claire, see, so I decided to sneak up here while Zoey was asleep and make sure she still loved me. Perfectly logical, Mr. Passmore.*

Did Zoey's father own a gun?

"Zoey?" A shade louder. She was heart-breakingly beautiful. Just the vision of her face, the face he loved, brought a lump to his throat. How could he have done what he tried to do with Claire? Because he was mad at Zoey? It seemed an inconceivably sleazy thing now.

He touched her hair, a tangle of shadows against the white

pillow. Her forehead was damp with perspiration though the room was cold.

"What?" Clear, but uncomprehending.

"It's me, Lucas. Don't freak, okay?"

"Lucas?"

"Yes."

"What are you doing here?" Not angry, just confused.

"Kind of a long story," he whispered.

"I just had a terrible dream," she said, weirdly alert without sounding entirely awake. "My parents were getting divorced."

He stroked her forehead, feeling a fresh wave of tenderness toward her. "Just a dream, sweetheart."

She drew back, making room for him beside her. He slid into the bed, kicking off his shoes and shucking his coat. He could feel her warmth in the sheets. Zoey laid her head on his chest. Lucas wished his heart wasn't pounding so ferociously. For a while neither spoke.

"It wasn't a dream," Zoey said in a different voice.

"Of course it was."

She wrapped her free arm around him, holding tight to his chest. The top of her hair, wispy blond tendrils, tickled his nose. "My dad is moving out tomorrow."

Was this still a memory of her dream? No, she was fully

awake now. "God, Zoey," he said. "Is this . . . like, real?"

He heard her sniffle and realized she was crying. He began stroking her hair. Zoey's parents—Mr. and Ms. Passmore—getting divorced? No way.

And yet it might explain so much more. Had Zoey known this was coming? Was this the reason she'd seemed so distant these last few days?

"How long—when did you find out?" he asked.

"I don't remember. It's all just kind of . . . " The answer trailed away. "I'm very tired," she said. "I have to be asleep now."

"I'll leave," Lucas said. He started to get up.

But she didn't relax her grip on him, and after a while he heard her deep, regular breathing and knew that she was asleep.

FOUR

NINA GEIGER LOOKED UP FROM the TV in the family room as the front door opened. She craned her neck to see, although she was pretty certain who was coming in. It wasn't like there were a lot of alternatives. Quickly she shoved a sketch pad she'd been drawing on under one of the throw pillows.

"'Zat you?" she yelled over the sound of the TV's laugh track, mumbling a little with the unlit Lucky Strike planted in a corner of her mouth.

No answer. Which meant it was definitely Claire. Nina fumbled around on the couch cushion, under the bag of no-fat and no-flavor-either potato chips. She found the remote control and muted the sound.

"Claire. I have to talk to you."

Claire appeared in the doorway. "Are you sure you have to?"

"Boy, you're getting home late," Nina said. "The coven meeting run long?"

Claire looked at her watch. "That makes five seconds of my time wasted. If you have something to say, get on with it. I'm tired."

"Okay, look," Nina said, trying to be conciliatory for once. "It's something I'm allowed to tell you. I mean, Benjamin said it was okay if I told you because it's not a secret or anything, but still you're not supposed to run around making a big thing out of it."

"That's another ten seconds."

"Benjamin and Zoey's parents are splitting up," Nina said.

"What do you mean?"

"I mean, not to get into all the gross details, but it turns out both Mr. and Ms. Passmore are a lot more interesting people than anyone ever thought," Nina said. "Think *The Young and the Restless.* Think *General Hospital.* I mean, Chatham Island *is* Port Charles."

Claire hesitated, obviously not convinced that Nina was telling the truth. She stepped into the room and, after a moment's more hesitation, sat in the easy chair. "Okay. You got me."

"This is totally serious," Nina said. "I mean, I really shouldn't be joking around, but this morning on the ferry Benjamin told me part of it, and then just a little while ago he called up sounding depressed and gave me the rest."

"Zoey didn't call?" Claire asked.

"No. But Benjamin and I talk about everything." It was true, and it gave Nina a little rush of satisfaction to be able to say it.

Claire curled her lip. "I never knew Benjamin to be so open about anything. You must have dragged it out of him."

"I guess he's open when he has someone he can trust," Nina said. Yes, it was a cheap shot, but then Claire had delivered a few to her over the years. Besides, a really cheap shot would have been telling Claire that Benjamin had finally said the three magic words. Throwing *that* in her face would be a cheap shot. It would be more fun if she saved that up for just the right moment.

"So the Passmores are separating," Claire prompted.

"Yes. Mr. P. is supposedly moving out tomorrow. They're going to keep the restaurant going for now, though."

"Why is this happening?"

Nina raised a suggestive eyebrow. "In a million years you'll never guess."

"Mr. Passmore forgets to put the toilet seat down?" Claire suggested.

"Funny. No, no, I told you—think soap opera. And Ms. Passmore is Brooke Logan."

Claire stared at her. "Are we talking unfaithful?"

Nina nodded. Okay, she shouldn't be finding this juicy.

After all, it was her best friend's and her boyfriend's parents. But Chatham Island was usually a pretty dull place and gossip like this didn't come along every day. "And guess who the other man is?" She said "other man" in a low, dramatic voice.

"Jeez, it's not Jake's father, is it?"

Nina was outraged. "How did *you* know?"

Claire shrugged. "Mr. McRoyan's that way. Everybody knows."

"I didn't. Besides, it was deeper than that. It turns out Mr. McRoyan and Ms. Passmore had a *thing* like nineteen years ago or something. This is back before the P's were married. Mr. P. takes a trip to discover Europe, and Ms. P. discovers Mr. McRoyan, who must have been cuter back then unless Ms. P. just has no taste. But, whoa, then Ms. P. discovers she's pregnant with none other than . . . our mutual friend Benjamin."

"By Mr. McRoyan?" Claire suggested, horrified.

"Nah. Although that would have added even more juice. No, Ms. P is pregnant and Mr. P. is the daddy, so Ms. P. dumps Mr. McRoyan. Flash ahead nineteen years. Ms. P. discovers that oops, Mr. P. was discovering more than just Europe. He was also discovering a fellow American. He discovered her so much that *she*, this other woman, was also pregnant. In fact, she has a kid. Now Ms. P. learns this, is very pissed, decides it's payback time, and apparently ends up doing the nasty with Mr.

McRoyan just as Zoey comes home early from Vermont."

"Payback." Claire nodded. She smiled her rare, wintry smile. "Awfully juvenile to think that sleeping with someone is a way to pay back your boyfriend."

"Husband."

"Right," Claire said, with an odd sardonic twist on the word. "Husband. Wait. This other woman was pregnant, too?"

"Give the girl a prize. It turns out Benjamin and Zoey have a half-sister."

"A half-sister by Mr. Passmore and some other woman. You're right, this is a soap opera," Claire said. "What's next? Someone's evil twin shows up? How is Benjamin taking this? Never mind, I forgot. Benjamin would never show any kind of real emotion over something this personal."

"He's pretty upset," Nina said. "He feels torn between his mom and dad, and also mad at both of them. But at the same time, he kind of looks at it as not being the end of life on this planet or anything. Mostly he worries about Zoey. She's the one who, you know, walked in on her mom and Mr. McRoyan."

"Benjamin told you that's how he feels, or you're guessing?"

"Of course he told me," Nina said.

Claire nodded. "Okay."

"I asked him if I should come over and be with Zoey, but he said no, everyone was exhausted."

"I can imagine," Claire said, sounding genuinely sympathetic.

"It's a major bum. I really liked their parents," Nina said.

"Liked, past tense? They're not dying, they're just getting divorced. Everyone does it." Claire's voice had caught on the word *dying*.

"Yeah, I know, but it sucks anyway. Especially for Zoey," Nina said, feeling a renewed sadness. It wasn't like anyone was dying, Claire was right. Not like *dying* at all. "You know Zoey," Nina said, trying not to let her thoughts veer where they had already veered. "She lives in a dream world. She never thinks anything bad is going to happen."

"Uh-huh. Too bad she doesn't have the firm grip on reality you have, living there inside your happy psychotic delusion."

The insult lay flat, without sting. Nina just nodded in acknowledgment. The details of the story might be juicy and even funny, but the effect they were having wasn't funny at all. Zoey must feel like she really was losing her parents in a way. And that was something that neither Nina nor Claire found at all funny.

"I hope Zoey's all right," Nina said. "I mean, you know. I guess it's kind of like it was when—" Damn. She shouldn't have gotten into this. Her eyes were filling with tears.

"Zoey'll be fine," Claire said softly. "Benjamin, too. We

survived, you know, losing um, you know, losing Mom, and . . . and, and that was worse than just being divorced."

Nina smiled ruefully at her sister. "Yeah, you can tell we survived fine by the way both of us are crying now." She squeezed her eyes shut and wiped the tears as they coursed down her cheeks.

"Tell Zoey and Benjamin if there's anything our family can do—"

"I remember when people were trying to be all nice to us."

"I know. It didn't help. Nothing helps, I guess."

Nina nodded agreement. "But Zoey can handle it."

At three A.M. Christopher's alarm went off. He hadn't been asleep more than a couple of hours, but he woke without resentment. He had work to do. The same work he got up for every day before the sun rose. A routine. It could be grueling at times, he often wished he could work less, but this morning the routine was sweet beyond imagination. To simply be doing what he always did. To be able to slip back so gratefully into his normal life.

So damned close to destroying everything. Another pound of pressure in his right index finger and his life would have changed forever. It was frightening how easily life could be taken and thrown away. It was like walking a tightrope, high in the air above the cheering crowds one minute and the next, with a single wrong move, a long, helpless fall.

He was going to have to watch the rope more closely in the future, to concentrate more on avoiding a mistake. Like losing Aisha. That was another mistake he had very nearly made. But she had come for him, trying to rescue him like the cavalry in an old movie, showing up at the very last minute with bugles blowing, horses at full gallop.

He made himself a pot of strong French roast coffee and fried some eggs. He needed the protein energy.

Outside, it was pitch black and dead quiet. Even the surf was subdued, barely surging over the sand. He climbed on his bike. He'd definitely have to buy an island car soon. It was getting way too cold to be pedaling around at three thirty in the morning.

He collected and divided his newspapers at the ferry landing. Weymouth papers, mostly, but also *Portland Press Herald*s, *Boston Globe*s, and *Wall Street Journal*s.

His last stop was always Gray House, the bed-and-breakfast Aisha's parents owned. It was the last stop because it involved a very tiring climb up the steep length of Climbing Way and he preferred to be rid of all unnecessary weight.

He leaned his bike against the fence and picked up the last papers. Ms. Gray had been extremely nice while he was recovering. Since then he'd been careful to set the papers precisely on the porch where no one even had to step outside to get them.

After placing the papers, he walked around the side of the big house to Aisha's bedroom window. It was dark, of course. She was asleep like any sensible person would be at this hour.

Still, it gave him a deep pleasure thinking of her safe and warm in her bed, just her beautiful face poking out from beneath the comforter. Her springy explosion of hair tumbled all around.

What kind of a fool had he been not to realize how great she was?

He went back around to the front, crunching pine needles underfoot and pulling up the collar of his jacket. The wind was always a bit stronger up here on the ridge.

He heard a soft click and looked to see the front door open, just a darker rectangle of shadow within shadow.

"Hi." Aisha's voice.

"Hi," Christopher said, flushed with excitement. He trotted over to her. She was wearing a long, sheer dressing gown and slippers.

"How are you doing?" she asked.

"I feel like a guy who miraculously survived a near-death experience," he said. "Like I was standing right in front of a speeding train and at the very last minute it somehow swerved and missed me."

Aisha laughed happily.

"I also feel like I've been the moron of the universe, in a lot of ways." He looked at her significantly.

"You have," Aisha said complacently. "But I can't stand out here and listen for as long as it would take you to make all the apologies you owe. I just thought you might be cold."

"I am a little," he said.

Aisha moved closer and put her arms around him. She kissed him deeply, then again, and again once more.

"Warmer now?" she asked.

"Much, much warmer."

"Good."

"Much."

Aisha smiled. "Do you have to cook tonight?"

"I'm supposed to, yes. Um, but afterward, I mean it's Friday night and all—"

"Okay. What do you want to do? It will be too late to take the ferry over."

Christopher sighed. "I know this will sound hopelessly dorky, but to tell you the truth, Eesh, I'd be happy if all I could do was just sit and look at you."

"That doesn't sound so dorky," Aisha said softly.

"You know, you got to kiss me, but I didn't get a chance to kiss you. And it would only be fair."

Aisha looked at him skeptically. "Is that how it works?"

"Uh-huh." He took her in his arms, holding her close, and kissed her. "Now we're even."

"Wouldn't want any unfairness," Aisha said in a voice that went from a squeak to a sudden throaty lowness.

"Tonight?"

"Tonight."

"And the next night?"

"Then, too."

Christopher rode away, possibly on his bike, although as he sped effortlessly down the long slope it felt like he might just be flying.

POLICE AND FIRE LOG

BY DAN SMITH

Fire and rescue vehicles were dispatched to 1127 Pearl Street and successfully brought a kitchen grease fire under control. The residents had evacuated the building, and there were no injuries.

Police units responded to a security alarm at Gifts by Terence, 809 Mainsail Street, and discovered that the premises had been broken into. Officers on foot gave chase to two young white males but were unable to apprehend them. Losses to the business included a broken window and a gift basket containing jams, cheese, and sausages.

Police units responded to a disturbance at 4310 Brice Street involving two juveniles. Early reports that a gun was involved in the altercation proved to be false when a careful search revealed no weapons at the scene. No arrests were made.

Fire and rescue vehicles responded to a call for medical assistance at The Breezes assisted-living facility. One person was taken to Weymouth Hospital emergency room with an apparent heart attack.

———————

Late last night Weymouth police units in concert with units from the state police rounded up a total of four members of the Aryan Defense Element, including two juveniles only recently released from state custody. A number of weapons were seized along with a quantity of hate literature. The Aryan Defense Element is a known white-supremacist gang originally thought to be based solely in Portland. The arrests came after several recent racially motivated attacks in the Weymouth area. Police sources say they acted on information from an informant within the gang.

———————

Fire and rescue vehicles responded to a 911 call stating that a person identified only as "Charles" had climbed a tree and was in danger of serious injury. Units arriving on the scene retrieved Charles—an orange tabby cat—and returned him to his owner.

Lucas Cabral

For a guy, life is always about having to do things you don't want to do and not being allowed to do things you do want to do. Maybe it's that way for girls, too. I don't know, not being one. But for a guy it's always—be tough, be brave, be manly, never show one minute of weakness because if you do, you're marked for life. You act weak or pathetic and it's like someone might as well tattoo the word victim on your forehead because that's what you are from then on. Sometimes it would be nice not to have all that pressure. It might be nice to just once, when something terrible happens, be allowed to start blubbering and weeping and running around all depressed. But what you have to do is kind of shrug it off. Play through the pain, as all the jocks say.

And at the same time, everything you do want, you're not allowed to have. Can't drink, can't smoke, can't do drugs, can't have sex. The first three I can live without. But the truth is, number four does kind of occupy your mind when you're a guy. It occupies it the way...well, did you ever hear about the Donner party? Those people who starved to death in the mountains back in the Old West days, and it got so bad they ate their relatives? You can imagine how often they thought about food?

That's how often I think about sex.

So here's the deal. Your girlfriend wants you to be all sensitive and open and understanding and never to pressure her, but if you do all that, then guys think you're a wuss. Besides, if you ever honestly tell a girl what's on your mind, she'll think you're a pervert. So you have to be somewhat open and mostly honest with girls, but not ever let other guys find out. Which, when you think about it, is fairly insane.

I try to kind of walk the line. I mean, I truly love Zoey, and it makes me feel good when I can talk to her and tell her how I feel about things. But at the same time, I have to be tough. I can't just let her make all the big decisions.

I think girls have it easier. Maybe not, but it seems that way.

Zoey

I've often thought it would be great to be a guy. Not that I am in any way unhappy being female. I am glad I'm a girl. I'm just saying it's easier being a guy, especially in relationships. It's like they have so much less to think about and worry about. For them it's so much about just having sex. I mean, it must be nice to have everything reduced down to such a simple perspective, you know? No complexities or worries, really. Just on this mission to have sex. Night and day.

Okay, yes, I know I'm exaggerating, but it's like, when you're a girl, things are complicated right from the start. The biggest difference is that we can get pregnant, so it's not just like, hey, sex is another form of entertainment. I've heard guys—not Lucas, but guys I've known—say sex should just be another fun thing to do on a Saturday night, like seeing a movie or shopping. I don't know if they really believe that or just say it to sound tough and cool for their friends. Probably they wish it were true. Only going to see a movie doesn't result in you getting pregnant or catching a disease. So, see, there is that little difference.

You mention this to a guy and he just shrugs and goes, uh, well, I'm on a mission to have sex because I have all these hormones. Plus I have to do it or my friends will think I'm lame. See, it has to be easier being a guy and getting to just think about all the fun aspects of things without having to get all serious and depressing with the realities.

In a way I feel like guys get to be kids longer than girls. It's like we have to grow up faster, which sucks.

FIVE

ZOEY WAS FIRST AWARE OF the fact that her radio alarm had gone off. Zoey was next aware of the fact that her pillow seemed unnaturally hard and was rising and falling slowly.

She opened her eyes and was surprised beyond belief to discover Lucas, arm crooked back behind his head, the pillow of his chest rising and falling slowly. There was a little wet spot on his shirt where she had drooled.

He stirred, one eye blinking open, shutting, then both eyes opened suddenly.

"What am I doing here?"

"That's just what I was wondering," Zoey said. She realized one of her legs was still entwined with his and quickly disentangled herself. "How did you get in here? Am I awake?"

"Oh." He sat up, wincing in pain, and rubbed at his neck, which he held forward at an odd angle. "I just came by to see you last night. You fell asleep on me."

"I did?" That didn't seem likely, but she did have a vague, dreamlike memory of something . . .

"Yeah, remember? You told me about, you know, about your folks."

"Oh. Right." Zoey tried self-consciously to push her hair into some kind of recognizable shape. Her folks. Yes, for several seconds she'd managed to forget about that. She hoped Lucas wouldn't notice the wet spot on his shirt.

"You look beautiful in the morning," Lucas said, smiling in spite of the fact that he couldn't sit all the way up.

"No, I don't." Another halfhearted attempt at straightening her hair. She kept her distance in case she had dread morning breath.

"Actually, you do." He looked around the room, twisting his neck and grimacing. "I guess I'm wearing my same clothes to school. I can sneak out past your parents if you look out for me."

"You don't have to sneak," Zoey said quickly. "I don't care what my parents see. They have no right to tell me how to live my life."

Lucas raised his eyebrows but said nothing.

Zoey smiled ruefully. "I know I sound like I'm being bitter, but that's not it. I'm just growing up. I've just figured out some stuff."

"They're still your parents," Lucas said with a diffident shrug.

"They're Jeff and Darla," Zoey said dismissively. "I have an extra toothbrush if you want."

"Really? You keep a supply, do you?"

"I always switch to a new one every month, so I have next month's still in its little box. Now you've learned one of my deep, dark secrets. It's pink," she added apologetically. "I change colors every month, too."

Lucas nodded. "Probably floss every day, too."

"Twice, actually."

"Well, I approve of good oral hygiene."

"Um, Lucas?" Zoey asked hesitantly.

"What?"

"Are you . . . you didn't take off your pants or anything, did you?"

Lucas grinned and threw back the blankets. Zoey saw wrinkled Levi's.

"You slept all night in jeans and your shirt and me crushing you?" She ran her fingers through his matted hair, an even bigger mess than hers.

"I didn't want to wake you up. You seemed very tired. You fell asleep instantly. Like a light switch."

"I was exhausted. I haven't slept in a long time, with all this stuff going on." She looked at him closely. "I've probably been a jerk to you lately."

He smiled sheepishly. "It's okay. I was a bigger jerk." For a moment he looked like he had something else to add, but he said nothing.

Zoey looked thoughtfully around the room. Sunlight forced its way around the edges of the shade. In the dormered window where she had her desk, she noticed the bare side walls. Normally they would have been cluttered with Post-it notes bearing her favorite quotes. But she had thrown them all away. Along with the journal where, over the years, she had written the first chapter of her romance novel more than twenty times. And the journal her mother had kept, starting with Zoey's birth and up through all her subsequent birthdays. All gone in a cleaning out of memories of things now past.

She felt sad, despite the sunlight. Today her father was moving out of the house. She wondered if she should skip school, stay home and help somehow. But was that the right thing? What exactly was the correct protocol when your father was leaving his home?

As if he'd read her mind, Lucas asked, "Are you going to school today?"

Zoey sighed. "If I stay home, I'm afraid I'll just make things worse. My dad—" Her words were choked off by a rising lump in her throat.

Lucas took her hand and held it in his lap.

"He's moving out," Zoey said. "Maybe I should help him. Only I'll just end up crying and being mad. And I feel like, I don't know, like I'm just halfway sane right now and I don't want to go back into all that. You know?"

"Yeah, I know. You have to keep yourself together in all this."

"Maybe I'm just being a coward."

Lucas shook his head. "This will be bad for your father, too," he said. "You think he wants to have to do this with you watching and crying the whole time?"

"But I can't stand the idea of him walking out of here, out of a silent house with no one even to say good-bye." She brushed wretchedly at a tear. "Damn, that's enough. I've cried enough."

Lucas started to put his arms around her, but she held him back. "Don't, please, or I'll just lose it completely. I have to get out of this house," she said with sudden decisiveness. "I can't be here today. I can't, I'm sorry."

"Sometimes I feel myself slippin', but I guarantee you I'll never fall. . . ."

Benjamin had a world-class stereo system and didn't have to rely on radio potluck to wake him up. The CD he'd picked and programmed the night before came on at the appointed hour on the chosen cut, and Clarence "Gatemouth" Brown and his guitar sang out from speakers around the room and in his adjoining private bathroom.

He knew it was kind of a cliché that a blind person would turn to music, but even if it was just a compensation for the lost world of sight, it still wasn't a bad compensation. His CD collection, all neatly arranged in racks, labeled in his own Braille stickers, covered the whole range of music from baroque to opera to big band to rock to blues. About the only thing left out was country, unless you counted Keith Urban and Faith Hill.

This cut ran about six minutes, during which he climbed out of bed, wearing only a pair of boxers, brushed his teeth, ran the electric razor over his face (not that this was strictly necessary every day), and climbed into a regrettably cool shower. Zoey had beaten him to the hot water again.

"Nobody but nobody can have good luck every day," Gatemouth pointed out wisely.

Benjamin raced the rapidly diminishing hot water, rinsing finally in something barely above ice water.

He half-dried himself and ran for warm clothing, shivering and cursing under his breath. But a surprising number of his hangers were empty. In fact, it would take some searching to put together anything like a normal outfit. Fortunately, he kept his clothing options limited, sticking to dark browns, dark blues, grays, and blacks, with the occasional plaid shirt. That way he was less likely to end up wearing something bizarrely mismatched.

He and his mother had worked out a system with the hangers so he could manage it all himself without the humiliating need of asking someone to pick his clothes for him.

Oh. Of course, he realized. No wonder the closet was nearly empty. His mother had been a little preoccupied these last few days.

He felt a momentary annoyance, but fought the impulse to get angry. It was pretty irrelevant, really. Although it could be seen as an omen of things to come. It was the kind of thing that reminded him that no matter how well he coped, he was still dependent in some things. He still couldn't separate whites and colors to do a load of wash; a minor, silly thing to worry about, but still . . .

"Stop it, Benjamin," he ordered himself. He was treading too close to self-pity, and that was definitely not allowed. He found his remote control and replayed the same song. He sang along with the music. "Sometimes I feel myself slippin', but I guarantee you I'll never fall. I hold my head up high and wade through water, mud and all. . . ."

"You will never be a blues singer," Benjamin admitted.

"Just too damned white."

There was a tapping on his door.

"Come in." He muted the music.

"It's me." His mother.

"Hi."

"Look, Benjamin, I thought maybe we should have a little talk."

"Okay. But I don't have much time before I have to head for the ferry."

"So you . . . you *are* going to school?" She sounded surprised.

"That was the plan," he said. "It's a school day."

"I thought maybe you'd feel like you had to stay home. You know, for your father." Her voice quavered.

Benjamin shrugged. "If I thought I could help, I guess I would. Is that what you wanted to say? You want me to stay home today?"

"No. Just the opposite. I was going to tell you that you should go to school. I think you and Zoey both need normalcy now, as much as possible."

"Did you talk to Zoey?"

A long pause. "No. I don't know that Zoey would listen to much I have to say. I think she's very, very angry at me."

"Gee, I can't understand why," Benjamin said sarcastically.

He instantly regretted his tone. He didn't want to get angry. And he didn't want to hurt either of his parents. They were already doing a good job of that themselves.

"Anyway," his mother said heavily. "I wish you'd make sure Zoey goes today, too."

"I don't tell Zoey what to do." Despite his best efforts he was beginning to get annoyed. His mother was just grinding him the wrong way.

"You *are* her big brother."

"I'm two years older and still in the same grade," Benjamin pointed out.

His mother wasn't making it easy for him to maintain his calm. She really should just go away now. She really should let him just finish dressing and getting ready to get the hell out of this house.

"That's not through any fault of yours, Benjamin. You know, I guess in some way you're going to be the man of the house—"

"Shut up," Benjamin snapped, suddenly viciously angry. "Just shut up. My father is *the man* of this house. I'm not *the man* of a damned thing. I'm a nineteen-year-old guy who's trying to get through twelfth grade without being able to see a blackboard or read half the books. I'm smart enough to just about manage it. And I'm clever enough to make people like me instead of laugh at me, and treat me like an equal instead of punching me out for the sheer hell of it, and isn't that wonderful. I'm Benjamin the Blind Wonderboy. But that's all I can handle, Mom, so don't dump your problems on me and start telling me I'm *the man* around here, whatever the hell that's supposed to mean."

"Sorry. I meant it as a compliment."

"Great. I'm flattered. I have to finish getting ready for school."

"This isn't easy for me, either, you know," his mother said.

Benjamin unmuted the music. His hand was trembling.

"Nobody but nobody can have good luck every day. . . ."

SIX

LUCAS TORE AT THE STUBBORN wrapping of the toothbrush, finally got it open after some muttered curses, and applied toothpaste. He had been in Zoey's bathroom before, but never this early in the morning and after having just spent the night sleeping with Zoey.

Sleeping with Zoey. That had a nice sound. Sleeping with Zoey. Yep, a very nice sound.

He realized he was grinning at his reflection in the bathroom mirror. *Just* sleeping, he reminded himself, which wiped the smile away.

Still, it seemed like they were back on more normal terms, Zoey and him. She'd sort of apologized for being hard on him, and now that he knew what had been going on with her, he could forgive very easily. If only she'd told him earlier. Only, of course, they'd been fighting, so naturally she hadn't told him. But if she *had,* then he wouldn't have been so upset, and he would have understood *why* she had been acting way too friendly to Jake. After all, his father was involved in the whole divorce mess, too. If he'd known all that . . .

Damn. He froze, looking at his suddenly pale reflection. If only he'd understood all that, he wouldn't have gone off with Claire and made out and tried to do a whole lot more. The memories came back sharp and clear. And with the memories came two feelings. One was definitely guilt. The other was, unfortunately, a kind of lingering excitement. Which led directly back to guilt.

Okay, so he had gotten some superficial physical pleasure out of making out with Claire. Obviously. She was a beautiful, sexy . . . cold-blooded, ruthless, almost reptilian girl. Who now had the power to destroy his fragile relationship with Zoey anytime she wanted to just by opening her mouth. A relationship that, even with all its frustrations, was the most important thing in his life.

He spit and rinsed. "She won't say anything," he muttered to the wary-looking face in the mirror. No. He could trust Claire.

Yeah, right. Oh, certainly he could trust Claire.

He opened the bathroom door and peeked out. The coast was clear. He dashed quickly to Zoey's room.

"Ready?" she asked.

He made an exaggerated smile, showing off his sparkling

teeth. "Now is it time for a morning kiss? I think it should be a regular thing we do whenever we sleep together."

Zoey smiled halfheartedly, and followed it with an equally halfhearted kiss. "Let's go or we'll miss the ferry."

"Hey, are we going out tonight?" Lucas asked. "I mean, I guess you wouldn't want to, probably."

"No," Zoey said. "I won't feel like going out tonight."

Lucas tried not to look disappointed, but he must not have been too successful because Zoey put her arm through his and gave him a kiss on the cheek. "How about tomorrow night?" she said.

"Saturday night! Absolutely."

They tramped down the stairs and ran into Benjamin in the entryway. Zoey winced, obviously embarrassed at having to explain to her brother why her boyfriend was there.

Lucas held a finger up to his lips. He fell into step as silently as he could behind Zoey and Benjamin. After a few minutes he'd say hi to Benjamin, like he'd just walked up.

"Hey, Zoey," Benjamin said.

"Good morning, Benjamin," Zoey said.

"You know, Zoey," Benjamin said as they set off down the street, "I've been thinking over what you said the other night; you know, about how Lucas is probably just overcompensating for feelings of inadequacy as a male and possibly even latent homosexuality? I think that may be true."

Lucas made a disgusted sound. "Okay, very humorous."

"Like I can't tell the difference between one person coming down a flight of stairs and *two* people," Benjamin said cockily. "Like I can't hear your big galumphing boots. And not to be cruel, but someone here didn't shower this morning."

"He came over early," Zoey said.

Benjamin shrugged. "I'm not Mom or Dad. Come to think of it, Mom and Dad aren't exactly Mom and Dad anymore. Did Zoey tell you about the Passmore scandal?"

"Yeah," Lucas said. He felt very uncomfortable being part of a conversation about their parents. He had always genuinely liked Mr. and Ms. Passmore. In fact, Zoey's family, living in what had seemed like idyllic family bliss just down the hill from his own screwed-up family, had always been a kind of example of how things could be. *Might* have been, if his own father weren't a tyrant and his mother too weak to resist him.

"I told Nina, too," Benjamin said.

"How did she take it?" Zoey asked.

Benjamin smiled, a sweet, tender expression. His voice, which had been hard and cynical, softened by several shades. "She was fine. You have excellent taste in best friends, Zoey."

Lucas and Zoey exchanged a look. Lucas looked quickly

away. The image of Nina in his mind was replaced by the image of Claire.

Claire. Guilt mixed with memories of pleasure, followed by dread. Claire wouldn't say anything, he told himself again. Why would she?

"Did you see Mom or Dad this morning?" Zoey asked Benjamin.

"Mom. We kind of got into it. She wanted me to talk you into going to school today."

Zoey nodded and shot an embarrassed glance at Lucas.

"You guys want me to leave?" Lucas volunteered. "I mean, you know, family stuff and all."

"No, no," Benjamin said. "We're not going to have a big talk or anything. Tell you the truth, I'm sick of the whole subject."

"I'm going to go see Dad after school," Zoey said. "Find out where he's staying and maybe bring him something. Cookies or something."

"I guess that would be a good idea," Benjamin said. "Maybe I'll go with you. I want to find out about this girl. This half-sister."

Lucas looked quizzically at Zoey. Zoey looked down at the ground. Benjamin stopped, sensing this new tension.

"Zoey, there's no point in trying to keep that secret," Benjamin said. He turned his sunglasses in Lucas's general direction. "Turns out our father has supplied us with a half-sister."

Lucas had absolutely nothing intelligent to say to that piece of news. Zoey and Benjamin had a half-sister? It was starting to seem like he'd been wrong about the Passmores being so normal.

"Whoever she is, she means nothing to me," Zoey said. "That all took place a long time ago, before I was even born. Dad wasn't much older than we are now when it happened. At least when *he* screwed up he was young, unlike Mom."

"Zoey, don't get into choosing sides between Mom and Dad," Benjamin said.

Lucas had begun to feel extremely uncomfortable.

"What Daddy did happened nineteen years ago," Zoey said coldly. "What our mother did happened last week. Don't forget, I saw it. It was . . . Look, she betrayed Dad, you, me—" Her eyes were hard in a way that Lucas had never seen before. "I don't like sneaking and secrets and betrayal."

Lucas sucked in a deep lungful of air. He put his arm around Zoey, comforting her, feeling her angry trembling.

Sneaking and secrets and betrayal. He replayed the phrase over in his mind. Yes, sneaking. Yes to secrets, too. And a betrayal that would have been a lot worse if Claire hadn't put a stop to things.

Claire would keep quiet, he told himself. Because if she didn't, it would be the end of the one real love in his life.

SEVEN

"IT'S THE BIG LINE OF goo," Nina announced with some satisfaction as she surveyed the length of the cafeteria line. "More
goo per square foot than has ever been brought together in
one place. The home office of goo. Goo central. Warm goo,
cold goo, goo the temperature of spit. Wait, that *is* spit. Goo
with and without sauce. It's a celebration of goo. A monument
to goo."

"So you're saying *goo*?" Benjamin asked tolerantly.

"Well, the main course today seems to be paste studded
with bits of dog food."

"That's the Friday special," Benjamin agreed.

"The vegetable is green, but the bad news is, it's carrots."

"But seriously, folks." Benjamin laughed, and Nina felt that
semi-delirious feeling that came over her all too often when she
was with Benjamin lately. Something between the early symp-
toms of flu and the giddy-moronic feeling when her dentist

gave her nitrous oxide. Objectively speaking, it was basically an unpleasant feeling, except that it was intensely pleasurable.

He was just behind her in line, and when she stopped for the person in front of them, he bumped into her. She bumped back, playfully, and the half-sick feeling just got worse. Or better. She accepted a plate from the cafeteria ladies.

"Yours is up," she told Benjamin. "About two inches left. Just follow the smell."

He retrieved his plate and again bumped into her. This time Nina had stopped suddenly for no reason except that she wanted him to bump into her. *Very juvenile*, she scolded herself.

They were at the end of the line. This was one of the few places where Benjamin could actually use a hand. He could negotiate a lot of things using his remarkable memory, but the configuration of the lunchroom changed every day.

She guided his hand to her arm and led him to an empty table. As soon as Benjamin sat down, two sophomore girls sat down nearby, looking far, far too innocent to be innocent. Nina gave them a dirty look. Then she glanced over to her usual table. Zoey, Aisha, and unfortunately, Claire.

"Maybe I'll sit with you today," Nina said.

"You know I'd love that," Benjamin said. "But I don't think you should mess with tradition."

"Yeah, tradition," Nina said unenthusiastically. She and Zoey and Aisha and sometimes Claire had been eating lunch together for years, uninterrupted by boyfriends for the most part. She'd thought it was a great idea back in the days when she was the only one without a boyfriend. "Well, there are two girls here at the table to talk to. A pair of sophomores, and only one of them has really bad leprosy."

Benjamin laughed again, and the two girls gave Nina cold stares.

"Hey, we're going out tomorrow night, right?" Benjamin asked.

"Sure. Not tonight?"

Benjamin sighed. "I don't think so. Zoey and I are going to see our dad at his new location."

Nina winced. "Ouch."

"Yeah. But tomorrow? I mean, if you can spare the time. It's Richie Felix's birthday party."

Nina grinned. "I totally forgot. Richie's birthday party. Remember last year when Melanie Amos hit that guy over the head with a bottle like she thought she was in a cowboy movie or something and he had to go get stitches?"

"And how many major boyfriend-girlfriend fights were there?" Benjamin asked. "I mean, I'm only counting ones where objects were thrown."

"Too bad Richie's such a strange kid. He has the world's most bizarre parties."

"You and I calling someone strange?" Benjamin said.

"Yeah. Well, your food's getting cold and that isn't going to help."

"Okay, sweetheart. I'll see you later."

Nina leaned over and put her mouth beside Benjamin's ear. "I have to tell you a secret."

"What?" he whispered back.

"I love you."

"I love you, too," he said.

That stupid feeling was back, and Nina realized she was grinning like the kind of sappy little dip who made her sick. If she'd been looking at herself right now, she'd roll her eyes and make some smart, cutting remark. But it wouldn't matter, she realized, because when you were in love it didn't matter what anyone else on earth thought or said, because pretty much everyone aside from Benjamin had temporarily ceased to exist.

"I am making myself sick," she muttered under her breath as she reluctantly carried her tray toward her usual table. She wiped the grin off her face and adopted a very cool expression that gave nothing away.

She took the seat between Claire and Zoey. Claire was shaking her head in disgust. Both Aisha and Zoey were batting their lashes at her.

"What?" Nina said grouchily.

"She's beaming again," Aisha told Zoey.

"Eyes shining, dopey grin, face red," Zoey confirmed.

Nina scowled. "What are you guys talking about?" She took a cigarette from her purse and planted it, unlit as always, in the corner of her mouth.

"Yeah, the cigarette is sure to hide that dweeby grin," Aisha said, rolling her eyes.

"I never thought I'd have to use the word 'Nina' and the words 'aww, isn't that sweet' in the same sentence," Zoey said.

"I'm not at all surprised to have to use the word 'Nina' and the words 'I may throw up' in the same sentence," Claire said. "Can we get past this and go on to the next step—Nina's daily ritual of abusing the food?"

"Funny you should ask," Nina said, glad to have the subject changed. She fumbled in her book bag and produced a sketchbook. She opened it to a black line drawing and shoved it in front of Claire.

Claire nodded thoughtfully. "Well, now I'm all the way sick." She pushed her food away. "You know, I'll never get fat as long as you're around, Nina. It's like a diet, almost."

Aisha grabbed the sketchbook, looked it over, and laughed.

"I'm thinking what I'll do is Xerox off like a hundred copies and spread them around the cafeteria Monday," Nina said, laughing at the possibilities.

"You know, that's a sickening cartoon," Aisha pointed out, "but it's kind of good, too."

"It is good," Zoey confirmed. "Since when do you draw?"

"It's just a little cartoon." Nina shrugged. "Any idiot could draw it."

"And one idiot did," Claire said.

"No, not *any* idiot could draw it," Aisha argued.

"No, you're right, it would take a particular idiot," Claire agreed.

"I'm serious," Aisha said.

"You know what you ought to do," Zoey said. "You should take it to Mr. Schwarz and see if hell put it in the school paper. We're short this week. I'd talk to him for you, but I'm not exactly his favorite student right now."

Nina knew Zoey had recently refused to do a story on drug use by the football team, because the story would have implicated Jake. And since it had just been one incident, Zoey had argued it wasn't a real story.

"I thought your teacher agreed it wasn't enough of a story," Claire said. *Still looking out for Jake*, Nina noted.

"He did, but he's still pissed," Zoey said. "He thinks I was influenced by the fact that I care about—" She paused, swallowed, and backed up. "I mean, that I used to care about Jake." She quickly turned her attention back to Nina. "But I'm serious, Nina. You should show that to Mr. Schwarz. We've never had a cartoonist in the paper."

Claire colored and concentrated on her food.

"Maybe I will," Nina said. She gave Claire a triumphant look. "Then I won't just be an idiot, I'll be a published idiot."

But there was no answer from Claire. Claire's eyes were far away. An expression that, in anyone else, Nina would have taken for sadness.

Jake fell in beside Zoey as she climbed the stairs from the cafeteria up to the second floor for their English class. She was walking alone, looking distracted, lugging her books and notebooks like they were a great weight.

"Hey, Zoey," he said, taking the steps two at a time to catch up with her.

She paused and waited for him, leaning against the rail to stay out of the flow of kids going up and down, a thin, almost fragile figure to Jake's eyes, her wispy hair as usual not quite forming any recognizable style.

He felt an urge to touch her, to hold her hand, but resisted. Things weren't that way between them, not anymore.

"Hi, Jake," she said, forming a smile.

Suddenly he felt almost bashful, at a loss for words. "I was just . . . I just wanted to check and see if you were okay."

"I'm doing okay. My dad's moving out of the house." Her lip quivered, but she overcame the emotion. "He's always saying he can't get to sleep because there's too much noise from all of us, so I guess it will be good for him."

Jake nodded. "I'm sorry to hear that. I always liked both your folks."

"Me too. I mean, your parents. Did anything—?"

He shook his head uncomfortably. "No. My mom is one of those people who doesn't ever hear anything or see anything she doesn't want to see, you know? Besides, she's not like your mom. She'd be totally lost on her own. What can she do aside from bake pies? Your mom is so much more independent. Maybe that's why my dad—" He waved the thought aside. It was just too gross to get into the whole question of why his father and Zoey's mother would end up having an affair. He knew there was supposedly a history there, going back to a long time ago, but they were the people they were today, and it wasn't nineteen years ago. It was now.

Zoey reached out and put her hand over his. It was a perfectly innocent gesture of comfort for a friend, Jake believed, but there were two facts that made that belief hard to sustain. First was the fact that the touch had a profound effect on him. Second was the fact that Claire chose that moment to pass by. Her dark eyes were cold and accusing, and Jake responded by jerking his hand away guiltily.

"Claire!" he called out.

Zoey turned, flushing pink.

A rushing group of freshman guys obscured Claire for a moment. Then she stepped forward with a look in her dark eyes that would have made Jake take a step back if he hadn't already been pressed against the railing.

"Hi, Jake. Hi, Zoey. Is this a closed meeting of the mutual support society?"

"I was just asking Zoey if . . . if she was okay," Jake said.

"And is she?" Claire asked. The words were silky, but cracked like a whip.

Jake nodded.

"Good," Claire said. "And have you checked with Louise Kronenberger lately to see if she's okay, too?"

Jake flushed. He wasn't easily intimidated, but Claire was capable of an ice-cold fury that was just scary. In a part of his mind he couldn't help but admire her. "Not lately," he said.

"Too bad, because I like to make sure absolutely everyone is okay. Zoey, Louise, Lucas." She turned on Zoey. "Is Lucas okay, too?"

Zoey was blushing darkly, her face set in resentment. "Yes, he's okay," she said through gritted teeth.

"Just okay?" Claire demanded. "I'm a little surprised. I found him much, much better than just okay."

.

Claire hadn't meant anything by it, Zoey told herself for the thousandth time in an hour. All through English, Claire's snide remark had distracted and bothered Zoey. Which was probably just what Claire had intended. Claire had seen her touching Jake, and she obviously wasn't ready to tolerate any unfaithfulness on his part.

Well, Zoey could hardly blame her. Infidelity wasn't her favorite human failing right now, either.

So Claire had taken a shot. It hadn't meant anything. How could it have?

Maybe she was referring back to the old days when she and Lucas were girlfriend and boyfriend. That was probably it.

Besides, when would there have been time or opportunity? Unless . . . had Lucas been on the afternoon ferry Thursday? No. She didn't think so. And Claire?

But that was stupid. Aisha hadn't been on the ferry, either. There were a million innocent reasons why Lucas might have stayed late on the mainland. And another million why Claire might also have stayed late.

And Lucas had come to her straightaway, even sneaking up to her room. The memory warmed her. She was being dumb. She was being stupidly suspicious. Just because her parents had cheated didn't mean she should go around suspecting everyone else in the world of being unfaithful. Lucas wasn't her father, after all. And she wasn't her mother.

Lucas had come to see her, comforting her in the night, reminding her that there were still good things in the world. Those weren't the actions of a guy who had cheated on her.

Claire stole a glance across the room at Zoey. Zoey looked preoccupied, even troubled.

Well, what did you expect, Claire? she asked herself. *You wanted to lash out, and you did a swell job.* Stupid. Inexcusably stupid. What would telling Zoey about Lucas accomplish? Break the two of them up? Oh yes, that would be brilliant. Then Zoey would be free for Jake. *Yes, Claire, brilliant.*

Not to mention the fact that it was a cheap shot at Zoey, who had enough problems in her life right now. So she'd managed to be stupid and cruel at one time.

What was the matter with her? She was acting like a jealous little ninny. So Jake had gotten drunk and slept with Louise. She and Jake technically weren't boyfriend and girlfriend at that point. Technically.

Claire realized she was squeezing a pencil so hard it was in danger of snapping. With a will she relaxed her muscles.

Technically not boyfriend and girlfriend, because Jake had been busy trying to get away from Claire. She'd had to manipulate him into coming back. Manipulating was something she was good at. Unlike Zoey, who just had to look sweet and winsome and guys would fall in love. Guys didn't fall in love with Claire, at least not *that* way. Why? Was Nina right? Was Claire some sort of inhuman ice princess? Was she really ruthless and self-serving? Was that why Lucas remained fixated on Zoey, despite everything? Was that why Jake still nursed his private love for Zoey? Was that why Benjamin, who had once seemed so desperately in love with Claire, now acted like he was lucky to have escaped her?

Did Jake still love her at all, even a little? They were supposed to be going out Saturday night. Richie Felix's party. Their first real date since the ski weekend. They'd probably end up spending at least part of the evening with Zoey and Lucas. Which should be very interesting, at least.

Jake peeked from under his hand at Zoey, then shifted his gaze to Claire. Day and night. Sweet and sour. Good and evil. No, that was too strong. Claire wasn't evil. Claire was just . . . he didn't know. What was Claire exactly?

Self-contained, like she needed no one. Like the whole rest of the world could disappear tomorrow and she'd shrug it off. A perfectly beautiful creature made of stainless steel and diamonds. Indestructible, unapproachable, unstoppable.

She wasn't without feeling, she had proved that. Not without a capacity to care, because she had cared about him, perhaps still did. But her feelings and emotions were under lock and key, allowed out only when she chose to show them, turned off like a light switch whenever she wanted.

And Zoey? Zoey struck him to the heart with her vulnerability. She *was* her emotions.

Had Claire been telling the truth? Was there something between her and Lucas? It wasn't impossible, he realized sadly. And after Louise Kronenberger, he wasn't in a very good position to complain. Still, if Claire was being unfaithful, he should be very angry. He was in love with Claire, after all.

Wasn't he?

And was Claire in love with him? She'd certainly acted like she was jealous. But in love? Well, maybe something she thought was love.

But of course, Claire's only true love was Claire.

BENJAMIN

It isn't that the idea of my parents divorcing didn't hurt me; it did. But I guess, unlike my sister, I'm more prepared for bad things to happen. I guess the reason for that is fairly obvious—when I lost my sight it was like a bolt of lightning out of a clear blue sky, so I <u>know</u> that bad things can happen. I know it on a deep, emotional level that Zoey doesn't yet.

And maybe even before that I was more of a realist; I don't know. Maybe it's just the way I am. Not cynical, exactly, but guarded. A little bit hunkered down. Tensing up for the next beating but already telling myself it's okay, Benjamin, you'll ride through it, and thinking ha, I can take whatever the world wants to hit me with.

No, I never expected my parents to get divorced. But it didn't devastate me. The funny thing was that even during that terrible, awkward scene where they made the big announcement, I was mostly just concerned for Zoey. And oddly enough, my thoughts were less on what was happening to my family than on this new person . . . this supposed half-sister.

That probably sounds cold of me. But I'll tell you—I've

done bitterness and despair. Been there, done it. It's a big damn hole that almost swallowed me up some years ago when I woke up in a hospital bed, opened my eyes, and realized that it was going to be nighttime for the rest of my life.

I don't go back to those feelings for anyone or anything. I take a wide path around them because I've learned some respect for the power of depression.

Now I focus on what I can do and what I still have, not what I've lost. And I think, well, it could have been worse. So in a weird way I guess I'm a sort of optimist. Just out of self-preservation.

You think about it and you realize that irrational hope is the most rational thing in the world.

EIGHT

THAT AFTERNOON BACK ON THE island, with a sky hidden by a low, gray blanket of cloud and the empty beach and bay at their backs, Zoey and Benjamin approached a shabbily exotic Victorian building.

"This is where Christopher lives," Zoey said. "Second floor of the tower. I mean, there's a tower, on the right," she clarified. "A Sleeping Beauty kind of thing, with a pointed roof."

"Really?" Benjamin asked. "I'll have to take your word for that. You know, Dad *is* Christopher's boss, or at least one of them. It's going to be tough for Christopher to ever call in sick. Bet he's pissed."

Normally Zoey appreciated Benjamin's seemingly unfailing wit, but she was a long way from being able to see anything funny about this. "I so much don't want to do this," she said.

"Wait till Thanksgiving and Christmas," Benjamin said darkly.

"Oh, God. I hadn't even thought about that."

"Well, now that you're feeling even more upbeat, let's go on in," Benjamin suggested. "Visit Dad in his brand-new bachelor pad."

Zoey led him up onto the porch and opened the front door. Aisha had told her not to bother knocking at this door since no one ever came down from the individual apartments to answer it. Inside was a stairway, rising up in a curve from the dusty, dim entryway.

"What do we have?" Benjamin asked. "Aside from dust and mildew; I can tell that myself."

Zoey shook her head. "It's a dump," she muttered.

"Yeah, well, let's not tell Dad that. Besides, how bad is it, actually?"

"Like something from an old black-and-white detective movie."

"Cool," Benjamin said impishly. "Maybe Dad can become a hard-boiled private eye."

"Not really very cool," Zoey said tersely. "I guess he's upstairs. Here, that's the railing."

"Hmm. A substantial banister." He ran his hand along the smooth wood. "I love a substantial banister."

Zoey was tired of trying to be nice. "Benjamin, if you're acting this way because you think I need to be cheered up, forget it."

"I didn't realize I was bothering you." He started up the stairs cautiously, the way he always had to be in unexplored territory. "A left curve beginning at the fourth step, one, two, three, four, and we straighten out again. Am I still annoying you?" he asked playfully.

"I just don't see much humor in this."

"There's humor in everything, Zoey, or just about everything. Seventeen steps and we're up. Must have nice high ceilings in the building."

"Okay, we're in a hallway, maybe four different doors," Zoey explained.

"Left," Benjamin said confidently.

"How do you know?"

"Listen," he urged. "Keith Urban. *It's gonna hurt bad before it gets better.* Playing on the stereo. I think the old man raided my CDs."

Zoey looked at him sharply. Was this some kind of a joke? But no, Benjamin looked much more serious now, even a little sad. And when she concentrated, she heard the music.

"Jeez, Zoey," Benjamin said under his breath. "Kind of a depressing song to be listening to." He let out a sigh. "I'd feel so much better about this if he was listening to . . . I don't know, like one of his old Stones albums. Something tougher. Divorce and country music. Man."

Zoey led the way down the hall, following the music, which grew loud as they reached the door. She took a deep, steadying breath and tried out a cheerful smile that wasn't going to last two minutes. She knocked.

"Let's just hope he doesn't have a woman in there," Benjamin said, reverting to black humor.

The door opened. Their father's face was eager, hopeful, for just a second before he recognized them and his expression crashed. Zoey realized he'd been hoping the knock was his wife, not his kids. He made an attempt to revive, trying his best to work up a devil-may-care look, but in the end he turned away quickly, hiding the pain that he couldn't keep from his face.

"Hi, Daddy," Zoey said. She pursued him, caught up, and managed to plant a clumsy kiss on his cheek.

"Hey," Mr. Passmore said, his ragged voice loaded with desperately fake cheer. "I didn't expect visitors so soon." He waved a hand around the room. "I haven't exactly got the place decorated just yet."

He was wearing a sweater Ms. Passmore had given him for his birthday. Zoey took in the room, trying not to linger too long on the opened suitcase full of rumpled clothing, the sagging bed, the dirty window opening onto the beach, a view that instead of making the room more attractive just seemed to add to the seedy sense of decay.

"Pretty grim, huh?" Mr. Passmore said with a self-deprecating look.

"It could use some flowers or something," Zoey said.

"Yeah." He nodded, as if this was a profoundly important suggestion. "Your mom always says that. You know, flowers . . . and, you know." He looked around again, unwilling to meet Zoey's eyes. "I guess some over there." He pointed to the low counter that separated the minuscule kitchen from the rest of the single room. "Some of those, what are those white flowers? You know, all the little petals and everything."

"Chrysanthemums," Benjamin said, surprising Zoey. "I remember them," he explained. "Roses and chrysanthemums."

"Flowers," their father said, nodding.

Silence descended, and Keith's sad lyrics still swelled clear, speaking of lost loves and futility.

Zoey fought the urge to turn off the offending music.

"I'm guessing this song was written *before* he got with Nicole Kidman," Benjamin said dryly.

"I suppose it is kind of depressing," Mr. Passmore said. He stared blankly at the CD player.

"It's a depressing situation," Benjamin said.

"Sorry."

Zoey was on the verge of telling him it wasn't his fault, a sort of automatic urge to offer comfort. But of course it was his fault, almost as much as her mother's. "Maybe things will still work out," Zoey said.

Her father's eyes were filled with tears. "Yeah," he said, sounding strangled.

Zoey saw Benjamin clench his fist involuntarily. His mouth was a tight line as he struggled to control his own emotions. Benjamin couldn't see the tears, Zoey realized, but he had heard them in that single desperate word.

"Well, we just wanted to see where you were," Zoey said.

"I'm right here."

"God, Daddy, what am I supposed to say? I hate this!" Zoey cried. "You shouldn't be . . . here . . . you should . . . ." Sobs had broken up her rush of pointless, meaningless words.

Her father opened his arms and took her to him. She cried, spilling her tears on his shoulder. And then she felt her father reach out and take Benjamin into the same embrace.

Claire took a slow walk around the circumference of her widow's walk, feeling agitated, even emotional. A storm, that's what she needed. A major, serious, blow the damned lights out, drown the streets, knock the branches off the trees storm. That would clear her mind.

But all she saw as she looked around from her high, private perch was gray cloud, lying so low it was like she could reach up over her head and touch it. It spread from far beyond Weymouth, still sparkling with car headlights and traffic signals, across the bay, over the island, far out beyond the range of sight above the Atlantic.

North Harbor was settling into darkness. Darkness had already crept under the sparse shrubs, down the narrow alleys, up the eastern walls. The sea had gone from gray-green to the color of molten lead, and to the east the sky was already black. The green warning light at the end of the breakwater was on. The sweeping beacon from the lighthouse would be coming on shortly, warning boats away from the island's northern point.

Normally Claire would have found something of interest even in this tiresomely consistent weather pattern. The idea that the sun was still up there, shining brightly above the clouds far to the west, and that away to the east the tops of those clouds were silver with moonlight . . . that usually would have held a certain poetry for her.

But this evening peace was hard to find. She was feeling foul and dangerous. Angry, with no real target in sight aside from herself. Was it just that Nina's happiness was getting on her nerves? That would have been way too petty. Was it that whole stupid episode on the stairs with Zoey and Jake?

Yes, that was part of it. She'd blown up in an attack of pure, spiteful jealousy. Pitiful. Tonight he was away with the football team, playing a road game in Lewiston. But tomorrow night they were going to that stupid party. How was she supposed to act? Should she just abandon the last of her pride and ask him outright, Jake, do you love me? Do you care at all, really, deep down?

She shook her head violently, throwing off the feeling, but not losing the underlying sense of anger.

She took a last, unsatisfied look around and descended through the hatchway, climbing the ladder easily from long practice.

She checked the little weather station she kept. Barometer unchanged. No wind to speak of. Temperature thirty-seven degrees.

She flopped down at her desk and turned on her computer, typing in the address that took her to the website she liked for its weather features and for access to certain research.

She pulled down the menu, and went to the weather maps. Slowly a map formed on her screen, a map that showed unbroken gray cloud cover from a hundred miles out in the Atlantic, extending inland over all of New England.

"I could really use a storm," Claire told the screen.

She bailed out of the weather maps and was on the verge of leaving the site altogether. But her eye was drawn to the menu for the site's chat room. She had homework to do, but she was too distracted to study. Nina would already have occupied the

TV and seized the remote control.

Claire clicked on the chat icon, and a prompt appeared asking her to pick a handle.

"A name," she muttered. She considered for a moment before typing in W–e–a–t–h–e–r G–i–r–l.

A grid came on screen, a series of channels. She scanned forward and stopped at one labeled 17-TEEN ONLY.

Enter.

	[17] Teen Only
Babyface	i dint say you were a jerk
Babyface	i was saying you sounded like a jerk
Beck	i'm a loser, baby
\<DooMeeeNow\>	babyface if I sound like a jerk i must be a jerkand that's why
Bad2daBone	your right, Beck. Hehe hehe.
\<DooMeeeNow\>	i'm pissed off at you, babyface
(:Z!ppy:)	Hi.
!MoFo!	Lol, Bad2.
Beck	chew me, Bad2. you too mofo.
Babyface	peace, DooMeee. chill, okay, take a prozac.
Babyface	take 2 prozac.

Your Receipt

Regina Public Library

Customer ID: **********6594

Items that you checked out

Title: Thomas & friends. Sodor's legend of the
lost treasure the movie
ID: 39085200335822
Due: June-01-19

Title: The Baby-sitters Club. The truth about
Stacey a graphic novel
ID: 39085901881561
Due: June-15-19

Title: The Islanders. Vol. 4, Lucas gets hurt ;
and, Aisha goes wild
ID: 39085901313276
Due: June-15-19

Title: Where is Walt Disney World?
ID: 39085902313218
Due: June-15-19

Total items: 4
May-25-2019 15:01
Checked out: 4
Overdue: 0

We are open in 2019 on Family Day, Easter
Monday, Victoria Day and Saskatchewan
Day.
www.reginalibrary.ca

It took Claire a few minutes to begin to get the basics of what was happening. It was like trying to listen to half a dozen different conversations at once. And none of them was exactly interesting.

	[17] Teen Only
Yeezus	Hey Beck step off man or i'll kick yer a$$.
Flyer	Hi. The usual brilliant conversation, I see. Using
Beck	Yeezus you wuss
Flyer	the information superhighway to its fullest potential.
!MoFo!	age and sex check!
<DooMeeeNow>	are there any girls here? any horny females?
Flyer	Gee, DooMeee, with that handle and such a subtle come-on I'm sure there are
Beck	16, male
Flyer	several females who'd be interested in you. Not HUMAN females maybe . . .
Yeezus	17, more male than Beck
Babyface	15, girl
<DooMeeeNow>	studly 16

| !MoFo! | 14, dude |
| **Flyer** | 17, male. Now can we not have another age check for at least five minutes? |

Suddenly there was a beep and a smaller box, superimposed and divided in half horizontally, appeared. It showed the name FLYER at the top.

[1] Flyer
How about you, Weather Girl? Not talking?

Claire was alarmed. How did Flyer know she was there watching? She hadn't said anything. She clicked on the box and typed "How do you know I'm here?" Enter.

The answer came quickly. There was a way to use the pull-down menu to find out who was monitoring the conversation. He was interested in her handle. "Why Weather Girl?"

Well, Claire decided, this was idiotic. Now she felt trapped in a conversation with some guy whose name she didn't know, whom she could not see, who, for all she knew, might live three thousand miles away.

Nevertheless, she typed in "I'm interested in weather."

"Why?"

"Because" . . . Why was she explaining herself? On the other hand, why not. People almost never asked her *why* she enjoyed weather. They usually just nodded, figured she was eccentric, and went on to the next topic. "Because it has such power to affect us and remains something we can't control. Because it's this huge system, all interconnected so that katabatic winds in Antarctica, and warm spots in the Pacific, and evaporation off the Caspian Sea all work together in incredible complexity."

"Oh, my God. Someone on here with an actual brain," Flyer said. "It's almost a miracle. Complete sentences. Punctuation, even."

"Thanks. I guess."

"No, thank you. I've spent a lot of time scanning this site for someone with half a brain, and I found someone with a whole one."

"You do this a lot?" Claire asked.

Suddenly a second box appeared. This time it was someone named Long Johnson. "Hey, weathergirl. tell me what you have on."

Claire stared at this for a moment, then hit the escape button and returned to Flyer.

"Hey, Flyer. Some guy just popped up and asked me what I

have on. What's that about?"

"Perv," Flyer wrote back. "We get them sometimes. Just ignore the guy; he'll go away. Answering previous question, yes, I do this fairly often."

Claire considered that for a moment, along with the creep who'd asked her what she was wearing. It was very likely that the people on the site were techno-nerds and creeps. On the other hand, *she* was on the site.

"Where are you, Flyer?"

"I'm in Manchester, NH, charm city. Your profile shows you're in Portland."

Close enough, Claire decided. She wasn't going to give away any more than that.

"Damn," Flyer typed back, "I have to go now. My mom is yelling something about dinner. But please, please come back on tomorrow. I'll wait for you."

"Why?"

"Because you sound interesting, Weather Girl."

"By the way, why the name 'Flyer'?"

"I'm getting my pilot's license. Have to go, but come again tomorrow, okay?"

"If I have time."

"Bye, Weather Girl."

"Bye, Flyer."

The box disappeared. She was back to the main screen, where Beck and !MoFo! were now insulting each other. She bailed out and turned off the computer.

Odd. Very odd. She doubted she would do it again.

NINE

THE KITCHEN WAS EMPTY, BENJAMIN was sure of that. He listened closely to the sounds of the house, wanting to make sure no one else was within range to overhear what he was doing. From upstairs he heard a creak; Zoey in her room. From the living room, the faint sounds of the television. His mother.

He paused to consider. His mother might get up at any moment and come to the kitchen for something to eat or drink. And that would be a little embarrassing.

Oh, well. It was either take his chances with the kitchen phone or be overheard using the upstairs hall phone.

He sat down at the table, placed a pad of paper and a ballpoint pen in front of him, and lifted the receiver. He dialed information.

"Yes, do you have listings for Kittery? The McAvoy residence. Sorry, I don't have a first name." He sighed. "Okay, better give me all six, then."

He grabbed the pen and, using the hard tip, began pressing

dots into the paper, a sort of Braille shorthand. He had an excellent memory for numbers, but even he couldn't recall six phone numbers. He hung up the phone, tore off the sheet, and turned the paper over. Now he could read off the dots with his fingertips. He dialed.

"Yes, is this the McAvoy residence? Oh, hi. Look, my name is . . . um, Jack. I'm a friend of your daughter Lara . . . You don't have a daughter? Gee, sorry, I must have the wrong number."

He went on to the next number and got an answering machine. He didn't leave a message. On the fifth call he got lucky. This McAvoy residence *did* have a daughter, and yes, she was named Lara.

"Well, ma'am, I'm an old friend of hers and I was just wondering if she was there this evening?"

No, she wasn't. Where had he known her?

"It's been a long time," Benjamin said smoothly. "I knew her in junior high."

Why was he calling her up now, after all this time?

Hmmm. Excellent question. "To tell you the truth, I know it's silly, but in eighth grade I borrowed a book from her and I just came across it in some old boxes and I wanted to return it."

He was rather pleased with himself for having come up with that on the spur of the moment.

But mom—he assumed it was Lara's mother he was

speaking to—didn't see why Lara would care about an old book. It occurred to Benjamin only then that this woman on the other end of the line had once been his father's secret lover in Europe. Where in Europe, he wondered vaguely. Paris, maybe, or Venice.

"Yes, I know, but I can't keep something that doesn't belong to me," he argued. "It just isn't right."

Mom McAvoy couldn't exactly argue with that. If he'd leave his number, she'd pass it along to Lara. She might be down next weekend.

"Down?" Benjamin pursued hopefully.

Yes, down from Weymouth.

"She lives in Weymouth now?" Benjamin said.

That wasn't really any of his business, but if he wanted to leave a number . . .

Benjamin gave her the first number that came to mind, which happened to be that of a used-car dealer whose annoying TV ads had drilled the number into his brain, and spelled out his name J-a-c-k B-a-t-e-s.

He hung up. So. Lara McAvoy, the mysterious half-sister, lived in Weymouth. How convenient. He dialed information again. "In Weymouth, please, the number for Lara McAvoy, or initial L. McAvoy."

Just one number this time, under L. McAvoy. He took a

deep breath and let it out slowly. He dialed. Four rings before the phone was picked up. A brusque male voice.

He pitched his own voice as low as it would go. "Uh, yeah, is this the Lara McAvoy residence?"

Yeah, she lived there, so what?

"This is UPS; we have a package for her, but the address label is torn. Looks like Third Street, or it could be Blakely; not our fault since the label is improperly attached."

It wasn't either of those addresses, the voice said. Not even close.

Benjamin held his breath.

The voice gave him the correct address and hung up the phone.

Benjamin settled the receiver.

729 Independence, apartment 402. Amazing. He practically walked past it on his way from the ferry landing to school every day. All the time, his half-sister right there, unknown to him. Wasn't life full of little surprises?

If only he could see her, this half-sister. If only he could see her face, and find the similarities between her face and his own. There should be some similarity if they shared the same father.

People had always told Benjamin that he'd gotten his mother's good looks—her cheekbones, her eyes. No one had ever said he looked like his father. He had an uncle, his father's brother, who used to joke about it, saying how lucky he was to look like his beautiful mother and not like his scruffy dad, ha ha ha. And he'd never thought anything of it before. But now he had done the math and whatever his mother said or believed, it was possible that his father wasn't his father at all.

If his father was indeed his father, then a keen eye should be able to find some similarity between Benjamin and this Lara. He crumpled up his Braille notepad, counted the steps to the trash can, and dropped it in.

Late Friday night, and Aisha was finding it a little difficult walking down Climbing Way wearing shoes with heels, and a little cold walking through the night with her legs bare below the hem of her dress. Stockings didn't exactly keep out the October wind. But she'd asked Christopher if she should dress up and he'd said sure, why not? She'd taken it almost as a challenge and had gone all out.

She'd sort of overlooked the fact that with the death of the family's island car, she would have to walk down to the restaurant dressed like she was on her way to dinner at the White House, her leather jacket doing nothing at all to keep her legs and toes warm. Then, as she passed through downtown, she'd encountered the problem of heels on cobblestones.

She was cold but still excited when she arrived at the door

of the restaurant. The sign on the door said CLOSED, but she went inside, grateful for the warmth. She took off her jacket and hung it on a peg. The restaurant was empty. A single candle burned on one corner table, flickering from the crystal, casting shadows on the white linen tablecloth. The only other light was the cheerful golden glow from the fireplace. She fluffed her hair and straightened her outfit.

"Christopher?" No answer. Louder, "Christopher?"

The swinging door to the kitchen opened, revealing a rectangle of brilliant fluorescence, then closed again. Christopher appeared, looking like he, too, was on his way to the White House for dinner.

"Hi," he said.

"Hi, back."

"You look beautiful," he said.

"You look okay, too."

He came closer, then stopped. "If I come any closer," he said, "you'll look just way too good."

"I'll take my chances," she said.

He took her in his arms and they kissed. He was the first to pull away. "Hey, I'm not just your little love toy," he said playfully. "I have an evening planned here."

"Oh, really?"

"This way, please." He led her to the small, candlelit table and pulled her chair out for her. She sat down and he yanked the napkin neatly from the table, unfolded it, and laid it in her lap.

"You didn't eat much for dinner, did you?" he asked suspiciously.

"You told me not to. I'm starving."

"Excellent."

"Where's *your* chair?" she asked.

He shook his head. "No, tonight I wait on you alone." He reached behind her and she heard the slushy sound of ice. He produced a bottle and showed it to her. "Moët & Chandon Brut. Unfortunately, we don't carry Dom Perignon. Or maybe it's fortunate, since DP costs four hundred a bottle in most restaurants."

"Champagne?"

"Of course, champagne. No one's driving tonight," he said with a conspiratorial wink. He unfastened the cage, wrapped a clean napkin around the neck, and twisted the cork neatly, a muted pop.

Aisha looked around a little nervously.

"Don't worry, miss," Christopher said, pouring her a glass of the wine. "I told Mr. Passmore what I was up to. He went for it. He's very susceptible to anything romantic right now, poor guy. I guess you know about the whole divorce thing."

"Yes," Aisha said. "I really—"

"Hush," Christopher held up a hand. "Nothing sad or depressing tonight."

"Absolutely," Aisha agreed. She took a sip of the champagne. "Excellent. The finest champagne I've ever tasted. Of course, the only other champagne I've ever had was at my aunt's wedding."

"Good. Then I'll bring on the first course."

"Aren't you going to have some?"

"I am your servant tonight," he said.

"You mean you'll do anything I want?"

"Yes. Anything."

"Mmmm. That certainly gives me something to think about," Aisha said. "Kind of a change in attitude for you, isn't it?" She asked the question playfully, but his answer was utterly serious.

"Yes, it is," he said. "I got kind of a second chance at life yesterday. I decided in this life I'd be a nicer person."

"You were always a nice person," Aisha said with feeling.

"Not always to you, though," Christopher said. "As of tonight that's changed."

"And now you'll do whatever I want?"

"Well, for tonight, anyway," he said.

"Then you'd better kiss me," Aisha said.

He leaned down and kissed her for a very long time, a time

that banished every memory of cold and left Aisha wondering whether the all-body tingle she was feeling came from the tiny sip of champagne.

He straightened up.

"Don't go," she breathed.

"Hey, I have a risotto going in the kitchen," he said. "Even for you I don't ruin a risotto."

"Risotto? You mean like that Rice-a-Roni stuff?"

His look was one of pure horror. "Aisha, because I love you I'm going to forget you said that."

"Um, would you say that again?" Aisha said.

He looked puzzled. "You mean 'risotto'?"

"You know what I mean."

He came back to her. And then he knelt beside her, bringing his face level with her own. "You mean, 'I love you'?"

"Yes. That was it."

"I do love you, Eesh. I was slow to figure it out, but now that I have, I promise never to forget it."

Friday Night

Nina lay in her bed and talked to Benjamin on the phone for half an hour. While she talked, she drew in her sketchbook. After they had talked for half an hour, it took fifteen more minutes to say good night. Benjamin had sounded distracted but not depressed. Distracted was good in Benjamin—he liked to have things to think about. After she hung up the phone, Nina lay awake in bed with the lights out for a while, playing a CD he had loaned her. It was baroque guitar, not exactly her usual thing, but Benjamin liked it and she wanted to understand everything about him. When she finally turned it off, she had to resist a powerful urge to call him back. Instead she told the darkness again that she loved him and went to sleep.

Claire lay against her mountain of carefully arranged pillows and read a book called *The Last Wilderness*. It was about Antarctica. It was Claire's goal to go to Antarctica when she'd finished college. It was the greatest place on earth to study weather at its most severe. The first year she'd stay just for the austral summer, maybe at Palmer base or McMurdo. Then, with more experience, she'd get to winter over. As far from civilization as a human being could get. As cold, hostile, and alien an environment as could be found. She had turned a dozen pages of the book before she realized she hadn't retained any of what she'd read. Her mind wasn't on Antarctica. It was on Jake, not far but very near. Simple, straightforward, never subtle, not even especially intelligent Jake. Almost a dumb jock, really. Not especially handsome to her eye, or particularly sexy. Just a dumb jock she wished loved her.

Aisha tried to sleep but couldn't, not even after the big meal and the champagne. The meal had been followed by what seemed like hours of long, slow, lingering kisses that had left her buzzing and giddy. Christopher said he had changed, but fortunately there were some things about him that hadn't changed at all, and the memory of those things kept her in a drifting, half-sleeping, half-waking state, smiling into the dark, sighing into her pillow. It was really Aisha who had changed, she realized. What had happened to the girl who dismissed moony-eyed romanticism as juvenile? What had happened to Aisha-like-a-rock, the girl who couldn't be distracted by mere guys from the more important issues of life? She seemed to have completely forgotten what those more important issues might be. The important issue now was that in a few hours Christopher would come by on his rounds and she would get to see him again.

Zoey fell straight asleep, exhausted. She woke after an hour and lay staring up at the ceiling. She'd had a dream. She didn't remember the details, but it had left her feeling sad and defenseless against her emotions. She wanted her old life back. She wanted her father and mother together in the next room. She wanted to erase what she had heard and learned, and especially what she had seen. She wanted to forget her mother screaming hysterical accusations at her bedroom door. She wanted to forget the image of her father in his apartment, looking like he'd had his heart torn out. She wanted to go back to being the girl who smiled more and laughed more and feared for nothing. The girl who collected quotes and wrote her endless first chapter of her never-to-be-finished romance novel. And, as incongruous as it was to feel this way, she wanted to wake up like she had that morning, with her head resting on Lucas's chest, to hear his heart beating and feel his arm around her.

Zoey

I read a quote by Oscar Wilde. I used to collect quotes and post them over my desk in the dormer because I thought that way I would learn to be wise and understanding. But this quote just shows what a silly idea that is. Oscar Wilde said "Children begin by loving their parents: after a time they judge them; rarely, if ever, do they forgive them."

It was so right on target with what has been going on in my own life. I had loved my parents. Then I had judged them. Now I have no desire to forgive them. But the problem is that Wilde was being humorous. He was a sarcastic, ironic man who said many very clever things that were designed to make people laugh and say, oh, that Oscar, he's so witty.

For him it was a laugh; for me it's just the truth. Nothing funny about it. I will never forgive my parents, especially my mother, for what they did. I know I'm supposed to be all mature and reasonable and understand that they are just people, after all. Just people who occasionally screw up. But they aren't just people. They're my parents. Wait, forget that. Just say that they are parents, period. That means they have to deal with being parents. And that means they have to make sure their kids have a family. And if that gets in the way of what they want, too bad.

My mom told me I might be sorry one day for the way I
had judged her. But no, I don't think so. See, I'm living with
the results. I'm the one whose family is screwed up. I'm the one
who had to go visit her father in his pathetic little apartment.
Why should I forgive?

I will get on with my life, I've decided that. I will do the best
I can not to let this mess me up, but forget about forgiveness.

TEN

ZOEY CALLED AISHA AT NINE forty-five on Saturday morning and announced that she had a shopping mission to perform. By ten forty-five the two of them were dressed and pounding on the door of the Geiger home. Claire answered, looked them over, and refused their invitation. They found Nina in her room, drawing on a sketch pad, headphones blasting Jack White so that she hadn't heard their knocking. In a small, distracted voice she was singing along to the song.

Zoey and Aisha crept in and without warning jumped on her bed. Nina tore the earphones from her head.

"You two are going to give me a heart attack!" Nina yelled. "I could have peed on myself."

Aisha grabbed the sketch pad and whistled. Nina jumped up, looking horrified, and yanked the pad away again. "Hey, you can't look at that."

"What was it?" Zoey asked Aisha.

Aisha batted her lashes coyly. "It looked like a drawing of someone we all know."

"Hmm. A *male* someone?" Zoey asked, wonderfully entertained by the way Nina was blushing.

"A cute male someone," Aisha confirmed. *"With* sunglasses, but *without* shirt. Also, small heart in the corner with the names Nina and Benjamin in it. Very junior high, although the drawing was pretty good."

Zoey smiled at Nina. "Where is the tough, unsentimental girl we all once knew?"

"I'm trying to develop my skill as an artist," Nina argued unconvincingly.

"And you just thought you'd start with boy nipples as a subject," Aisha teased. "When have you seen Benjamin without his shirt on, anyway? Seems kind of suspicious to me."

"When we all go swimming down at Big Bite," Nina said, now several shades redder than usual.

"And in your dreams, when you wake up going unh, unh, oh Benjamin, more, more, oh yes, Benjamin, oh yes, yes—" A pillow swung with some force interrupted Aisha's rendition. "Hey!"

"Don't make me use this again," Nina warned, holding the pillow like a weapon.

"It's okay," Aisha said. "I know love makes people do strange things. Like hitting people with pillows." She gave Nina a dirty look.

"Is there a reason why you two came by to torture me?" Nina demanded.

"I have a shopping mission," Zoey said solemnly.

"A shopping mission?" Nina echoed.

Zoey reached into her bag and pulled out a piece of paper. "Exhibit A: the list." She dug into her wallet and held up a credit card. "Exhibit B: my dad's MasterCard."

"Excellent," Nina said. "The mall zone?"

"We will crawl the mall," Aisha said.

"We will empty the mall," Zoey said. "By the time we're done, there will be no mall."

"What's the mission, anyway?" Nina asked as she shucked off her rumpled clothes and scrounged for new rumpled clothes on the floor of her closet.

"I went over to my dad's apartment again this morning, early. It's kind of not-very-decorated or set up, so we made out a list of stuff he needed."

Nina exchanged a look with Aisha. "That must have been kind of—what's the word?" Nina said.

"Awkward?" Aisha suggested. "Strange?"

"Yeah, at least," Nina said. She found a sweater and slipped it on over her head. When her head poked through she added, "Didn't it bother you a little?"

It had bothered her terribly, Zoey admitted to herself. She shrugged. "I'm trying to adjust, you know? It's pretty bad and all, but still, he needs towels and a scritchy thing for pots and pans and some curtains."

Aisha shook her head sadly and gave Zoey a doleful look.

"Stop it, you guys," Zoey said impatiently. "I'm trying to act like this is all perfectly normal."

Aisha shook her head again. "If my parents ever broke up, I'd feel like killing myself. Wait a minute," she added in alarm. "I didn't mean that. I mean, don't kill yourself or anything."

Zoey smiled. "Good thing you added that last part, Eesh, or I might have just run out and hanged myself."

"I guess you don't want to talk about it, huh?" Aisha said.

"What is there to talk about? People get divorced all the time. Look at all the kids at school whose parents are divorced."

"Easier to count the ones who *aren't*," Nina agreed. "Still, you know, I guess it's not something you think will happen to your own parents."

"No," Zoey said, staring blankly at Nina's desk.

Nina sounded uncomfortable and made a show of paying

attention to her hair in the mirror. "I mean, when my mom died it was like that. You always think that kind of thing happens to other people."

Zoey heard the quiver in Nina's voice, and it unleashed the emotions she'd worked so hard at suppressing all morning. "Damn. Here goes my makeup." She brushed away a tear.

Nina sat beside her on the bed and put her arm around her. "I know it doesn't help, but I'm really sorry this had to happen."

The tears came freely now and she realized that both her friends had their arms around her, and both of them were crying as well.

"God, Nina, your mom dies, my parents get divorced . . ." Zoey shook her head.

Aisha drew away. "I almost feel guilty," she said.

Zoey made a blubbering laugh. "It's okay, Aisha."

"Yeah, you're probably next," Nina said.

Zoey and Nina both began giggling through their tears. Aisha didn't find it nearly as funny, which just made Zoey laugh all the harder.

There was a knock on the door and Mr. Geiger stuck his head in. "Say, Nina, if you're going over . . . to . . . the . . . mainland—" He fell silent and stared uncertainly at the spectacle of three girls, tears streaming down their cheeks, taking turns giggling hysterically and sobbing pitifully. "Never mind." He closed the door quickly.

Lucas lay flat on his surfboard, riding the annoyingly gentle swell, waiting for one more half-decent wave and wondering whether his feet were frostbitten. He was just going to have to move to California or Hawaii someday. East Coast surf was never that great, and here in Maine it was almost impossible. He'd gotten about four decent waves in the two hours he'd been freezing out here. Four decent waves and the fifth had been a long time in coming, but if he wasn't mistaken, it was rolling in right now.

He turned toward the shore, judged the timing, and began paddling to match speed with the wave. The leading edge of the surge caught him and he was up, nimbly pulling his numb feet under him, standing, wobbling, fighting to stay up.

An outcropping of bleached granite was just ahead, marked by explosions of water. This was the fun part. He shifted his weight and cut right, against the grain, coming as close to the rock as he could, flying past, but so near he could almost have reached out and touched it.

The wave broke on the gravel shore and Lucas rolled off the board into the surf. He came up laughing happily and saw a figure standing on the beach, shaking his head in derisive amusement.

"The things you white boys will do for fun," Christopher said.

"You should try it sometime," Lucas said. He squeezed water back out of his hair.

"Pretty weak waves, aren't they?"

Lucas nodded. "Yeah, but see, I add the extra element of playing tag with the rocks. I could easily have had my brains bashed out."

"Then it all makes sense," Christopher agreed. "You up for something?"

"What?" Lucas began peeling off his wet suit and putting on his warm, dry clothes.

"There's a car I'm thinking of buying. I thought maybe since I know zip about cars you'd come look it over with me."

"A real car or an island car?"

"Island car. I just need it for delivering my papers in the morning. It's getting slightly cold for the bike. Plus I can use a car to make pickups for people at the ferry."

Lucas grinned. "Also, it's hard to use the backseat of a bike for making out."

"You forget, *I* have my own apartment."

"*You* forget—Aisha walked in on you there when you had

that other girl with you." He finished dressing and bundled his wet suit into a zipper bag.

"That's not going to be a problem in the future," Christopher said.

Lucas looked at him more closely. He'd seen that look before. On himself, for one. "So you and Aisha are all straightened out now?"

Christopher's grin was part smugness, part dreaminess, part memory. "Mmmm, definitely." He sighed, grinned wider, then sighed again. "We've decided just to make it a thing between us only. I mean, you know, just see each other."

"Christopher, you're too much of a dog to be serious."

"Things change," Christopher said.

"Sometimes for the better, sometimes for the worse," Lucas said. He tossed Christopher his bag. "I'll carry the board." They started across the beach, climbing up to the road.

"Yeah, we're practically an old, boring, stable couple now, like you and Zoey," Christopher teased.

"Well, I don't know how stable Zoey and I are," Lucas said. Surfing, even bad surfing on an indifferent ocean, always drove every other concern out of his mind. He'd started years earlier, when it had been an escape from his father, and in a way from his own confused, angry mind. Now it was like he was walking back into reality.

"Maybe you should back off a little," Christopher suggested. "You know, you keep pushing Zoey, she'll just get more stubborn."

Lucas laughed. "Says the voice of experience. It's not about that. It's not about sex."

"It's not?"

"This part of it isn't about sex," Lucas clarified. "Okay, it's about sex in a way, but it's not because I've been trying to pressure her or anything. It's more about . . . something else."

Christopher leered. "*Who's* the something else?"

Lucas looked around guiltily. "You can't tell Aisha, all right?"

Christopher stopped. They had reached the edge of town, and Lucas leaned his board against a tall wood fence. "Tell Dr. Shupe," Christopher said. "Just because I can't be a hound anymore doesn't mean I go around telling male secrets to members of the opposite sex."

"See, I was pissed at Zoey because of, you know—"

"Oh, yeah, I know." He wiggled his eyebrows suggestively.

"I was also pissed because I saw her hugging Jake. Which Claire also saw. But neither of us, me or Claire I mean, neither of us knew about this whole thing with Zoey's mom and Jake's dad and all this divorce crap, so we were just pissed off because it looked like Zoey and Jake were . . ." Lucas trailed off and

124

took a deep breath. He scrabbled his wet hair violently with both hands. He focused on a rough patch on the wax coating of his surfboard.

"Don't go stupid on me," Christopher said impatiently.

"Look, I was mad at Zoey, Claire was mad at Jake, we ended up going for a drive . . ." He picked at the patch of peeling wax.

"You and *Claire*?" Christopher's jaw actually dropped open. "You and Claire? Wow. Huh. So, what did you do?"

Lucas waved a hand dismissively. "Made out a little."

"Kissing?"

"Uh-huh."

"Tongue?"

Lucas nodded.

"Were any buttons or zippers involved?"

Lucas shrugged noncommittally.

"Little tiny snaps?"

"We didn't like do *it* or anything," Lucas said, putting an end to the inquiry.

"Does Zoey know?"

"Yeah," Lucas said sarcastically, "I went straight to her house and told her the whole thing in complete detail."

Christopher looked at him with a mixture of envy and pity.

"You are so screwed, boy, if she ever finds out."

"I thought maybe I *should* tell her. I mean, you know, get it all out there. I think she'll let it go," he added, sounding unconvincing even to himself.

Christopher sneered. "Yeah, right. You must have gotten salt water in your brain, man. Check it out—her parents are getting divorced because her father was screwing around like twenty years ago, right? And her mother was doing payback with Mr. McRoyan. Now along comes Lucas. Lucas *thinks* Zoey was screwing around with Jake, so Lucas tries a little payback with Claire. You see any problem there, Lucas?"

"It's not *exactly* the same," Lucas said weakly.

"Very, very close, dude. If you think Zoey is going to be all forgiving about you and Claire Geiger in the backseat of her daddy's Mercedes . . . man, you are dumb."

[1] Flyer

You came back.

[2] Weather Girl

I didn't have anything else to do. Nothing on TV on Saturday afternoon.

[1] Flyer

I'm glad you came. I soloed this morning. Meaning I took my first flight without an instructor.

[2] Weather Girl

Congratulations. Weren't you nervous?

[1] Flyer

A little. If I had crashed, it would have been very embarrassing. My father was a naval aviator. Now he flies for United.

[2] Weather Girl

So I guess flying's in your blood, huh?

[1] Flyer

My dad wanted me to do it. But actually it turns out I do enjoy it a lot.

[2] Weather Girl

Can I ask you a slightly personal question?

[1] Flyer

Sure. I may even answer.

[2] Weather Girl

Your dad flies commercial airlines but you live in Manchester?

[1] Flyer

See, I knew you were smart. He flies out of Boston. My mom and my dad are separated.

[2] Weather Girl

Sorry. I have a friend going through that now. Actually, two friends, her and her brother.

[1] Flyer

Tell them it does get to seem more normal after a while. Not like it's no big deal, exactly, but it does get more normal, having your mother in one place, your father somewhere else.

How are they doing, your friends?

[2] Weather Girl

I don't really know.

[1] Flyer

You mean they don't want to talk about it?

[1] Flyer

Are you still there, WG?

[2] Weather Girl

I'm here.

[1] Flyer

Is something the matter?

[2] Weather Girl

No. I was just thinking.

[1] Flyer

What were you thinking?

[2] Weather Girl

I don't know how my friends feel about this divorce because I don't know how they feel about anything. I didn't ask. And I'm not exactly the person everyone comes to with their problems. I don't know why I should be telling you this.

[1] Flyer

Because I'm just a line of type on a computer screen, WG. I'm a safe person to talk to.

[2] Weather Girl

I guess that's it.

[1] Flyer

So, not very popular, huh?

[2] Weather Girl

Actually, I guess I am popular in some ways. It's just not something I care about. I mean, I have friends; they just don't open up to me very much.

[1] Flyer

Do they think you'll disapprove?

[2] Weather Girl

No. I guess they just don't think I'm very sympathetic. Or maybe they think I'll use things they tell me for my own advantage.

[1] Flyer

You're very complicated, aren't you?

[2] Weather Girl

You could say that.

[1] Flyer

I like complicated.

[2] Weather Girl

Thanks. I have to go now.

[1] Flyer

You have to?

[2] Weather Girl

Have to get ready for tonight.

[1] Flyer

Oh. Major date?

[2] Weather Girl

A date. I don't know how major.

[1] Flyer

Just my luck; you have a boyfriend.

[2] Weather Girl

For now. We'll see.

[1] Flyer

That sounds interesting, but I guess we'll talk about that another day. By the way, my name is Sean.

[1] Flyer

Still there, or did you already sign off?

[2] Weather Girl

I was deciding whether I should give you my name. But I realized you wouldn't even know if it was my real name. So: it's Claire.

[1] Flyer

Claire. Perfect. It's exactly right.

[2] Weather Girl

Maybe that's not my real name.

[1] Flyer

No, I think it is.

[2] Weather Girl

Why?

[1] Flyer

Because I think you want to be sincere with me.

[2] Weather Girl

Sincerity is not the first thing people who know me think of when they hear my name mentioned.

[1] Flyer

All the more reason for you to want to be sincere with me.

[2] Weather Girl

I like the name Sean.

[1] Flyer

I like the name Claire. Even if it isn't your real name.

[2] Weather Girl

I have to go.

[1] Flyer

Bye.

[2] Weather Girl

And that is my name, by the way.

[1] Flyer

Good-bye, Claire. Tomorrow?

Weather Girl has signed off . . .

ELEVEN

"NINA, GET YOUR FACE OUT of the mirror," Claire demanded. She struck a three-quarter profile and checked the effects of the foundation on her cheekbones. Then turned and checked the other side. She was in a bra and panties, while Nina wore a robe. *Claire's* robe, of course, lifted from the hook on the back of the bathroom door.

"It's my mirror, too." Nina leaned into Claire, pushed her, and captured several additional inches of the bathroom mirror.

"By the way, excellent cosmetic technique," Claire said snidely. "You could quit school and get a job preparing corpses for burial." Whatever had happened to the good old days when Nina spent Saturday nights lurking in the house watching *Game of Thrones*, and Claire had the bathroom to herself?

"Preparing corpses? Could I practice on you?" Nina casually swiped Claire's mascara.

"Don't *touch* my mascara, Nina. That's mine. Damn it, Nina, you always get the applicator all gummed up." Claire rolled her eyes and made a little guttural noise in her throat that was a signal of exasperation.

"I'm thinking about getting my nose pierced," Nina said, looking at herself critically, a picture that included the ubiquitous Lucky Strike, already stained with dark lipstick.

"Nose piercing is out," Claire said. "Lip piercing is much cooler."

"No way. Where did you hear that?"

"It was in *Seventeen*," Claire lied smoothly. "What you do is pierce both lips, upper and lower. Then you put one earring through both holes."

Nina made a face. "Oh, very cute, Claire."

"Is there some reason you can't go buy your own makeup?" Clair asked irritably. "Is there some reason you have to use mine?"

Nina shrugged. "You have better stuff."

"That's because I don't buy mine in five-gallon jugs at the discount drugstore," Claire said, snatching back her blusher. She made a second grab for her mascara, but Nina was too quick.

"I can't deal with buying makeup at the department stores in the mall," Nina said. "Those Clinique girls scare me. White coats, plastic faces, unnatural thinness." She shuddered. "I see them and I start thinking *Invasion of the Bodysnatchers*. Like they're selling beauty products that contain microscopic organisms that take over your mind. I mean, let me ask you—have you ever seen a Clinique girl eat? Aliens never eat, Clinique girls never eat. Coincidence?"

"Nina, why are you here? You're going out with Benjamin, who couldn't care less what your face looks like. Fortunately for you," she added.

"Hey, let me ask *you* something. Why would you wear a bra like that? I mean, doesn't the lace itch?"

"I'm going to a party. Some people believe it's a nice idea to dress up for a party. Others," she added dryly, "believe in wearing clown makeup and disguising themselves as street people."

"But who's going to see a bra? Unless there's something going on I don't know about?"

"Nina, there is so much going on that you don't know about I wouldn't know where to start," Claire said. She made another grab for the mascara and this time caught it. "Aha!"

"I'm just saying if no one is going to see it, why not wear something comfortable?"

"Like your Doc Marten's steel-tipped bras and your Woolworths' ten-for-a-dollar pull-'em-up-to-your-ribs panties?"

"Does Doc's make bras now? Damn, I didn't know," Nina said.

"You know, the Felixes' house is pretty big, so maybe we could agree to stay on different floors all night."

"I thought maybe Benjamin and I would just follow you and *Joke* around all night. Are you still going with him, by the way? Aisha said she saw you on the stairs the other day at school giving him the evil eye. I explained it was the only kind of eye you have."

"Would I be going to this party with him tonight if we weren't still seeing each other?" Claire answered evasively.

"I just thought after he and Louise—" Nina let the implication hang.

So. Wonderful. Now it was common knowledge that Jake had slept with Louise Kronenberger. Claire had the strange experience of watching her own face in the mirror as she mastered her emotions. A twitch in the muscles of her jaw. A coldness in the narrowing of her eyes. "I decided to give him a chance to make it up," Claire said smoothly. "You should be grateful."

"Why should *I* be grateful?"

"Because I don't know all that many guys, really. Jake, Christopher, Lucas . . . Benjamin. If I broke up with Jake, I might have to take one of *them*." She turned a cool, confident stare on Nina. "And Benjamin and I always did get along well."

She'd fully intended the remark to be hard, and even mean, to warn Nina off the topic of Louise permanently. It was a nice little threat that would exploit Nina's insecurity with guys, and Nina's lingering sense of inferiority. It should have backed Nina off like the warning of a rattlesnake.

Except that Nina just laughed. Not a fake-tough laugh, but a genuine, not-worried laugh. "Go ahead and try, Claire. Anytime you want." Then she laughed again.

Claire was startled. She actually took a step back before recovering her composure. "Confident, aren't you?" she said lamely.

Nina nodded. "Yes. See, I don't manipulate Benjamin like you do Jake, so I actually know how he *really* feels. He loves me. I love him."

Claire stopped herself just short of saying *oh yeah?*

Was it her imagination or had Nina grown taller lately? There was definitely something new there. She was still weird Nina, still the annoying, occasionally bizarre Nina. Still the ludicrous unlit cigarette, the permanent bad hair day, the defiantly bad taste in clothing. And yet a different Nina, to be so confident about a guy.

Especially since Claire was confident of so little.

She tried to come up with a suitably clever, biting comeback, but ended up just handing Nina a tissue. "Here," she said. "Your lipstick's smeared there."

✦ ✦ ✦

Lucas waited and watched like a hawk from the living room of his house. He checked his watch. Seven twenty-five. The ferry was at seven forty, and Aisha hadn't walked past. And yet it was certain that Aisha would pass his house on her way down to meet Christopher and the rest of the gang at the ferry. Christopher intended to surprise them all, especially Aisha, with the truly awful car he'd bought that afternoon.

Except Aisha was notoriously late for everything and she might come tearing by at the last minute at a dead run, which would be no good since he really wanted to talk to her before she saw Zoey.

He really wanted to talk to Aisha. Aisha had seen him on the ferry with Claire on Thursday night. Nothing necessarily fatal there; after all, there were a hundred good reasons why he might have stayed late on the mainland and ended up taking a late ferry home. Same with Claire. There was just the one ferry, and if they had each had separate, perfectly sensible reasons for staying late in Weymouth, well, then, they'd have had no choice but to take the same ferry home.

Right?

Except that talking to Christopher that afternoon had made him nervous. Christopher was of the definite opinion that Zoey would not be understanding. Not at all. And with them all at the same party tonight, crossing on the ferry together, Aisha might just casually blurt something about Thursday night.

Lucas didn't want to have his life ruined by a casual blurt if he could help it.

There she was! Walking past, swinging her arms nonchalantly, wearing sneakers and carrying a pair of leather shoes in her hand, whistling as she went. He jumped up and tore for the door, closing it carefully behind him. His father was a commercial fisherman and was already asleep in preparation for a day that began in the early hours of the predawn.

"Aisha! Hey!"

"Lucas." She stopped and tilted back to give him a critical look. "Looking good, looking good. Haircut?"

"No," he said, panting a little from his burst of speed. "Decided to use a brush."

"Radical," Aisha said.

"Looking forward to the party?"

"I went the last two years," Aisha said. "A cross between a good soap opera and a boxing match."

"Missed them," Lucas said. "What with, you know, being in Youth Authority."

"Too bad. You can't miss Richie Felix's birthday parties. He's kind of a creep, but his parties are great."

Aisha seemed in a much better mood than Lucas had seen her in lately. Downright care-free. Obviously, what Christopher had said was true—the two of them were getting along well. Over the previous few days, especially, it had seemed to Lucas that Aisha had been acting snappish and preoccupied. Come to think of it, she and Christopher had looked half-wasted that night on the ferry. He fell into step with her.

Now he remembered. How many days ago had it been? Hadn't she asked him if he'd helped Christopher buy a gun? Yes, she had asked him that, but he'd been too into his own problems with Zoey to pay much attention—beyond denying it, of course.

"So, Aisha, everything work out okay with you and Christopher the other night? You know, Thursday?" he asked, taking a shot in the dark.

Aisha froze and stared hard at him. "What do you know about that?"

He shrugged.

"It all worked out okay," Aisha said tersely. She pursed her lips and shook her head regretfully. "You know, it would be cool if we could all just kind of forget it, you know? I mean, Christopher's past it now. He doesn't want to talk about it."

Obviously, Lucas noted. He'd spent several hours with Christopher that morning and the dude had said nothing.

Lucas nodded sagely. "Cool by me. Everyone's entitled to a mistake without it having to become gossip of the week." Did that sound too blatantly self-serving?

"Did you tell Zoey about it?" Aisha asked.

"No. Did you?"

"She's a good friend and all," Aisha said, "but this is kind of major stuff. I mean, Christopher could have been arrested, and I don't want people thinking he's some gun-carrying nut. He's not," she added fiercely. "He was tempted, but everyone gets tempted."

"No prob," Lucas said. "As far as I'm concerned I don't know anything." *More true than you know, Aisha,* he added silently, although he was getting some ideas. "In fact, I never even saw you guys on the ferry Thursday night. You weren't there, *I* wasn't there."

Aisha smiled and gave him a quick hug. "You're a good guy, Lucas."

Actually, I'm a low-rent jerk pulling this crap, he reflected. *But whatever it takes.* Christopher was right—this was not the time in Zoey's life when she was going to be understanding about him making out with Claire. Definitely not. But so far this had worked out very nicely. Now, if the rest of the evening just went as smoothly, he'd go on being a happy young man.

TWELVE

ON THE FERRY RIDE FROM the island to Weymouth they all sat together like the old days, a circle of friends, spread haphazardly around a big part of the upper deck.

Still, Nina realized, things had changed. In the old days she would have been the extra tagalong. She and sometimes Aisha, back before she'd met Christopher. Zoey would have been with Jake, Claire with Benjamin, Lucas . . . well, Lucas would still have been in the Youth Authority. And Nina would have come along as a sort of portable class clown to make jokes and then later to disappear when the couples started making out.

She slipped her left hand into the pocket of Benjamin's jacket. He smiled. She smiled too, foolishly. He found her hand and entwined his fingers with hers. They sat there, some distance apart from the rest, listening to the others talk, Nina stealing secret glances at Benjamin and wishing they weren't with the group because she very, very badly wanted to kiss him.

"We could kind of slip away downstairs," Benjamin whispered.

Nina's smile widened. Evidently Benjamin was thinking along her same lines. Was it true that people in love could read each other's minds? "What would we do down there?"

He shrugged. "Discuss the situation in the Middle East?"

"I'd like that," Nina said huskily. "You know how much I enjoy international relations."

"I guess the others would think it was tacky," Benjamin said, deeply regretful. "It's getting harder and harder being around you."

"Oh, really?" Nina snickered.

Benjamin laughed. "You know what I mean," he whispered. "Stop that," he chided sternly when she kept giggling. "You know perfectly well what I meant was that it's hard being with you and trying to act in a decent, civilized way when what I really want to do is pretty much just make out constantly."

"Me too," Nina said.

"Yeah."

"Uh-huh."

"Hmmm." A sigh.

"The moon came out, by the way," Nina reported, tilting her head back. "It's about half full, shining in a circle with clouds all around. If you want to know precisely what *kind* of clouds, you'll have to ask Claire."

"I don't need to know that badly."

"Good answer," Nina said. It confirmed for her the confidence she'd expressed to Claire. Benjamin *was* over Claire. Really and truly.

"You look beautiful in the moonlight," Benjamin said. "I mean, as I imagine you. The breeze lifting the ends of your hair, your eyes deep in shadow, mysterious but with the light from the stars and the moon reflected there, your lips—"

Nina cleared her throat. "Claire and Zoey and Aisha would think we were being disgusting if we went downstairs and made out."

"Yes. All that stuff is supposed to come at the *end* of the date. I mean, if all we do on a date is kiss and so on we might as well have stayed home."

"You're right. Let's swim back right now."

Benjamin shook his head. "Actually, I have kind of a plan for tonight, if you don't mind."

"A plan?"

"Just a little side trip before we hit the party. It's not exactly a date-type thing. More like a detective-type thing."

"Oooh. Cool. Then afterward?" Nina asked.

"After the detective part comes the romance part. That's how it works."

"And . . . and of course the romance part, that will be the *hard* part." Nina began giggling again. "I tried not to say it, but I couldn't stop myself."

"I'm very shocked, Nina, really. You are so immature and childish," Benjamin said. "And if I don't get to kiss you within about eight seconds, I may die."

"Downstairs. You go first. I'll follow in a minute so it will look casual."

Zoey huddled deeper down in the neck of her sweater and drew her hands up into the sleeves of her coat. It was freezing on the ferry, and her behind was numb from contact with the metal bench. Lucas, Jake, and Christopher were talking about cars, and had been ever since Christopher had revealed his new pride and joy, a car that was frightening even by island standards.

She and Claire were studiously avoiding any conversation at all. Naturally, Claire hadn't apologized for her extraordinary outburst on the stairs Friday, because Claire had almost never been known to apologize for anything. Which left talking only to Aisha, and Aisha was in some kind of waking dream state, humming to herself and occasionally sighing and saying things like "Wow, it's such a beautiful night."

"It's mostly just about horsepower," Jake said.

"I'm just saying with the Viper you've got the horsepower,

sure, but that's not the only important thing," Lucas said.

"I'd still rather have a 'Vette," Christopher said.

Claire was looking morose, Zoey observed. She was paying no attention to the guys and instead just focused on some indefinite point in midair. Like she was a million miles away.

She wasn't even paying attention to Nina and Benjamin, who were sitting a little distance away and periodically erupting in giggles.

Zoey couldn't believe how happy Benjamin seemed. How could he? Was he immune to all that was happening to their own family? It almost made her angry; in fact, it did annoy her. It wasn't right. There should be a period of mourning for the death of their family.

"Zero to sixty in less than four seconds," Lucas said.

"That's like you're standing still and then one one-thousand, two one-thousand, three one-thousand, four one-thousand, and boom, you're doing sixty," Christopher offered.

"That would be so excellent," Jake opined.

Zoey noticed that Claire had focused on Nina and Benjamin. There was a bemused expression on her face that gave way slowly to an expression of sadness.

Nina had evidently made some joke, because now Benjamin was laughing, and Zoey bridled at the laughter. How could Benjamin be so cold about what was happening to their parents?

To their family? He'd been affected by the spectacle of their father weeping yesterday, but he'd shaken it off in a way that Zoey could not.

Benjamin got up and made his way toward the stairs. Nina fidgeted in a bad parody of indifference for all of about five seconds, then sprang up and went after him.

Claire rolled her eyes and happened to meet Zoey's gaze.

"That was subtle," Claire said dryly.

Zoey managed a weak smile of acknowledgment.

"True love," Claire said with profound sarcasm. "Can't beat it." She looked at Jake, who was entirely engaged with Lucas and Christopher, then looked away again with the sad expression Zoey had noticed earlier.

Zoey looked at Lucas. It hadn't been long since she and Lucas were as nauseating as Benjamin and Nina were now. What had happened to change that?

He had wanted to push their relationship further than she'd been willing to go. That had been the start of it. But she was to blame, too. For neglecting him while she'd become preoccupied with the drama of her parents. He'd asked her—had it only been a couple of days ago?—when she'd spent a sleepless night, still reeling from the worst of the blowup between her parents, whether she still loved him. And she'd said she didn't know.

Yes, there was blame enough to go around. She slipped her

cold hand over his. He turned away from Jake and looked at her in surprise. She smiled. He squeezed her hand.

At that moment Jake fell silent. His eyes met Zoey's and Zoey looked away. Claire turned sharply to look out at the dark sea. And floating up from the lower deck came a pearly laugh, suddenly smothered, then renewed an octave lower and quieted again.

"What are we looking at?" Benjamin asked.

"We are looking at a four-story building, Benjamin. Red brick, to be precise. On the bottom floor is a musical instrument shop called Strings. Also a little restaurant or coffee shop or something called Downtown Deli," Nina said.

"I'm guessing it's a delicatessen, then."

"I said it was a restaurant, Benjamin," Nina said. "Don't get all technical on me when you haven't even told me what we're doing here."

She watched his mysterious smile grow wider. He'd been acting strange ever since they'd gotten off the ferry and left the others behind. "We are in search of lost sisters," he said.

"Zoey? She's down at . . . Oh. Really?"

He nodded. "I was able to find out her address. This is the place, unless you're playing tricks on me and we're actually standing outside a McDonald's. 729 Independence, apartment

402. She must live on the top floor."

Nina looked up at the highest row of windows. "Four, five, six windows. Two have lights on."

"You see an entrance anywhere?"

Nina looked around. "Maybe it's around the back. No, wait, there it is. It's just a little dark, so I didn't see it at first."

"We need a story," Benjamin said. He stroked his chin thoughtfully.

"What kind of a story?"

"A story for why we're wandering around in this apartment building, in case anyone sees us."

"We don't want to just tell people the truth?"

Benjamin pushed his shades back up on his nose. "Not yet. I want to spy out the situation first."

"Cool. I've never spied before," Nina said. "It adds an edge of excitement to my life."

"Mmmm. We say we're looking for Barney and Betty."

"Who are Barney and Betty?"

"You know, the Rubbles. They live next door to Fred and Wilma. But we say they live at 739 Independence. Seven *three* nine. That way, if anyone questions us they'll just go, 'hey, you're in the wrong building, this is seven *two* nine.'"

"Barney and Betty. Cool. Now what?"

"Now we go in. You lead the way."

Nina guided his hand to her arm. "You know what we could do, if anyone asks us what we're doing. I could pretend to be blind, too. Then they'd say 'no wonder you're lost, it's a case of the—"

"'—blind leading the blind.' Uh-huh."

Nina led him up to the doorway and gave Benjamin a dirty look, which, naturally, was lost on him. "You know how long I've waited to be able to use that line? The blind leading the blind. For years I've waited for the right setup." She tried the door and it opened. Inside, a stairwell leading straight up. "Stairs."

They climbed carefully. "Okay, we're on the second floor. Swing around right and we have another flight."

"What's it like in here? Smells like someone's been cooking with curry. I hate curry."

"What's curry taste like?"

"Like curry, Betty," Benjamin said.

"Very funny, Barney. Okay, swing right again and we have still more stairs."

"Someone's coming," Benjamin hissed. "I just heard a door open up on the next floor. Run up ahead and see if you can tell which door. I'm going back down to the second floor."

Nina raced up the rest of the stairs and craned her neck around the corner. A guy and a girl were just coming out of one of the apartment doors. The guy was cute in a scruffy garage-band kind of way. He had major Patrick Stump hair. Nina's first thought on seeing the girl was that she looked familiar. Probably she'd seen her around on the streets. Nina went past this area twice a day on school days.

The girl spotted her. "Looking for something?" she asked, sounding a bit belligerent.

"Um, yeah. The uh, um, Fred and Barney. I mean, Barney and what's her name. Wilma. Betty. Barney and Betty."

"Not on this floor," the guy said sarcastically. "Try Bedrock."

He and the girl brushed past. "Yeah, Bedrock, ha ha," Nina said. "They hear that all the time."

The couple disappeared down the stairs. Nina ran over to the apartment they'd just left. 402. So, it *was* Benjamin and Zoey's half-sister. Unless Benjamin had the wrong apartment. Or unless these were people who'd been visiting the people who actually lived in the apartment.

She waited till the couple was down the stairs, then ran after them. She found Benjamin at the far end of the second-story hallway, pretending to examine a fire extinguisher.

"Hey, it's them," Nina announced breathlessly. "At least I think it is."

"Where are they now?"

"Should be down to the street by now," Nina said.

Benjamin grinned. "Then the game's afoot!"

"A foot?"

"The game's afoot! Haven't you ever read Sherlock Holmes? Whenever something major's happening, Sherlock says it to Dr. Watson and off they go."

"The game's afoot!" Nina repeated.

"Except I'm Sherlock. So I get to say it. Let's go before they get away."

Nina led him quickly down the stairs and they burst out onto the street. Nina looked left and right, then spotted the couple walking away at an easy pace, arm in arm. "They're heading downtown, back toward Portside. Maybe half a block ahead of us."

"Okay, we follow. But try and be cool about it. Don't let us get too close."

"No prob, Sherlock." Fortunately, the Saturday night street traffic was fairly heavy, with the pedestrians growing thicker as they got closer to the fashionable Portside district.

"What does she look like?" Benjamin asked.

"I just saw her for a few seconds," Nina said. "Brown hair."

"I have brown hair," Benjamin said thoughtfully.

"No, you don't, you have blond hair," Nina said, lying automatically.

Benjamin sighed patiently.

"Okay, she has brown hair, a little lighter than yours. Lots of it, kind of a trashy, puffed-up do. Blue eyes, I think."

"Zoey has blue eyes," Benjamin observed thoughtfully.

"She's tallish. Dresses kind of bar-slutty, no offense if she is your half-sister. I'm seeing a very short mini and cowboy boots."

"You don't approve?"

"A mini with boots? Please. It's a major fashion *don't*. I think I read it in *Glamour*. Oops. They're stopping to look in a window. Here, sit." She pulled him down beside her on a wooden bench. "Look innocent. I have an idea." She grabbed his face and kissed him.

"That's how you look innocent?" he asked wryly.

"There they go. Up. Darn, I can't really see them now in the crowd."

"Damn."

"I'll continue leading you in the same direction they were going in," Nina said carefully. "But since I can't really see them . . . it's almost a case of the blind leading the blind. Ha!"

"Are you happy now?"

"Ha!"

THIRTEEN

"SHE TOLD ME TO WALK this way," Jake sang.

"Talk this wa-a-ay," Lucas chimed in.

Zoey and the rest heard the party before they had even turned the last corner onto the street, Aerosmith almost vibrating the pavement underfoot. The Felixes had a great three-story town house right in the Portside neighborhood. Loud music wasn't much of a problem because no one expected to be able to sleep on a Saturday night anyway.

"You know, Richie's a dork," Aisha pointed out, "but the boy does have cool parents."

"Cool?" Christopher said, disbelieving. "They're way past cool. They must be deaf."

"They won't be there," Zoey explained. "Richard has these parties a couple of times a year. His folks check into a hotel for the night and hire a bouncer to make sure things don't get out of hand."

"No way." Christopher laughed.

"A very strange family," Jake said, mercifully cutting short his singing career. They walked as a group up to the door and huddled on the steps. Jake rang the doorbell.

"Like anyone's going to hear the doorbell," Claire pointed out.

But the door opened, letting out a blast of music and revealing a man with a wild mane of blond hair and a build like a professional football player. Behind him was a tall, leggy woman with blue eyes and a skeptical, downturned smile.

"Hi," Zoey said brightly.

"Yeah, whatever," the man said sourly.

The two of them brushed past without another word and headed down the street.

"Looks like the bouncer just took off," Christopher said.

"No, they're Richie's parents," Zoey explained.

They had left the door conveniently ajar, so Jake led the way inside.

A dark entryway opened onto a hallway, which in turn ran past several rooms and eventually on to the kitchen at the back of the house. An open stairway led from the hallway.

In the entryway: people. On the stairs: people. In each of the rooms as Zoey made her way along the hallway: more people. Everywhere people, low lights, loud music, shouted conversation. The last room on the right held a bed piled four feet high with coats. The kitchen held a fifty-gallon Rubbermaid trash can filled with ice studded with bottles of Coke and Mountain Dew. There was a table loaded down with crackers, cheese, brownies, chips and dip, all fairly well destroyed.

Richie appeared suddenly behind Zoey, startling her.

"Thanks for coming!" he shouted.

Zoey nodded. "Wouldn't miss it."

"Hey, you seen my parents?"

"They just left." Zoey pointed back toward the door, hoping sign language would help.

"Excellent." He grabbed Tad Crowley, who was walking by. "Tad. The 'rents are out of here. Bring in the keg."

Zoey looked around for Lucas, but they had all been split up in the tide of bodies in motion, pulled away by friends or just the tidal surge. She saw Jake reach for a Coke.

"Brew's on its way," Richie told Jake.

Jake shook his head, and Richie shrugged and went off in pursuit of a girl Zoey didn't recognize.

Jake leaned close to Zoey in order to be heard. "I think I'd better be a good boy and stick to the legal stuff."

Zoey nodded.

"Where'd everyone go?"

Zoey shrugged. She tried an answer, but now it was Calvin Harris and the already loud music rose another notch. She leaned close to Jake, putting her hand on his muscular shoulder for balance. "I think I saw Aisha and Christopher heading upstairs. I don't know about the rest. Too dark to see."

"If *you* want a beer, go ahead," Jake said. His lips actually brushed Zoey's ear. Two junior guys came racing through and nearly bumped into Zoey. Jake pulled her out of the way, his hand casually on her waist. He didn't remove his hand. Zoey didn't take her own hand from Jake's shoulder.

"I don't drink very often," Zoey said.

Jake made a self-deprecating face. "I think I may have a problem with alcohol, you know? So I better play it safe. Last time I got drunk at a party I ended up . . ." He prudently let that drop. "Wouldn't want to do anything stupid. Or even say anything stupid."

"Everyone says stupid things," Zoey said dismissively.

For a frozen moment Jake's expression became somber. His serious dark eyes met hers with a look of confusion, hesitation. His mouth opened as if he were going to speak, then he clamped it shut, literally biting his lower lip.

Suddenly he drew his hand away. Just as quickly Zoey took her hand from his shoulder.

"Well, I guess I'd better go find Claire!" he shouted, no longer standing so near as to be heard easily.

"And me, Lucas. I mean, I'd better go find Lucas." She threaded her way from the kitchen and along the hallway, miming hellos as she went, pretending to be able to hear shouted greetings and shrugging at shouted questions. At the foot of the stairs she turned and looked back. Jake was alone, as if an invisible force field kept him apart from the crowd surrounding him. He was looking down, shaking his head slowly.

Zoey climbed the stairs and nearly ran into Lucas, who was coming down at the same moment.

"Hey, I was looking for you," he said.

"I was looking for you, too."

He took her arm and drew her back upward. "Come upstairs; it's a little less loud."

Zoey followed him up and the intensity of the music did diminish somewhat, at least enough that screaming was no longer necessary. Upstairs were several bedrooms feeding off a central hallway. One room reeked of pot smoke. Louise Kronenberger poked her head out, a joint hanging from her mouth. She held it out for Zoey.

"Don't think so, Louise," Zoey said.

Louise giggled happily. "Come on, Zoey, it might loosen you up. You might actually have fun."

Lucas crooked his finger at Zoey. "The relatively normal people seem to be down here."

Zoey bridled. Louise's snide remark about loosening up had rankled a little. Now Lucas was leading her where? To the boring room? To be with the normal people? She grabbed his arm and stopped him in the hallway.

"Am I boring, Lucas?"

He gave her a deprecating look. "Why, because you don't get high? I don't get high, either."

"I don't do lots of things," Zoey said.

Lucas shrugged dismissively, but Zoey noted he hadn't exactly denied what she was implying.

"I wonder sometimes if maybe you'd be happier with a girl who was more, you know—"

"More like Louise? I had a shot at Louise, remember? No big accomplishment, since basically every guy in school has a fair shot at Louise, but I blew her off."

"Okay, some other girl," Zoey said. "What if we're not right for each other?"

Lucas's smile disappeared. "What are you saying?"

"Nothing, I was just thinking maybe I kind of hold you back.

Maybe you'd be happier if I weren't your girlfriend." It had started as a teasing, nonserious conversation, but now it was deadly earnest.

"Zoey, I love *you*. Not some other girl." He glanced around self-consciously, lest some male overhear him.

"I love you, too, Lucas," Zoey said. She felt troubled, like she was sliding down a long, slippery slope, but she couldn't stop now. "But you must look at other girls sometimes."

"Of course I *look*," Lucas said. "Everyone *looks*. That doesn't mean anything."

"When you see other girls, don't you sometimes think, I'll bet she'd be easier to get along with than Zoey is?"

"Only when you're having PMS," Lucas said.

"I'm serious. Don't you think, I'll bet that girl would be more fun, or more cool, or maybe she's prettier, or maybe she'd, you know, have sex?"

Lucas's eyes narrowed. "Are you saying this because you're thinking about other guys?"

"Of course not."

"Like maybe you're thinking some other guy has more money or has a cool car or maybe this other guy wouldn't be trying to pressure me into sleeping with him?"

"We were talking about *you*," Zoey said impatiently. "About what you want."

"I want you," he said simply.

"Just me?" She looked searchingly at his face.

His eyes darted away, then returned to meet hers defiantly. "Just you, Zoey."

"It's important for me to know, Lucas. To be absolutely sure. I mean, sometimes people seem like everything's okay, like they're a happy couple and all that, then you find out that's not the way it was."

"You mean like your parents?"

Zoey nodded in mute acknowledgment. Of course that's what she meant, although she hadn't been thinking about it consciously.

"You know, maybe your dad really does still love your mom and she loves him. I mean, maybe it was just one of those things that happened."

"Just happened? My mother just happened to sleep with another man?"

"There was a lot of history there," Lucas pointed out. "She'd just found out your dad had a kid by some other woman nineteen years ago and never even told her. She was pissed. She wanted to get her pride back after the way your dad treated her."

"Yeah, she really has her pride now," Zoey sneered.

"People do stupid things they're sorry for later," Lucas said. He looked down at the floor and shook his head, reminding Zoey of Jake.

"Don't expect me to forgive her," Zoey said. "If two people supposedly love each other, they don't do things like that, betraying the other person behind their back."

"Maybe you're wrong," Lucas said earnestly. "Maybe that is the way people are."

"Then they're jerks," Zoey said harshly. "I would never do that to you."

"No, I guess you wouldn't."

"This looks serious," Christopher said, passing by.

Lucas looked relieved. "No, no, just talking."

"I lost Aisha in here somewhere."

"Here I am." Aisha appeared and wrapped her arms around Christopher from the back. "Let's go downstairs and dance. The DJ said he'd do some dance tunes."

"You guys want to come?" Christopher asked.

"Maybe in a little while," Lucas said.

"I guess I'm being kind of a drag, huh?" Zoey said. "Sorry. This whole divorce thing has kind of preoccupied me."

"I understand," Lucas said.

"We're not my parents," Zoey said. "I do understand that. I

mean, it's stupid to start being suspicious about everyone. Especially you," She slipped her arms around his sides and pressed against him.

Lucas kissed her.

FOURTEEN

"THE PORTSIDE TAVERN," NINA SAID. "They just went inside."

Benjamin paused to consider. "What's it like inside?"

"I've never been in there," Nina admitted. "Supposedly it's kind of funky. They serve food and all. Plus there's a band, I think."

"Maybe we wouldn't be too conspicuous." He didn't sound convinced.

"Yeah, a high school junior and a blind guy in the Portside Tavern, that wouldn't attract any attention," Nina said.

"Okay, look. How about if you park me somewhere and you go in. See what they're up to in there. Probably just drinking or whatever. Listening to music."

Nina felt a little nervous at the prospect of leaving Benjamin out on the street alone on a Saturday night, but there was no way to mention it that wouldn't just make him mad. "Okay. Do a one-eighty. About four steps. There's a bench."

She waited until Benjamin was seated, looking very casual behind his shades though she could see the tension in the way he crossed his legs. *Tense at being out alone on a rowdy street?* she wondered. More likely just excited by all the detective play-acting. That was Benjamin, she realized fondly. The boy did love a mystery he could pick at.

She went through the front door of the Portside. Fortu-nately, there was no bouncer since it was still early in the night and the big crowds wouldn't be along for an hour or so.

The room had a low ceiling and bare brick walls that made it feel like you were in someone's basement. There was no band, just recorded music. Bad music, Nina noted.

The restaurant area was partly full, but most of the people were crowded around the bar. Including Lara and her pre-sumed boyfriend, the guy with the hair. From the way the bartender greeted them, it was obvious they were known here. One of the cocktail waitresses went over and said hi to Lara. The boyfriend—Mr. Hair, as Nina thought of him—gave the waitress's butt an appreciative look.

Drinks appeared. Lara and Mr. Hair tossed them back like pros. Two more appeared. These went down just as quickly. Then Mr. Hair went off with the cocktail waitress in the direc-tion of the kitchen. Lara didn't seem at all concerned. In fact, she barely seemed to notice.

Nina realized she was standing around looking exposed and obvious. She decided to head toward the ladies' room like she was on a mission. As she passed by, Mr. Hair and the waitress emerged from the kitchen. The waitress went straight toward the bathroom, entering just behind Nina.

Now that she was in the bathroom, Nina decided she'd better look as normal as possible. She took one stall while the waitress took the other. While Nina made the experience as realistic as possible, she listened and heard small crackling sounds from the next stall—tin foil or plastic wrap maybe. Probably opening a tampon, she decided.

Then there was a sniffing sound, unusually prolonged. A sneeze. A curse. A long sniffing sound again.

Nina flushed and left quickly. Lara and Mr. Hair seemed to be ready to go. Both refused another drink from the genial bartender. Mr. Hair reached across and shook the bartender's hand. The bartender gave him a wink and went on about his business.

Nina fell into step a few feet behind the couple. Outside she found Benjamin on the bench, still looking very casual, calmly gazing around as if he was interested in the people passing by. It would have taken a close observer to notice that his gaze never exactly followed anyone or focused on anything especially interesting, but instead was frequently aimed at a section of blank wall.

"Let's go, Holmes," she hissed. "The game's feet are heading across the street."

"What did you find out?" Benjamin asked, taking her arm.

What had she learned? Nothing exactly, although she was having the beginning of a suspicion. "Not much. They had a couple of drinks. Mr. Hair—"

"Mr. Hair?"

"The boyfriend."

"Oh."

"Mr. Hair goes off with one of the waitresses for like a minute, then the waitress goes to the john, where she was either trying to inhale tampons or doing a couple lines of coke. Could be crank. Or it could be NeoSynephrine and she has a stuffed-up nose."

Benjamin nodded thoughtfully. "The way you describe it, it could be coincidence."

"Yeah, I know. Also, he shook the bartender's hand."

"A long handshake? A handshake that made you think 'hmm, there's something significant in that handshake'?"

"A handshake that made me think 'hey, that guy's slipping that bartender something he doesn't want anyone else to see.'"

"And they were both drinking, right?"

"Bada boom, straight down the throat, no waiting," Nina confirmed.

"Yeah. Interesting. Lara's only nineteen, supposedly. Shouldn't be able to drink in a bar like that. Unless she knows someone."

"Ah, excellent point, Sherlock."

"Where are we heading now?" Benjamin asked. "By my count we're just down from the Chickenlips Saloon."

"And they just went inside. I'm on them. Here, squat down."

"Squat down?" he echoed.

"Squat. You're reading the front page of the newspaper through the front of the machine."

Nina left him and ran to catch up. Here, unfortunately, the bouncer was already on duty, and there was no chance that Nina was going to pass for twenty-one. She rejoined Benjamin.

"Doorman," she explained.

"Damn." He stood up. "It doesn't matter. If they come out in less than ten minutes, we'll have a pretty good idea."

As it happened, they emerged in just over five minutes.

"Off we go," Nina said.

"One more try, after that we drop it," Benjamin said. "I mean, it's night and we're trailing a guy we think may be a dealer. Some people would say that's not all that brilliant."

"Lots of people would say that."

Benjamin frowned. "Wait, unless I'm way off, there aren't any more bars on this street. From here on up it's residential, isn't it?"

"Yeah. You guessed it."

"Well, well. What a coincidence."

Claire danced with Jake

Claire was a precise, elegant dancer, always carefully understated, never wild. She could stay on the beat, but she gave no impression that the music affected her on an emotional level. Possibly because it did not in fact affect her much one way or the other. For Claire, dancing was a duty, something she had to do, like saying hello to people or laughing politely at people's jokes or any of the countless other basically irrelevant things she had to do to get along. She was determined to do well since it was unthinkable that she would ever be a dweeb. And it was a part of that duty to project a certain subtle sexuality, and so she did that, too. Still, the impression she gave was of a person who would be every bit as pleased to be reading a book, which was literally true.

Jake danced with more grace than people expected of someone with so much muscle, with legs as hard and big around as fire hydrants and shoulders that seemed to extend an unnatural distance in either direction. There was grace, but sheer size limited his movements, so that he danced carefully, always aware of people around him who might not want to be struck by a carelessly swung arm. In his own mind he looked like a dancing bear straight out of the circus, but at least, as dancing bears went, he was one of the more gentle ones.

✦   ✦   ✦

Aisha danced with Christopher

Aisha was not exactly embarrassing as a dancer, but close to it. She believed that underneath it all, dance was surely somehow a mathematical exercise that could be figured out by means of formulas—foot goes here and hand goes there. Hip out as arm moves down. This would work for as much as thirty seconds at a time, before the system would break down and she would come to an almost complete stop before trying a new variation. Her usual expression was one of concentration, succeeded sooner or later by frustration.

Christopher danced like a fugitive from a club in Ibiza. He was all liquid, effortless control, not just responding to the music but instinctively anticipating it, knowing what came next, there before it happened. Inventive without being showy. Athletic without being extreme. In fact, he knew full well he could be much better, but there was nothing to be gained by making other people look bad. Especially people who thought dancing was secretly a form of algebra.

Zoey danced with Lucas

Zoey danced small, almost shyly. She was a good dancer, but not innovative or demonstrative. Mostly she did what others did, kept her eyes on Lucas or on the floor, because looking into someone's eyes when you were gyrating provocatively was dorky. She was sorry that Benjamin wasn't here, because when he danced people mostly paid attention to him, unable to believe he could be so cool without being able to see. At least Claire was dancing, which guaranteed that most of the guys would be looking at her and not at Zoey.

Lucas hated dancing with all his heart. If he could just never dance, he would be happy. Someday, when he was in a steady relationship and didn't have to do the whole dating thing anymore, he would simply stop. When he was married, he would never go dancing. Never. Not for money. Not with a gun to his head. But it was a basic part of high school dating life, and he didn't quite have the nerve to just say no. He was jealous of people like Nina, whom he'd seen dancing at homecoming. Nina could just spaz out, totally lost to reality while she was dancing. Lucas was trapped in reality. The reality that he felt like the largest, most obvious dweeb on the planet when he had to dance.

FIFTEEN

CLAIRE KNEW IT WAS PERFECTLY natural and normal and to be expected that eventually Jake would dance with Zoey. It would have been strange if he hadn't. They were friends, after all. Besides, everyone traded partners during the course of a party. Only the most insanely jealous couples got upset at seeing their dates dance with someone else. It was even to be expected that guys might flirt with other girls, or girls with guys. That was all a part of life, especially at a party.

The problem was that while Jake and Zoey danced, neither of them flirted. It was a strange thing to be upset over, Claire acknowledged privately, and yet she was upset.

Jake was behaving with unnatural rigidity around Zoey. He was stiff and formal, not a smile or a laugh. Yet when Zoey was distracted by a girl she knew and turned away from him for a moment, Jake's eyes were on her, following Zoey's every movement. Not the usual check-out-her-butt glance. Nothing that crude and harmless. Instead he looked at her with a wistful longing, the way a person looked at something he had loved and lost and wished he could have again.

The DJ played a slow song, Sam Smith's "Stay With Me." Claire almost laughed. Perfect. Zoey was with Jake, looking around nervously, like maybe she shouldn't do a slow dance with him. Jake was standing there awkwardly, big arms at his sides, looking half-hopeful, half-afraid.

At that moment Claire believed she might actually hate him. He so wanted to take Zoey in his arms and dance with her. He so desperately wanted her to let him hold her.

Claire turned away, afraid she would lose her composure completely. She couldn't bear the thought that Zoey might look over and realize she was upset. She felt a sickening twisting in her stomach.

When Claire looked back, they were dancing. Both holding each other at a safe distance, Zoey smiling politely, uncomfortable but determined to act as if everything was normal. Jake . . . Jake looked like a big, stupid puppy who'd stolen a bone from the table and was beside himself with joy yet fearful his prize might be snatched away.

Claire tried not to look, but she couldn't help herself. There it was in Jake's face, the proof. Of course he still loved Zoey. Had there ever been a time, even for a minute or two, when he didn't? Had there been a minute or two in there when he had genuinely loved Claire?

How would she ever know? Claire asked herself. Her whole relationship with Jake had been born of her own careful manipulation. It had all been very clever on her part. Wonderfully intelligent, far outclassing poor Jake's efforts to resist her.

Only now, underneath it all, it was still Zoey he wanted. Zoey, who had kept ownership of his heart by turning on him and choosing Lucas.

She wondered idly how Lucas would feel about this, but that was pointless. Zoey had done nothing blameworthy in his eyes.

No, that wasn't the way to handle this at all. There was another way. A cold, ruthless, but effective way to take care of Jake's puppy love for Zoey.

It wouldn't make him love Claire. She was now prepared to accept that at least that was impossible. But it would ruin his little fantasy for a long while.

Jake released Zoey at the end of the short, too short song. Lucas had come back on the floor, and Zoey had let him put his arms around her. Jake's own arms felt empty now. He managed a smile for Lucas, an acknowledgment as close to graciousness as he was capable of.

It would have been uncool to say one tenth of what he felt.

Hopelessly uncool to express the way he still felt when he saw Zoey with Lucas. A man didn't act that way, and Jake was a man.

He looked around for Claire and saw her not far off, a pale, solitary figure that stood out from the crowd as if she were lit with her own personal spotlight. Beautiful, smart, strong Claire. She was the girl every guy in school fawned over. There were plenty who would toss their present girlfriends aside for half a chance at Claire. And she was *his* girlfriend. He was lucky; everyone said so.

"Hey, babe," he said. He put his arm around her waist just as Lucas had done with Zoey.

And Claire smiled, just as Zoey had smiled for Lucas.

"I missed you," she said.

"Me too," he said, trying to sound as if he meant it.

"Kiss me," Claire said.

He did. How could he not? And her lips were soft beyond belief, her mouth so sensual and inviting. And yet he felt as though Zoey must be watching them. In a way he hoped she was watching and feeling at least the smallest amount of jealousy.

"Let's go upstairs," Claire said, in her voice that accepted no argument. "I'm tired of all this noise."

She took his hand and led him away from the dance floor

and up the stairs, past the second floor to the third. The third floor was far enough away from the speakers to be relatively quiet. Most of it was semi-finished attic, with a wood floor and no partitions. Exercise equipment was scattered at one end, weights and an Exercycle and a Soloflex. At the other end of the room was a pool table, where no fewer than six people were wielding cues.

The exercise end of the room was darker, lined with dormered windows and inset benches. It was to one of these that Claire led Jake.

"Reminds me of—" Jake began, before deciding he'd better not go on.

"Zoey's bedroom?" Claire supplied. "Yes, I always liked that desk she has built into her window."

They sat together, facing each other, both with a leg kicked up onto the bench. Claire's skirt slipped up her leg. She swept her silken black hair back over her shoulder and looked at him with a frank, appraising expression.

"We're all alone now, more or less," Claire suggested.

He nodded. There was something wrong with this situation. On its surface Claire had just brought him up here to make out. Plenty of other couples were doing the same thing—and more—at various locations around the house.

Except that Claire didn't do things like this. Jake felt alarm bells going off, but what could he do? Claire leaned into him, glittering dark eyes closing ever so slowly, her lush lips open.

She kissed Jake with an intensity he had never known from her. She left him gasping for air. His heart was racing. Almost against his will a sly smile spread over his face. "That was nice," he admitted.

"Well, I like kissing you," Claire said.

"I like kissing you, too," Jake said truthfully. Whatever fantasies he harbored about Zoey, Claire was here, now, very close. Claire could kill at a hundred yards; this close she was irresistible. Even when he had been so haunted by the memory of what she had done to his brother, Jake had never been able to build up any sort of immunity to her.

Claire kissed him again, then pulled away, leaving him leaning forward into emptiness. She laid her hand on his face. "I guess our relationship has reached a point where we can be honest about how we feel," Claire said thoughtfully.

"I guess so." Again the warning bells, but softer, more confused this time.

"Well, look, Jake, I don't want to lose you, but I think it's time we cleared up some stuff that I may not have been totally honest about." She turned to look out of the window, her face lit by moonlight.

"Sounds major," Jake said jokingly.

She shrugged. "It is and it isn't. Of course you know that I know about you and Louise Kronenberger," she said. "You know, that you slept with her. Had sex with her."

Jake shifted uncomfortably. "Look, Claire, I was drunk, and I mean really, really drunk. Plus, you know about the whole thing that was going on then—I'd been doing drugs earlier that night, and the game, and getting suspended. And we weren't exactly going together, you and me, not really."

Claire made a wry smile. "I know there were mitigating circumstances. And I'm not blaming you. Not at all. I'm just saying since I know about you, it seems unfair for me not to tell you my little secret."

Jake swallowed. He gave her a hard, suspicious look. "What do you mean?"

"Well, it turns out I'm not exactly a virgin, either, Jake." She smiled like they were conspirators.

He froze. He had been right to hear warning bells. "Who was the . . . who did you do it with?"

Claire smiled impishly, an unnatural look for her. She was enjoying this. "Who do you think?"

"Benjamin?"

"No, not Benjamin." She laughed, as though that was somehow a funny suggestion. "Like I'd sleep with my sister's boyfriend; give me some credit. Of course not Benjamin."

"Do you mean this was—like recently?"

"Now don't get upset," Claire said.

"I just want to know, that's all," Jake demanded, his voice rising.

"Lucas."

"Lucas?"

Claire tried out the impish smile one more time. She added an insouciant shrug. "You have to admit he is kind of cute."

Jake looked like he'd been punched in the stomach. He was dazed and breathless. "You slept with Lucas. Like a long time ago, when you guys were going together?"

"It was just a couple of days ago," Claire said. "I mean, it was just fun. I'm not in love with him or anything. It was just sex. You know, like you and Louise."

"I didn't even remember that, Claire!"

"Sorry," Claire said huffily. "I didn't know that made it any different. I *do* remember." Now, she told herself—just the smallest little smile, eyes averted, like I'm remembering. A coy little smile that will eat at him forever.

She saw the shocked anger in Jake's eyes. And then, following the first emotion, came the slow dawning of calculation. Just as she had known it would. His next question would be . . .

"Am I supposed to believe this is all okay with Zoey?"

She could almost have slapped him at that moment. But that

would have been a superficial, temporary pain. "You know how straight Zoey is," she said. "She'd never be able to deal with it. Lucas didn't tell her, obviously."

"And you think I *can* deal with it?"

No, Claire said silently. *I don't think for a moment that you can deal with it. I think you'll never want to touch me again, believing that I slept with Lucas.* "What's the big deal?"

"What's the big deal?" Jake nearly screamed.

"Oh, it's okay if you sleep with Louise, but it's not okay if I do it with Lucas? You might try being a little more consistent, Jake." No more cuteness now. It was no longer necessary to be coy. The damage was done. "Not being sexist, are you? Okay for guys, but not okay for girls?"

"How could you do that to Zoey? And to me?"

She looked at him coldly, letting some small part of her inner rage peek through. "How could I do that to you, Jake?" Claire realized she was trembling now. The playacting was over with. She got to her feet. "Don't play high-and-mighty with me, Jake. You think I'm blind? You think I don't know you still love Zoey? And don't you think Lucas suspects the same about her?"

Ah, his eyes actually lit up at the possibility! Even now, he couldn't help it. So much the better. He deserved what he was getting.

"Lucas and I know all about your ever-so-chaste ongoing love affair. So we decided to have a little fun of our own." She leaned down close to Jake's face. "And it was fun, Jake. Lucas was wonderful. As Zoey will find out sooner or later, when she gets over playing junior nun."

Jake shot to his feet, bristling with rage and horror. "You bitch." His hands clenched into fists, but Jake wasn't the kind to strike out at her, no matter how outraged he was. Besides, beneath it all, he was constructing a whole new world of hope.

She watched as he walked stiffly away.

Damn him to hell. She was well rid of any guy stupid enough to fall for this cheap trick. Benjamin would never have fallen for it. Not Benjamin. Benjamin who, like the others, no longer loved her.

Claire threw herself back onto the bench and, in the privacy of the dark recess, cried tears of bitter self-loathing.

SIXTEEN

HIS BRAND-NEW HALF-SISTER, WAS, IN all likelihood, a drug dealer. Or, if not a drug dealer herself, then involved with one. She couldn't possibly be ignorant of what Mr. Hair was up to. Not unless she was an idiot. And so far no one in the family had turned out to be an idiot.

"You realize where they're going," Benjamin said.

"Duh. I mean, it's a good guess, anyway," Nina said.

"And can we possibly guess *why* they would be going to Richie Felix's birthday party?" Benjamin asked sourly. The music from the party was clearly audible. Bass was vibrating up through the cobblestones.

"They like to dance?" Nina suggested.

"Uh-huh. You know, I kind of feel like I don't really want to know who they're selling drugs to at this party. I mean, it's all people from school, people we know."

Nina made a doubtful noise. "I thought you wanted to know everything, Sherlock. There they go, by the way. Right inside. Didn't even bother to knock."

"Not always. I mean, do I want to know what kids at school are using drugs? Not really. Besides, I don't want to spy on *them*. I just wanted to see if I could get some answers about my alleged half-sister; you know, get a sense of things before I decide whether to meet her face to face."

"This is so *The Young and the Restless*," Nina said. "Half-sisters. Drug dealers. You are going to talk to her eventually, aren't you?"

Benjamin considered the question as they closed the distance to the Felix house. "I suppose. It's kind of a major decision, though. Let's hold back for a couple of minutes. We don't want to come in right after them. It might look kind of obvious."

"It's cold out here, though," Nina complained.

"Are you dressed warmly?"

"I'm wearing a warm coat, but I have nothing on underneath," Nina said.

He could hear the leer in her voice. Even though he knew she was teasing, the image still sent a pleasurable tingle through him. "Don't say things like that," he said with mock-severity. "Sherlock never had the slightest interest in women."

He felt her settle close to him, sharing his body heat. "I guess it is kind of huge," she said thoughtfully. "I mean, not every brother-sister thing is as nice as you and Zoey. Look at

Claire and me. We already know this girl's a possible drug dealer. Which means there's a chance she's almost as rotten as Claire."

"It's not just that," Benjamin said. "There's the whole question of how she'll feel about suddenly having an unknown family popping up in the middle of her life. Suddenly she'd have a half-brother and a half-sister and a biological father. Some people would consider that upsetting."

"You're so thoughtful," Nina said affectionately. "I was just thinking she might be the kind of person who'd want to borrow your CDs."

Benjamin laughed perfunctorily, but his thoughts were elsewhere. "Tell me again what she looks like," he asked.

Nina was silent.

"Are you there?" Benjamin prodded.

He heard Nina sigh. "Benjamin, I don't know whether or not she looks like you. She might, I guess, but I can't be sure."

"Oh. Was I being that obvious?"

"No, it's just that I know the way your twisted, devious mind works. You're thinking maybe your mom and dad lied to you?"

"Their record for honesty isn't all that great right now," he pointed out.

"Benjamin, you're being dumb. Your mom is your mom and your dad is your dad."

"Let me ask you something—do I look like my dad at all?"

Nina made a growling frustrated noise deep in her throat. "Okay, you look more like your mom. It's obvious to anyone that you and she look alike. Same nose, same chin."

"And nothing in common with my father?"

"You're both kind of cute, although he's actually much cuter, you know, if you like old guys."

"Mmm-hmm. So, the answer is no."

"Look, you also don't look like Mr. McRoyan, if that's what you're thinking. Not at all. This is dumb. So what if we decide Lara looks like you?"

He shrugged. It did sound a little farfetched. Maybe it was just the paranoia that came from never being able to see things for himself. "If she looks like me, then I guess I'll conclude that we are related. Meaning we have the same father and that my father is my father."

Nina was silent for a long time. Then, "You're a strange person, Benjamin. I used to think maybe underneath it all we weren't right for each other, that I was too weird or whatever. But you are plenty weird your own self."

"Let's go, Dr. Watson."

"First kiss me, Sherlock," Nina said. "If it turns out Mr. McRoyan *is* your real father, that will make you *Joke's* half-brother. I might not want to kiss anyone related to him."

184

"Seems pretty peaceful," Nina remarked, looking across the dance floor.

"What?" Benjamin shouted. "If you want me to hear you, you'll have to scream directly into my ear. Someone is landing a jet in here."

"I said it seems peaceful!" Nina yelled.

"Oh, yeah. This is peaceful, all right."

Various kids from school came over and said hello, exchanging unheard jokes and polite laughter. Richie appeared in his characteristically sudden way, startling Nina by patting her on the back. He mouthed words for a while, and Nina nodded and smiled in response.

"What did he say?" Nina asked Benjamin.

"Who? Was someone here?"

"Our host. Richie. He was telling me something. I thought you'd be able to hear with your Blind Boy superhearing."

Benjamin grinned. "I can't use my superpowers unless I'm wearing my Blind Boy costume."

"What's that? A red cape and Calvin Klein briefs?"

Benjamin put on a shocked expression. "A red cape? That's Superman. I'd never infringe on his trademark style. I think Blind Boy's costume should be mismatched plaids and polka dots and stripes."

"I like my idea better," Nina said. "Hey, there's Lucas!" She raised her voice and shouted his name at full volume.

Whether he had heard or just happened to spot them, he came over. "Where have you guys been?"

"We got lost," Nina said. "I let Benjamin try and lead us. We ended up out by the mall."

"Any major excitement yet?" Benjamin asked.

Lucas shook his head. "Nah. Kind of disappointing. I kept hearing how wild and unpredictable these parties are."

"Usually by now we'd have had at least two or three screaming breakups and an equal number of drunken fistfights," Benjamin confirmed.

Nina spotted a familiar head rising up the stairs. She put her mouth to Benjamin's ear. "Mr. Hair, going upstairs."

"We're going to go check things out," Benjamin said. "Is Zoey around?"

"She was just here. Had to go to the little girls' room with Aisha."

Nina led Benjamin to the bottom of the stairs.

Jake took the plastic cup greedily and swallowed the beer in several long gulps. That was five, and he was beginning to feel the buzz, a fiery sensation starting in the muscles of his neck. Tad Crowley was working the tap, draining beer into cups, setting the cups on the kitchen butcher block table.

"Let someone else get one," Tad said, shaking his head in bemusement. "It's a long night, Jake; pace yourself, man."

Lars Ehrlich came up suddenly and popped Jake playfully on the shoulder. He was grinning and pink, but his face grew more cautious when he saw Jake's face. "Hey, big Jake. If you want to get truly hammered, come on upstairs, man. I don't want to share with all these losers."

Jake shook his head resolutely. "No more drugs. I fail a piss test again and I'm history as far as the team is concerned."

"Plus, your dad will kill you," Lars said.

"My dad can go to hell," Jake snapped. "He's no better than anyone else. Worse. Give me another beer," he demanded of Tad. The days of worrying what his father would say or do were over now. They'd been over since he'd learned that about his father and Zoey's mom. His father was in no position to judge, not anymore. He was no better than Lucas. The same as Lucas, another behind-the-back cheap-shot artist. Lucas had betrayed Zoey, and his father had betrayed his mother. What was the difference?

Lars opened his jacket suggestively. Nestled inside, Jake saw a bottle of clear liquid. "Tequila," Lars said, wiggling his eyebrows. "It'll get you there faster than beer."

"My man, Lars," Jake said magnanimously. He followed Lars upstairs.

They found a corner of one bedroom. A couple was making out without much interest on the bed. Some older-looking guy with lots of hair and a pretty but slightly trashy-looking girl Jake had never seen were in secretive conversation with two of the school's more notorious druggies.

Lars cracked the seal on the bottle, took a swig, shuddered, and handed the bottle to Jake. Jake quickly raised the bottle and took two deep swallows that burned like fire all the way down. The effect was almost immediate. His head swam, and he had to steady himself by reaching out for the windowsill.

"See what I mean?" Lars leered.

But Jake wasn't interested in what Lars had to say. He was interested in wiping the lurid image of Claire with Lucas from his mind. It wasn't that he cared so much about Claire cheating on him. Maybe he even deserved it after Louise. Besides, Jake knew he was no paragon. Maybe once he'd believed he was someone special, but now he knew better.

No, it was Zoey who was special. It was the betrayal of Zoey that hurt. How could Lucas have done it? How could Claire? Both of them not fit to kiss Zoey's shoes. It would tear Zoey up when she found out.

He took another drink. It would tear her up, but at the same time it would be good for her in the long run to be rid of Lucas. Only how would she find out? That was the question—would she ever find out, or would Lucas just go on laughing behind her back?

No, no, no. That couldn't be allowed. The thought that Lucas could have betrayed Zoey and yet still have her all to himself . . . She had to be told. She had to be told the truth. And the sooner the better.

Aisha rummaged through the contents of her purse and finally, in frustration, upended it and dumped the contents onto the marble counter. Her eyeliner rolled into the sink. A pack of gum fell onto the tile floor of the cramped, over-bright bathroom.

Zoey bent down to pick it up for her. "Here. Your gum. What are you doing, anyway?" They were crammed into the tiny bathroom together. Actually, the two of them and the girl who was passed out and snoring in the bathtub.

"I'm looking for a tampon. I was sure I had one more in here." Aisha raked through the mess she'd made.

"I'll check my purse," Zoey offered. "Wait, here. No, sorry, that was Lifesavers."

"What flavor?" Aisha asked sarcastically. "I'd rather use peppermint if it comes down to that."

"Passion fruit," Zoey said with a smile. "Hang on, I'll see who's outside." She opened the door a crack and happened to spot Nina and Benjamin walking past.

"Nina," Zoey hissed.

"Hey, Zoey," Nina said. "Benjamin, your sister is here. Peeking out of the bathroom like a spy."

"Hi, Zoey."

"Hi, Benjamin. Um, Benjamin? This kind of just involves Nina," Zoey said.

"Oh, fine. I can take a hint. I'll just stand out here while you girls have all the fun."

Zoey grabbed Nina and yanked her inside, closing the door on Benjamin. "Aisha needs a tampon."

"I'll check," Nina offered. "But I think all I have is my wallet and cigarettes and gum." She extracted a Lucky Strike and popped it into the corner of her mouth. "No, wait, I have Lifesavers, too. Wintergreen." She held up the pack.

Aisha sighed. "We have Lifesavers. I don't need Lifesavers."

"Wait. Aha!" Nina held up the tampon. "What will you pay me?"

Aisha snatched it out of her hand. "You two can leave now."

"Hey, Eesh," Nina said, "I was watching Christopher downstairs dancing. He's good."

"You know how it is, all of us black people can dance."

"Yeah, right. I've seen *you* dance," Nina pointed out. "You know the Tin Man in *The Wizard of Oz*?"

"Please leave now," Aisha said, batting her eyelashes. "Please go away and find someone else to ridicule."

Zoey and Nina slipped outside into the hallway and rejoined Benjamin, who was carrying on a polite conversation with a sophomore girl Nina had seen hanging around him before.

"So what have you two been up to?" Zoey asked.

Benjamin responded by looking uncomfortable. Nina put on her blank look, the one she resorted to when she was avoiding telling the truth. Nina was the lamest liar imaginable.

"Actually, Zoey—" Benjamin began.

"Um, what were we up to?" Nina jumped in. "Nothing. We've been here the whole time, you just didn't see us."

"Nina, I think I might as well tell her," Benjamin said, looking amused but also a little nervous.

"Tell me what?" Zoey asked.

"I, uh, I located our half-sister. You know, Lara? Turns out she lives here in town."

Zoey froze. "Benjamin, what have you done?"

"We followed her. And now, oddly enough, it turns out she's here." He smiled winningly.

Zoey shot a glance at Nina, who just shrugged. "You told her who you are?"

"No," Benjamin said. "I haven't told her."

"You must have told her, Benjamin, or why else would she be here?" Zoey insisted.

"I'm not sure you really want to know *why* Lara's here," Benjamin said in an undertone. "She's here with her boyfriend, and unless we're really out of line somehow, it kind of looks like her boyfriend is in a certain illegal business that involves making a lot of stops around town."

"Damn it, Benjamin," Zoey said. "What made you go off and do this?"

"Chill out, Zoey. I don't take orders from you, *little* sister."

There was a warning edge in Benjamin's voice, but Zoey was too angry to let it go. "This is something that affects both of us, Benjamin. You should have at least asked me."

"It was important to me," Benjamin argued. "I wanted to know who she was and what she was like."

Zoey fought down an angry reply. Throughout the whole mess of the split between their parents, she and Benjamin had managed to stay on the same side, though his feelings differed from hers in some ways. She took a deep breath. "Look, I don't want to fight with you, Benjamin. It just caught me by surprise, all right? A couple of days ago I suddenly learn I have this so-called half-sister, then you cruise in and say, 'Oh, by the way, she's here at the party and I think she deals drugs.'"

Benjamin made a wryly sympathetic face. "You're saying

that's what? Kind of a surprise?"

"Yeah," Zoey said. She smiled, too, and saw Nina relax. "You're not going to introduce yourself, are you?"

"No. Not yet," he said. "Knowledge is power. For now I'm happy knowing who she is without her knowing anything about me, or us."

Zoey considered, curiosity warring with caution. Curiosity won. "Okay, so where is she?"

Nina pointed to a doorway just down the hall. "Tall, brown hair, not bad looking but slightly sleazy. She's with a guy who looks like Patrick Stump."

"Patrick Stump?" Benjamin asked.

"Lead singer for Fall Out Boy," Nina clarified. "Jeez, Benjamin, enter this century."

Zoey rolled her eyes. "I'm just going to take a peek."

"See what you think of her," Benjamin said seriously. "Take a good look at her."

Zoey started toward the door, feeling faintly ridiculous playing games. She looked in the door. There was a couple making out on the bed. There were two guys in the shadows of the far corner of the room. Just inside the door, two more guys she knew from school were huddled close to a couple, an older guy with lots of hair, and a girl.

Zoey just took a glance and turned away. So that was her

half-sister. Had she looked like a relative? She'd have to get a closer look.

Only now the two of them, Lara and her boyfriend, were leaving, brushing past without apparently seeing her. And at the same time, just over their shoulders, Zoey had recognized one of the two people sharing a bottle of liquor.

SEVENTEEN

"DAMN, HERE COME LARA AND Mr. Hair," Nina hissed. She grabbed Benjamin's arm and propelled him down the hallway. Unfortunately Marie Burnett was blocking their way, asking Nina something about Modern Media class.

"Hey, it's that same girl," Mr. Hair said.

"What is with Mr. Mifflin lately?" Marie wanted to know. "I mean, quizzes like every week?"

"Come, Watson," Benjamin said.

"Hey!" Mr. Hair yelled.

Nina and Benjamin stumbled past a surprised Marie and pelted down the stairs. But not quickly enough.

"Keith, what are you doing?" Lara cried.

What Keith was doing became apparent very quickly. He shoved past Nina on the landing and grabbed Benjamin by the neck. He pushed Benjamin rudely up against the wall. "You've been following me all damned night, pisshead."

"How could I be following you?" Benjamin said, sounding

as reasonable as he could while being choked.

Nina launched herself at Keith, but he brushed her aside with a sweep of his hand and she fell to her knees on the landing. Benjamin heard her cry out and swung with as much accuracy as he could—and at the close range, his accuracy was fairly good. His fist caught Keith on the side of his head. Keith released his hold, but there was no contest between a blind fighter and one who could see. Benjamin's follow-up swing caught air, and Keith sunk a fist into Benjamin's stomach, doubling him up.

Nina saw him fold and screamed, a sound that carried almost to the top of the stairs against the background noise of music and loud conversation.

Keith knelt over Benjamin and drew back his fist.

"No, you creep!" Nina yelled.

"Keith, don't!" Lara shouted.

Keith hesitated, fist still cocked. "He's been trailing us all night," he told her. "I have to teach this boy a lesson."

"Tell him to stop it," Nina said urgently to Lara.

Lara shrugged indifferently.

Benjamin took advantage of the momentary lull to lash out with his foot, which caught Keith in exactly the wrong place. At the same moment, Nina shouted, "Lara, he's your brother!"

Keith rolled back, clutching himself.

Benjamin struggled to his feet. He managed a swollen,

misshapen smile, stuck his hand out in the general direction of Lara and said, "It's true, I am your half-brother, and I'd really appreciate it if you didn't let your boyfriend kill me."

Lara stared at him closely. Keith was up again, mostly recovered. "You're blind, aren't you?"

"Blind?" Keith grunted.

"Yep, I'm your blind half-brother Benjamin. Later, if I'm still alive, I'll introduce you to your blond half-sister."

The shoulders were unmistakable. It was Jake, Zoey was sure of that. And from the way he was swaying unsteadily as he tilted the bottle up, he had been drinking for a while.

She hesitated. Jake wasn't really her concern anymore. He was with Claire now. What she should do was go and find her, ask her to talk to him. But Jake was still her friend, wasn't he, even if he was no longer her *boyfriend*?

Zoey crossed the room. Lars spotted her coming and started giggling guiltily. Jake turned slowly, and his eyes met hers. She had expected cheerful, bleary drunkenness. What surprised her was the intensity of his gaze.

"Jake," she said gently. "Why don't you come downstairs and dance with me?"

"Dance?" His eyes might have been focused, but the rest of him was swaying six inches to either side. "Can't, Zoey, sweet

Zoey. I have to finish this bottle." He held up the half-empty bottle of tequila.

So much for indirect. "Jake, you know you shouldn't be drinking," she said firmly.

He smiled wistfully. "Do you care, Zoey?"

"Of course I care, Jake. You're my friend, and I don't like to see you hurting yourself this way."

"Me?" he asked softly. "I'm not the one who's hurt, Zoey."

From outside the room Zoey heard shouting, the sound of a scuffle or fight. The sight of Jake stinking drunk was profoundly depressing, and she wished she could just leave this party now. Benjamin and her half-sister, Jake hammered and hurting, some idiot fighting in the hallways. Where was Lucas, anyway?

Jake took another drink, defiant.

"Jake, stop it. You can't drink."

"Sure I can. Didn't you just see?"

Lars belched loudly and added, "He can definitely drink."

She grabbed Jake's arm and tried to pull him away, but even drunk, Jake was far too strong to be moved. She released him.

"Jake, I'm asking you as a friend who cares about you to stop this. You're just hurting yourself. I don't know if you had some kind of fight with Claire or what, but this isn't going to help."

"Yeah, I had a fight with Claire," he admitted. "She told

me something interesting. You want to know what it was?"

"Probably not," Zoey said. She was losing patience. "It's personal between you two."

"Oh, no," he said, shaking his head emphatically. "It's not between just us."

A movement caught Lucas's eye. Yes, just what his instinct had told him—it was a fight. He had to squat a little to see what was happening on the stair landing. When he did, he was amazed to realize he was looking at Benjamin slipping to the ground with some guy standing over him, drawing back his fist.

Lucas muttered a curse and broke into a run. Halfway there, he saw Benjamin lash out with lucky accuracy, planting a foot in his tormentor's crotch. Lucas winced in automatic sympathy, then grinned in admiration. Benjamin had to know that the guy was just going to pound him twice as bad now. The boy was a piece of work.

He reached the steps and bounded up two at a time. There was a certain amount of loud talking, but to Lucas's surprise, the guy who had been pounding Benjamin now seemed to be just standing there, looking surprised. Standing there with legs together and a face that had a greenish tinge, but apparently not interested in carrying on the fight.

"Everything okay here?" Lucas asked.

Nina cocked an eyebrow at him. "If you're supposed to be the cavalry, you're late."

"Lucas, meet my half-sister, Lara," Benjamin said. "And her friend . . . Keith, right?"

"Keith," the guy said, gritting his teeth.

"Lucas Cabral," Lucas introduced himself. "I think I'll leave now." The situation looked under control, and like it involved private stuff that had nothing to do with him.

He'd find Zoey and ask her what this was all about. She'd taken off for the bathroom fifteen minutes ago, which, even for a girl, was a long time in the can. Especially since he'd seen Aisha return to the dance floor a few minutes ago.

He heard her voice and slowed down, trying to fix the direction. A door. He peeked around the corner. There was a couple making out on a bed. No, the guy had fallen asleep. In the corner Lars Ehrlich was sitting on the floor, hanging his head between his knees. Probably trying to keep from throwing up, Lucas decided.

Zoey was with Jake. Lucas bristled. She had a hand on his arm, trying to pull him away, but he resisted. "Hammered," Lucas said under his breath. "Plowed under."

He relaxed and hung back, just keeping them in sight. Jake didn't look much like a romantic threat right at the moment. In fact, it was obvious that Zoey was just trying to get him to stop drinking for a while. Lucas wondered whether Jake was an alcoholic. Could be. The guy didn't seem to know how to have *one* beer. When he drank, it was like slow-motion suicide.

Lucas had seen plenty of that type in the Youth Authority. Ninety percent of the guys in there were druggies or drunks or both. It was one of the reasons Lucas had so little interest in booze. Bunking with guys who would drink antifreeze to get drunk and then end up screaming about spiders on the way to the hospital in a straitjacket gave you a whole different perspective on alcoholism.

He stayed back from the doorway, out of sight, he hoped. No point in humiliating Jake any further by getting involved.

Zoey was talking to him, trying to be reasonable, a low murmur interrupted occasionally by some loud, slurred declamation from Jake.

It was impossible to be jealous. Zoey was just being Zoey, trying to make everyone feel better. Hard to be angry about that. Hard to feel bad about the fact that you were lucky enough to be going with a girl who was sweet and decent.

God, she was beautiful. God, he loved her.

"Oh, no," Jake said, shaking his head emphatically. "It's not between just us."

Lars had collapsed in the corner. "Jake, why don't we go

outside and get some fresh air?" Zoey asked.

"Yeah. Yeah, that would be nice, Zo; you and me, just like the old days. You and me." He raised his head and looked at her. "You know what, Zoey?"

"What, Jake?"

"I still love you, Zoey. You know that? Not Claire, never Claire. Always you."

"Jake, you're just drunk and you're mad at Claire."

"No. I love you. Leave that guy, that Lucas, and come back to me, okay?"

There was a pathetic, puppyish look in his eyes. "Jake, I'm with Lucas now," she said.

He formed a half-smile. "And Lucas is with Claire."

"No, I think you're a little confused," Zoey said condescendingly.

"He screwed her," Jake said.

Zoey was about to dismiss the remark, but there was something in the way Jake had said it.

"They did it in the front seat of her daddy's Mercedes," Jake said.

"What are you talking about?"

"Lucas and Claire. Claire and Lucas. Sex. It. You know. She . . . she . . ." He was swaying dangerously now. "She said she liked it. That's what she said."

Zoey swung her hand palm open and slapped him across the face, a reflex action. He looked at her in shock. Slowly he reached up to touch the reddening patch on his cheek.

"It's true, Zoey," he said, sounding hurt.

Suddenly Zoey was aware of Lucas at her side.

"What's going on here?" he demanded, poised warily, as if he expected some sudden move from Jake.

"Too late, Cabral," Jake sneered. "I told her about you and Claire."

Zoey saw a look of pure horror on Lucas's face. She felt as if all the blood had drained out of her in an instant. She took an unsteady step back.

"Zoey—" Lucas said, but had nothing else to offer.

"Get away from me," Zoey said.

"Zoey, no," Lucas pleaded.

"Get away from me!" Zoey screamed.

"Zoey, I love you!" Lucas cried.

Zoey ran.

Lucas reeled. He stared, horrified, at Jake. Jake wore a sickly look of triumph.

"What did you tell her?" Lucas demanded.

"I told her about you and Claire, you scumbag," Jake said.

Lucas flinched. Jake knew he had made out with Claire?

"Who told you about that?" he demanded, knowing the answer.

"Who do you think?" Jake said.

"Look, it was just one of those things," Lucas said desperately. He was furious with Jake, but what could he say? He'd been making out with Jake's girlfriend behind his back. He wasn't exactly in a position to act all outraged. And then there was the fact that Jake was more than drunk enough to swing on him.

"Just one of those things?" Jake laughed. "I'll tell Claire you said that. You screw my girlfriend and it's just one of those things. Hear that, Lars, this little piece of crap sneaks around and screws my girlfriend and hey, it's no big deal." He had stopped swaying and was focusing dangerously now.

"Jake, what are you talking about, dude? I didn't screw Claire."

A malicious smile spread over Jake's face. A smile with no hint of mirth. He slammed an open hand against Lucas's chest, shoving him back.

"Jake, I tried, all right?" Lucas said, holding up his hands placatingly. "We made out, I was mad at Zoey and Claire was there and one thing led to another."

Jake shoved him again, but with less conviction.

"Jake, that didn't happen. We didn't do it, man. Close but it never happened."

Behind the alcoholic haze, Jake's mind was working. "Claire said . . . Why would she . . . ?"

Lucas looked around in a wild parody of perplexity. "How in hell would I know why Claire does or says anything? But if she said we did it, she's lying."

Jake backed away a step. His brow wrinkled as he considered. Lucas was just as lost. Why would Claire lie like this? She had to have known if she told this story to Jake that Jake might tell Zoey. What motive did she have? Surely she hadn't just made up the lie without knowing where it would lead. Not Claire.

But that wasn't his problem right now. Right now his problem was what Zoey believed.

"Jake, I have to go, man. If you're going to pound on me, you have to do it now or let me walk. I'm not saying you don't have a right. It was low rent of me to be putting moves on Claire."

Jake nodded, but his real attention was far away.

"Sorry about this mess, Jake," Lucas said. "It was bad enough, but it wasn't what Claire said."

Again Jake nodded distractedly.

Lucas hesitated, torn between trying to settle this with Jake right now and the crying need to go after Zoey. He had to clear this up as fast as possible. He'd tell Zoey the truth. That would be bad enough, but she could forgive him for that, couldn't she?

But if she believed what Jake had told her, she would never, ever forgive him. Not after what had been happening in her family.

He ran down the stairs, passing Nina and Benjamin, who were still talking to the couple who'd been trying to beat them up just minutes earlier.

Nina grabbed him as he went past. "What happened? Zoey just went tearing out the front door."

"Later, Nina," Lucas said. He ran outside and instantly realized he'd forgotten his coat. The temperature had dropped below freezing. He checked his watch. Five till nine. If Zoey was heading for the ferry, she'd be gone in five minutes. If he ran, he might still catch her. He might catch her, and she might believe him.

And if not . . . If he lost her . . .

No. He felt a thrill of fear, and the awful feeling that he had already lost the race. He ran as if his life depended on it.

Jake found Claire where he had left her. She seemed subdued, looking out of the high window at the street far below. He stood, waiting for her to notice him, still trying to collect his thoughts. The physical effects of the booze were still powerful. Standing straight was an effort, but parts of his mind were beginning to clear. He felt terribly weary. Too weary to try to be clever.

"Hello, Jake," Claire said placidly, still looking out of the window.

"It was a lie, wasn't it?" Jake said.

Claire said nothing.

"Why, Claire? What was the point?"

Claire's thin ghost of a smile appeared and evaporated. "Do you love me, Jake?"

Jake just stared. "What . . . what's that got to do . . ."

"Do you love Zoey?"

His eyes met hers. He looked away.

"And how do you think she feels about you, Jake?"

He shrugged. How *did* Zoey feel about him? Better than she felt about Lucas, now that she knew about him and Claire. Only he was forgetting—that hadn't really happened. That had just been a lie Claire told him.

Claire stood up. "Think it through, Jake," she sneered. "You just told her a lie about her boyfriend. You just told her Lucas slept with me. A lie. A pathetic lie you told because you wanted her back. Think it through, Jake," she snapped, suddenly furious.

"I don't . . . You're the one who told me," Jake protested.

"Me?" Claire looked surprised. "Why on earth would I go around telling people I slept with a guy I'm not even seeing?

207

Why would I tell a lie like that?" She put her face close to his. Her beautiful, cold-eyed face. "Whereas you, Jake . . . You *would* make up a lie like that to get Zoey back. A low, contemptible trick to break up Zoey and Lucas, to take advantage of her vulnerability and get her to come back to you. How do you think Zoey will feel about you when she realizes you've done this to her, Jake?"

He looked at her in horror.

"You *and* Lucas," Claire said. "Both of you so in love with Zoey. What was I, Jake? What was I?"

Her voice had lost its dangerous silkiness. It was ragged with emotion. He was stunned to see tears in her lustrous eyes. Despite everything, he couldn't help but feel some distant strain of pity mixed in with helpless despair at what she had done.

Her eyes blazed. "Don't *you* feel sorry for me, you bastard."

"I didn't know—I didn't think you cared."

"Yeah, you're right," Claire said. "I don't care. I don't have feelings. I don't have a heart, Jake. I'm just a cold, manipulative bitch. Well, that's what you thought, and tonight that's what you got. You hurt me, Jake. And when you hurt me, you damned well get hurt back."

Lucas ran, through random, quick-melting snowflakes, down the cobblestoned streets, plowing through the groups of fashionable, yuppie-restaurant-crowd types, around the rowdy college-aged bar patrons.

The ferry's warning whistle sounded high and shrill. He ran full tilt, slipping on wet brick sidewalks, scrambling up, panting.

The ferry's whistle shrilled again. Too late, but he ran across the last street and slammed against the railing. The gangway was up and the ferry ropes cast off.

She was there, standing at the stern, looking down at him from her high perch.

"Zoey!" he cried out, rattling the railing in his frustration.

Her face was set in rigid lines of bitterness.

"Zoey, it isn't true!" he yelled. The ferry was pulling away, a dozen feet of water already between them.

Slowly and deliberately, Zoey turned her back and disappeared.

AISHA GOES WILD

PART TWO

Zoey

Halloween is coming up soon, supposedly the time to be afraid. Or at least to think about fear. Or maybe it's just a time to wear masks and eat other people's candy.

You want to know what scares me? Not monsters. Not aliens. Not the guy from the movies, the guy with the long razor blade fingernails. What scares me are needles. I mean, when I have to go to the dentist, it's the novocaine needle that bothers me most. Lying there on your back, your mouth open with that little sucking thing hanging from your lip, a bright light in your eyes, carrying on a conversation where all you can say is "uh-huh, unh-unh" and a kind of yodeling sound that means "I don't know." Then, up from nowhere comes the needle, floating, hesitating, then plunging right into your gum. A needle. In your gum. You want to scare me on Halloween, try dressing like a dentist.

But you know, it's interesting—to me the things that end up being really awful in my life aren't the things that I'm scared of. The bad things are the ones I didn't even see coming. Like when Benjamin lost his sight. Or like my parents getting separated recently. Or finding out that Lucas...

Anyway.

Anyway, those have been the really terrible things in my life so far. None had much to do with being scared.

You grow up as a kid scared of the monster who lives in your closet, or scared of the dark, or even like me, scared of the dentist. All that wasted fear, when it's just the day-to-day reality that ends up being awful.

ONE

ZOEY PASSMORE HAD SEEN LUCAS come running down the street, dodging through the slow-moving cars and around the dark-coated knots of restaurant-hopping yuppies. She had heard him shout out her name, the sound bouncing around the brick and cobblestone till it acquired a metallic twang. And at the last minute, as the ferry's second and final blast sounded, she'd had to stop herself from getting off the boat and running to meet him.

But she *had* stopped herself.

She didn't want to listen to his pleading and apologies. There would be no forgiveness for what he had done.

She had wanted to hide before he could see her, but she'd felt rooted to her spot at the stern. She looked down at him from high above as he slammed his hand in frustration against the railing while the ferry pulled away, putting inches, then feet, then impassable yards of inky water between them.

Only when he looked up, brushing his lank blond hair back

with a painfully familiar gesture, only when his dark eyes met hers, did she at last turn away.

Zoey waited until the ferry was well out into the harbor before looking again. From here, on the unlit deck, half-invisible under an obscured moon, she knew Lucas could no longer see her. But she could see him, a forlorn figure almost alone on the bright landing, small against the backdrop of Weymouth's aged brick waterfront buildings, even smaller against the looming backdrop of modern office high-rises behind them.

He hadn't left to go back to the party. But at any moment he would. Claire was still at the party, and he would surely go running back to her.

Zoey tried to suppress the images that leapt to the front of her mind. She'd always had far too good an imagination. Now it supplied her with all the pictures she didn't need to see: lurid shots of Lucas with Claire, sprawled across the leather seats of Claire's father's Mercedes. Her imagination even supplied the dialogue: *"Claire, you're so wonderful. So unlike Zoey. So much sexier. So much more adult."*

Although, of course, he probably hadn't *said* any of those things. He would have been too busy for conversation. They both would have been far too busy to talk, but oh, they would have thought a few things. The two of them, thinking about the people they were cheating on. Claire cold-bloodedly unconcerned for Jake. And Lucas . . . Lucas probably just thanking his lucky stars that he didn't have to wait around for Zoey to decide whether she was ready. Why wait for Zoey when he could have Claire right now?

At last, with the ferry well out into the bay, she could no longer see him at all. Now she faced the darkness ahead. Chatham Island wasn't yet visible except for the faint green light at the end of the breakwater and the white sweep from the lighthouse at the northernmost tip of the island.

She slumped back onto a cold steel bench and hung her head. Her blond hair streamed back, lifted by the wet, chill breeze. "Lucas," she whispered. But she didn't cry. She'd cried herself dry over the breakup of her parents' marriage. She had no more tears left.

Lucas had cheated on her, just as her mother had cheated on her father. And the result would be the same: it was impossible for any relationship to survive this kind of blow. She would never be able to trust Lucas again.

Nearby on deck, huddling together for warmth, a family. Father, mother, and seven- or eight-year-old son. They weren't Chatham Islanders or she'd have recognized them. They must be going on to Allworthy or Penobscot Island. They'd been shopping on the mainland and carried net stretch bags, like all islanders. The little boy's bag held a costume, the mask visible in its cellophane-windowed box. One of the X-Men, or something like that.

Halloween was coming up, two weeks away. A depressing thought, not because of Halloween itself, but because Thanksgiving and Christmas followed fast on its heels. The first Thanksgiving without her father at home. And what would have been her first Thanksgiving with Lucas.

Again the images flooded her brain, trailing disgust and jealousy and even, strangely, a sense of guilt in their wake. They mingled inextricably with the images of her mother on that terrible day when Zoey had come home early. Too early and seen what she should never have seen.

Without even intending to, Zoey went back to the railing and gazed at the far-distant landing, now just a bright dot, lost in the lights of the city. Perhaps Lucas was still standing there, realizing what he had lost.

Perhaps he was already back at the party with Claire.

The distant, dwindling light grew blurry. And Zoey realized that she hadn't yet cried out all her tears.

Lucas stood on the pier in an agony of frustration, watching the ferry disappear into the darkness. It was the last ferry of the night. They had all planned on going back home from the party on the water taxi, splitting the forty-dollar cost between the eight of them. He dug his hand in the pocket of his jeans and looked at what he drew out. Nine dollars and two quarters. Not enough.

And what could he say to Zoey anyway? Even if he had been able to explain, just what was he supposed to say? "No, I didn't *sleep* with Claire, we just made out"? That was a lesser offense, certainly, but still not something that would make Zoey rush into his arms, full of forgiveness.

And the truth was he *had* tried to get Claire to sleep with him. He had tried; there was no denying it. At the time he'd thought Zoey was getting back together with Jake. He'd thought he had some justification. But none of that was going to convince Zoey.

No, Lucas realized bitterly. He had been a jerk, and now he was paying for it. Paying with a hurt that was physical in its intensity. *His* fault. Claire was to blame, too, but the real fault was his. No big surprise, that. He had a talent for screwing up.

"So you're my brother," Lara McAvoy said to Benjamin. She squirted ketchup over her plate of fries and ate a long one in two bites. She was pretty, Nina decided, although you almost couldn't tell under the overdone makeup and white-trash hairdo.

Her boyfriend, Keith, sat back in the diner booth. Nina noticed that he looked less handsome under the harsh fluorescent overheads than he had seemed in the dim light of the party. Although he still had excellent rock-star hair.

Benjamin sat beside Nina, across the table from the other two. The fingers of his right hand rested where he could maintain contact with his coffee cup. That way he wouldn't have to feel around for it. He was aiming his opaque black shades in the direction of Lara's voice, giving his usual uncanny impression of being sighted, although of course he saw nothing at all, not even Lara's bold, curious stare.

"Yeah, I'm afraid so," Benjamin said. "I didn't intend to just spring it on you, but things were getting a little out of control . . ."

Nina stole a glance at Keith: the *thing* that had gotten out of control. But there was no acknowledgment. He just watched from beneath half-closed lids.

"And you say I have a half-sister, too, huh?"

Benjamin nodded. "Her name is Zoey."

"Well." Lara ate a fry.

Benjamin sipped his coffee. "Yeah."

"I knew I supposedly had a natural father out there somewhere in the world," Lara said. She laughed derisively. "I mean, I knew I wasn't related to that slug my mom married."

She certainly seemed to be taking it well, Nina thought with mild surprise. If Nina had suddenly had some guy pop up and go, "Hey, guess what, I'm your half-brother," she was sure she'd have reacted with something more emotional than french fry eating.

"Where does he live?" Lara asked.

"We all live in North Harbor," Benjamin said.

"North Harbor? Where's that?"

"You know, Chatham Island," Benjamin said.

Lara nodded. "Oh, right. That's one of those little islands out in the bay. I haven't lived around here all that long. I used to live down in Kittery until I moved out to get my own place."

"*Our* own place," Keith interjected sullenly, his first contribution to the conversation.

"Is it cool living on an island?" Lara asked. "I mean, do you guys party a lot out there?"

Nina stifled a sarcastic response. This was Benjamin's half-sister, after all. They shared the same father. And for that matter, so did Zoey, and Zoey was her best friend. This Lara girl might *look* like a bimbo and *sound* like an airhead, but surely, if she was related to Zoey and Benjamin she had to have some good qualities.

"I like the island," Benjamin said. "Um, so. What do you do?"

"You mean, like, for work?"

"Or school, or whatever," Benjamin said.

Lara shrugged. "I wait tables. I also do temp work sometimes."

Benjamin smiled. "See, it must be a family trait. My folks . . . which is to say, *your* folks, too, to some extent . . ." He took a deep breath. "Anyway, we own a restaurant on the island."

Keith perked up slightly at this. "Like, a good restaurant?"

Probably wants to know if the Passmores are rich, Nina realized. She wondered if Benjamin had thought the same thing. She saw the tiny, ironic smile, quickly suppressed.

"Just a little place for islanders year-round and tourists in the summer." He plastered an innocent smile on his face. "What is it *you* do, Keith?"

"I do whatever," Keith offered.

Uh-huh. Keith *sold* whatever. Whether he also *did* it was an open question, but Nina and Benjamin had followed them around long enough earlier that evening to be sure that Keith, at least, was in the business of selling drugs.

"Anyone mind if I don't smoke?" Nina asked. She retrieved her pack of Lucky Strikes from the bottom of her purse, shook one out, and stuck it unlit in the corner of her darkly lipsticked mouth.

Lara stared at her for a moment, then returned her attention to Benjamin. "So, like, you're blind, huh? You can't see anything?"

"All I can see are reruns of *Full House*," Benjamin said, straight-faced. "It's a weird kind of thing; totally baffles the doctors."

Nina laughed out loud, then stifled herself when it became clear that neither of the other two had gotten the joke.

"So, what am I supposed to say?" Lara asked.

"What do you mean?"

"I mean, like okay, so you're my half-brother, right? So, what does that mean?"

"I don't know that it means anything, Lara, except that now you know you have a half-brother and half-sister and a biological father." He shrugged. "Maybe if you need an organ donation someday . . ."

Lara thought about this for a while as she consumed a few more fries. "You're not just making this up, are you?" she asked finally. She gave Benjamin a strange, sideways look.

"Why would I make it up?"

She shrugged. "Sometimes people tell me things and I don't know if they're real or not."

Nina noticed Keith grinning wryly and chuckling to himself.

"Well, I'll tell you what, Lara," Benjamin said patiently. "No one wants to rush anything or force anything, all right? So how about if I give you my number at home. You think

223

about what you want to do, and if you want to, you can call me, okay?"

Nina fumbled again in her purse and produced a pen. She wrote Benjamin's phone number down on a paper napkin and handed it to Lara. Keith reached aggressively and took it, leaving Lara's hand poised in midair. She shrugged and ate another fry.

"We have to go," Keith said. He looked at Benjamin, then at Nina. "She'll call you if she wants anything."

Lara stood up and turned her sidelong, skeptical gaze on Benjamin. The look was lost on Benjamin, of course, who kept his shades pointed at the spot where she had been. "Is this all true?"

"All true," Benjamin said.

"Because I heard maybe you just made it up."

"Where did you hear that?" Benjamin asked reasonably.

For some reason Keith found the question funny. He laughed harshly and shook his head in merriment.

"I hear things about people," Lara confided.

"Oh, yeah," Keith agreed sarcastically. "You'd be amazed what Lara hears."

TWO

"IT'S NEVER SOME LITTLE SKINNY guy who you end up having to carry," Christopher complained. "No, no, it has to be some behemoth."

"Behemoth?" Aisha asked.

"Yeah, behemoth. It's a good word. It means great big dumb white boy who drinks too damned much."

Jake McRoyan was far too drunk to walk unaided. He had consumed a large volume of beer and a smaller, but still dangerous volume of tequila. Aisha had found him collapsed in a corner in one of the bedrooms at the party. He'd been moaning something about Claire being a bitch, which wasn't especially surprising. Jake and Claire had a strange, self-destructive relationship, it seemed to Aisha. Not at all like the mature, rational relationship she herself had with Christopher.

She'd gone to Claire to ask for help in getting Jake to move, but Claire had been coldly indifferent. That *was* a surprise. Claire had stood by Jake in the past when his drinking had gotten out of control. Maybe she'd reached the end of her patience. Claire wasn't renowned for her patience.

So Aisha had drafted Christopher, and now the two of them were half-leading, half-carrying Jake down to the pier to catch the water taxi home. Jake's knees kept splaying out, collapsing his legs. Then Christopher would grab him under his arms and prop him back up and Aisha would offer encouraging words: "It's only another few feet, Jake, come on."

Jake tripped over his own feet and nearly went flying. Christopher kept him from slamming against a concrete light post, but just barely. "Jeez, this guy is heavy," Christopher complained. "I'll bet he's two twenty-five. Damn big lumpy football player. If a guy's going to be a drunk and make people carry his ass around the streets, he ought to be under two hundred pounds."

At last they reached the pier and sloughed Jake onto a bench, where he promptly rolled off and lay crumpled on the ground, passed out.

"Well, he stays there, as far as I'm concerned," Christopher said. "I can't lift that dude. When it's time, we can drag him on board."

"No argument here," Aisha said. She had little enough pity for drunks, and because she'd had to carry Jake, she was sweaty and her clothes were rumpled and the image of a romantic interlude with Christopher on the trip back to the island seemed pretty unlikely now. "You know, I was kind of disappointed by the party tonight. I mean, I was at Richie's last two birthday parties and both times we had some kind of massive explosion or something. Breakups, fights, hair pulling. It was kind of tame this year."

"Maybe we just missed most of the excitement," Christopher said.

Aisha decided she didn't care if she was sweaty and frowzy. Christopher was too, so they were even. She wrapped her arms around his waist and kissed him. "We didn't miss *all* the excitement. I remember certain exciting moments."

Christopher kissed her deeply and slipped his hands inside her coat.

"Christopher, not out here in public," she chided, although without much conviction. "Someone might see."

"No one around but Jake, and he can't see anything right now," Christopher said.

Aisha closed her eyes and reveled in the pleasure for a moment, but when she opened them again, she noticed someone she'd missed seeing earlier.

"Stop it. There's Lucas," Aisha said, pushing Christopher away. "*Without* Zoey," she added in an undertone. He was halfway down the block, sitting and seemingly staring at a docked sailboat.

"What happened, they fight?"

"I don't know. Everything was fine early on, then suddenly I couldn't find Zoey, and Lucas was wandering around looking very bummed."

"Hey, Lucas!" Christopher shouted. "Come here and stop being lazy. Help me get Jake up off the ground. You been sitting there the whole time watching me drag this overgrown monster all the way down here?"

Lucas shambled over and without a word helped manhandle Jake back onto the bench.

"You know, I'm starting to think our man Jake here may have a little drinking problem," Christopher said.

"He doesn't drink all that often," Aisha said.

"Yeah, but when he does, he gets serious about it. I have the occasional brew myself, but no one has ever had to carry me down the street," Christopher said. He looked at Jake with distaste.

"He had a bad night," Lucas said quietly.

"If you're a drunk, you can always come up with some excuse," Christopher countered. "So what's his problem tonight?"

Lucas looked glum and shook his head. Then they heard the sound of heels on cobblestone. Claire, coming down the street in a chic cream wool coat that contrasted sharply with her long, jet-black hair.

Lucas's expression went even darker than it had been. He muttered a particularly foul curse word, moved off a short distance, and turned his back on all of them.

Aisha and Christopher exchanged a significant look. Lucas and Claire had a long history between them, but Lucas wasn't usually one for being quite so vicious.

"I have a feeling Jake's *problem* just showed up," Christopher said in an undertone.

Claire glanced coolly down at Jake and checked her watch. "It's five till one. Where are Nina and Benjamin?"

"And Zoey," Aisha amended.

"I believe Zoey left early and caught the last ferry," Claire said blandly. "Ah. There they are."

Nina and Benjamin were just coming down the street.

"Where have you two been?" Aisha called out. "You missed the dismal last few hours of the party."

"We've been spying and kicking ass," Nina said happily.

"We met my half-sister for the first time," Benjamin announced. He grinned complacently at the silence. "We had a delightful time. First we spied on her and her boyfriend, discovering that her boyfriend sells drugs. Then I was chased and pounded by said boyfriend. Then I got in a lucky kick to his balls. And we rounded off the evening with a long and fairly stupid conversation over french fries."

Aisha looked at Christopher. "Okay, I'm starting to think you're right. We missed most of the excitement."

When they disembarked from the water taxi, the seven of them went their separate ways. Claire, directly toward her home without a word to anyone. Nina followed her, but only after she and Benjamin said good night to each other for several minutes that involved a lot of kissing and false departures followed by more kissing. It got on Aisha's nerves a little because she'd have liked to have a similar long farewell with Christopher but Christopher was busy with Lucas, the two of them trying to get Jake off the boat.

"I'll probably still be awake when you come by later," she whispered to Christopher.

"I'll knock on your window," he said, smiling at the prospect.

"Knock quietly. My mother can hear things that no other human being can hear," Aisha warned.

Christopher and Lucas finally went off, half-dragging, half-carrying Jake and discussing the best way to sneak him into his bedroom without alerting his parents.

Aisha walked with Benjamin through the graveyard quiet of North Harbor, down dark, cobblestoned streets where the darkest alley, even at one thirty in the morning, was safe. Here on these streets Benjamin could get around almost as well as a sighted person, the darkness irrelevant to him as he kept his subconscious count of steps from corner to corner.

She left him at his house, asking him to tell Zoey to call her in the late morning after Aisha got back from church. From the Passmore home it was a long climb up the aptly named Climbing Way to the ridge that overlooked the tiny town. Aisha leaned into it, trying to ignore the complaints of her tired muscles.

Aisha lived in a bed-and-breakfast, a huge, painstakingly decorated old home that in summer rented rooms to tourists. This time of year there were no tourists and big parts of Gray House were empty. The family—her mother and father and little brother, Kalif—lived in a separate area upstairs with its own family room, bathroom, and kitchen. Aisha was the only one whose room was downstairs. It made for a feeling of isolation sometimes, but also of privacy.

To her surprise, as she entered the house on tiptoes, she saw a light in the guest living room just to the right. She peeked inside and saw her father, wearing a bathrobe and snoring in a wing-back easy chair.

Aisha crept over to him and saw that he had a book open on his lap. An illustrated book on birds.

She shook his shoulder gently. "Wake up, Daddy."

"Huh?" He opened his eyes. "What? Oh. I wasn't sleeping."

"Daddy, don't you think I'm a little old for you to be waiting up for me?"

He gave her a sleepy, disgruntled look. "I wasn't waiting up for you." He lifted the book. "I was reading up on cormorants."

"Sure you were," Aisha said.

"And by the way, the answer is no, you're not too old for me to wait up for you," her father said. "You'll never be that old as long as you're my daughter." He got up, groaning as he straightened his back. Aisha gave him a helpful pull.

"Did you have a good time?" he asked.

"It was okay."

"Good." He started off toward the stairs but stopped at the door. "Oh, someone called for you earlier."

"Really?" Aisha was intrigued.

"Yes. First he tried to tell me his name was T-Bone. But when I threatened to hang up, he decided his name was really Jeff Pullings."

"Jeff?" Aisha felt her stomach roll. Jeff was calling her? Now? "Did . . . did he say anything?"

"Yes, he said he had a gig." Her father gave her a knowing look. "That means a job for a musician. Gig."

"Yes, I know."

"Oh. Well, anyway, he said he's opening for Tea Stew and

232

Applejack in Boston this weekend and he wondered if you'd like to come down."

Aisha took a moment to translate "Tea Stew" into Tiësto. "Applejack" was Afrojack.

Then it hit her. Jeff's rap group was opening for two major acts like that? She'd always thought he was good, but this was *major*. At least, she was pretty sure it was major. She'd never paid all that much attention to music. In the morning she'd ask Nina. Nina would know.

"Thanks, Daddy," she said distractedly.

"Well, good night."

Aisha went to her room. She snapped on the lamp by her bed. The clock showed almost two in the morning. In another hour and a half Christopher would come by in his newly purchased island car, delivering papers. He would tap at her window and they would kiss on the front porch or in the warmth of his car, making up for the good-bye they'd had to pass up at the landing.

Christopher, the great love of her life.

So different from Jeff, the *first* great love of her life.

THREE

LUCAS AND CHRISTOPHER MANAGED TO drag and carry Jake from the landing across the ferry parking area, past the Passmores' restaurant, and along the curve of Town Beach. But they still weren't half the distance to Jake's house.

"Man, I was hoping to get an hour of sleep before I had to get up and go to work," Christopher complained.

"I gotta take a rest," Lucas said. He sloughed Jake's arm off his shoulder and the two of them tumbled Jake over the low concrete retaining wall onto the beach.

"We could just leave him there," Christopher suggested hopefully.

Lucas shook his head. "He's had a bad time of it tonight."

"He's hammered. How bad a time could he be having?"

Lucas slumped down gratefully onto the sand, resting his back against the wall. Christopher sat down wearily just on the other side of Jake.

"Why does this remind me of a scene from *Weekend at*

Bernie's?" Christopher asked dryly. "Two of us and a dead guy."

As if to deny that he was dead, Jake began snoring fitfully.

"So. What hit the fan with Jake here?" Christopher asked.

"Claire told him I'd slept with her," Lucas said.

"You slept with Claire?" Christopher demanded, simultaneously shocked and envious.

"No. I told you about it, Christopher. We kind of made out was all."

"Yeah, I remember that."

"So Claire told Jake we'd done *it*. Jake gets upset and proceeds to get roasted. Then he goes off and tells Zoey the big news."

Christopher was absently sifting sand through his fingers. "Why'd he tell Zoey?"

Lucas shrugged. "I don't know for sure. But basically I guess Jake still kind of likes Zoey. Maybe she still likes him, too, I don't know."

"Oh, so it's like he's warning her that you're a dog. He figures when she hears about this, she'll dump you and go running to him?"

Lucas sighed. "I don't know, dude. I'm too tired to figure it all out. Except that for whatever reason, Claire lied to Jake. Maybe she was trying to make him jealous. Maybe she just wanted to make him mad enough to kick my ass."

"Women," Christopher said without elaboration.

"Claire," Lucas said darkly. He dug his hand down into the cold sand. The tide was coming in, lapping closer and closer, inch by inch. But they were well up the beach, beyond the reach of the water.

"Maybe she told Jake figuring he'd be sure to tell Zoey," Christopher suggested. "Maybe she wants to break you and Zoey up."

"I'm sure she has some reason," Lucas agreed, "but with her, who knows? No one understands Claire, except maybe Benjamin." He nudged the unconscious Jake. "This poor dude, man, he's just helpless."

"So what are you going to do about Zoey?" Christopher asked. "Tell her, 'hey, babe, I didn't do it with Claire. I tried like hell but I didn't because she wouldn't let me'?" Christopher laughed cynically.

"I'm glad you're entertained by my life falling apart," Lucas said grimly. "Christopher, do you ever think maybe you're just the world's biggest screwup?"

"No, man," Christopher said. "You shouldn't think that way, either."

Lucas stared out into the darkness for a while. "You know what I have going for me if I lose Zoey?" he said at last.

"No. What?"

"Not a single goddamned thing, Christopher," Lucas said. "Not one single thing."

Christopher had no answer for this. He sighed and looked mightily uncomfortable, and at last Lucas forced a lighter tone.

"So. How about if we drag Jake down to the water? Cold seawater in the face might wake him up enough to stagger home."

Christopher climbed to his feet, brushing sand from his pants. "Worth a try."

"Come on, Jake," Lucas said gently. "Time to hit the cold shower."

Aisha sat in her room, on her still-made bed, with her personal photo album open on her lap. The lamp was on, casting a gentle yellow glow. She wore a long flannel nightgown, light gray with pink flowers. On the wall above her bed was a mounted poster of Einstein. On the opposite wall a poster of Stephen Hawking against the backdrop of his book *A Brief History of Time*. Over her desk were photos of Ronald McNair, the astronaut and physicist killed in the *Challenger* explosion, Barack Obama, and Dr. King.

In the book on her lap was a photograph of Jeff Pullings and her, hugging extravagantly. To Aisha's critical eye, she looked like a toothpick topped with lots of hair. Jeff was a head taller, hair cut in a stylish fade, muscular arms bare in a torn, sleeveless denim jacket that was open in front.

She could remember the day the picture had been taken. Aisha with Jeff and his friends, all on a Saturday hanging out by Faneuil Hall Marketplace. Jeff and three other guys had decided they were going to get serious making music, and armed with a turntable, a small amplifier, a tape player, and a lot of D-cell batteries, they were going to entertain the tourists at Faneuil Hall and, no doubt, be overheard by someone with connections to the music industry.

Aisha had thought at the time that it was a silly plan, but Jeff was three years older, an actual *senior* while Aisha was a lowly freshman, so she kept quiet.

As it turned out they played for a while, picked up nine dollars in donations, and finally got rousted by two good-humored cops. The police informed them that there was a city bureaucracy that had to be dealt with if you wanted to play music in public.

Unlike Jeff, Aisha had the patience to learn more. And three months later Jeff got a regular spot rapping in one of the T stations, Boston's public transportation system. During the week commuters on the system got a few minutes of a string quartet as they waited for trains. But on Saturday and Sunday the spot was turned over to Jeff, now, in honor of the "T," calling himself T-Bone.

That's what he was doing when Aisha and her family left Boston. Now he was opening for Afrojack and Tiësto. Or Tea Stew, as her father said. Jeff had come a long way. He was a success, against all the odds. And now he wanted to see Aisha again.

Aisha went to her closet and after some digging pulled out her old diary. In those days she had written her private thoughts down on paper, protected only by a tiny brass lock that had long since broken. Now when she felt like writing, she put it in her computer, protected by passwords. Only, she seldom wrote anything anymore.

Dear Diary: Got an A plus on the stupid math test today and Mr. Lass naturally made a big deal because it was the only perfect score in the class, which was so embarrassing. That little bitch Breonna (gag, retch) called me a mega-dweeb...

Aisha smiled ruefully and thumbed forward. Fortunately she'd gotten over being embarrassed that she was good in things like math.

Dear Diary: Guess who asked me out? Jeff PULLINGS!!!! He's a SENIOR!!!! I nearly screamed when he said it. No one EVEN believes it's true . . .

Dear Diary: Mother is totally MENTAL because I'm going out with Jeff. Like just because he's older he's only after one thing. Duh. Like guys my own age aren't just the same. And being older he's so much more mature, so he's not all gross about things. I am so absolutely in LOVE with Jeff. I think someday he'll be a famous musician and we'll be married and I'll be a model. Like John Legend and that Chrissy girl only not so dorky . . .

Dear Diary: Jeff just left this minute and I had to write about it instantly. It was so magical and amazing. He is so mature and so cool. We french-kissed for a really long time and I even let him touch under my bra!!! Scream!!!

Aisha closed the book. The fourteen-year-old Aisha seemed like another person. A slightly embarrassing person, gushing over Jeff like that. But there was one more entry she wanted to read again. She remembered the date.

Dear Diary: This was the night. The night when I absolutely became a WOMAN and not just a little girl.

That's what Jeff told me, that now I was his woman, not his little girl. In case you can't guess, dear diary, we finally—

There was a light tapping sound at her window and Aisha started guiltily. She slammed the diary closed and slid it under her pillow.

She caught her breath for a moment, then drew the curtains back. What she saw was a familiar, though distorted face. A Joker mask.

She opened the window. "Hi, Christopher."

"Why so serious?" Christopher asked.

"Wait, you're not Christopher," Aisha said, feeling guilty but trying to act normal. "You're so much prettier than he is."

Christopher pulled off the mask. "Very humorous."

"Now, what if I had screamed at the top of my lungs and woken up my father and mother?"

Christopher looked thoughtful. "Hmm. I guess I'd have had to run for it." He wiggled his eyebrows suggestively. "Can I come in?"

"No, you can't. I'll be right out."

Aisha closed the windows and drew the curtains again. She pulled on her galumphy L.L. Bean boots, leaving them unlaced, and her puffy green parka over her flannel nightgown. She hazarded a look at herself in the mirror and had to laugh. If Christopher could love her looking like this, he must really love her. What would Jeff think if he saw her in full Maine regalia, looking like a cross between Minnie Mouse and Frosty the Snowman?

She crept silently down the hall and opened the front door carefully. The air was a cold slap, making her face tingle, immediately finding its way under the hem of her nightgown. Christopher came up with the mask back on.

"Kiss me," he whispered.

"It's freezing out here," Aisha said.

Christopher pulled off the mask again, obviously a little disgruntled that she didn't find it as hysterically funny as he did. He put his arms around her, squeezing air from her parka, and pulled her close.

His first kiss was infinitely gentle.

Jeff had always been playful when he kissed her.

His second kiss was deeper, not aggressive, but yearning. She opened her lips.

She remembered the first time Jeff had ever french-kissed her. She'd been shocked and slightly disgusted. But later, when she'd gotten used to it, she'd found it incredibly exciting.

As she did now with Christopher.

As she had then with Jeff.

Christopher's lips were fuller.

Jeff's thinner. And there had been a rasp of whiskers.

Christopher was taller.

Jeff had been broader.

Christopher trailed kisses down her throat, lowering the zipper of her parka to expose more. "Let's go sit in my car," he said in a low whisper.

They walked across the yard to Christopher's shattered, horrible island car. Aisha glanced back nervously at the house. Fortunately her parents' windows were at the back. Unless they came into the family's private living room, they couldn't see the front yard.

Inside the car it was marginally warmer. The radio was on, playing scratchy, staticky, but unfortunately recognizable music. Tiësto. "Feel It In My Bones." Aisha snapped it off.

"You don't like the music?" Christopher said.

"It's not coming in very well," Aisha said.

Christopher smiled self-deprecatingly. "It's not exactly a great sound system. But the sad thing is, it's one of the best parts of this car."

"You think *this* is bad?" Aisha looked around at the interior, the sagging headliner, the fact that there were no backseats, the plastic wrap and duct tape that were the right rear window. "For an island car this is nothing. You still have a windshield."

"Don't be dissin' my ride," Christopher joked. "This is as big a piece of crap as anything on the island."

"No way. You have a muffler."

"Well, I have to since I drive around at night," Christopher said defensively. "But how about the paint job? How about the fact that one headlight points left and the other points almost straight up?"

"Hey, in *our* island car only one door opens. And our radio only gets one station, and that's a country station."

"Oooh. That is good," Christopher admitted.

"But I will say you have an excellent stench of mildew," Aisha allowed. "And I like the way the rear bumper is attached with yellow nylon rope. That's a nice touch."

"I'll show you a nice touch," Christopher said in a low, sexy voice.

"You wish."

There was a loud rapping on the roof of the car that made them both jump.

"Uh-oh," Christopher said. He lowered the window on his side. "Hi, Mrs. Gray."

"Well, hello, Christopher," Aisha's mother said.

"I was, uh, delivering the papers?"

"I see them there on the porch," Mrs. Gray said. "Also, I

believe I see my daughter. In your car. At three thirty in the morning."

"We were just saying good night," Aisha said.

"Then say it," Mrs. Gray said, putting some steel into her voice.

"Good night, Aisha," Christopher said, extending his hand formally.

Aisha shook it. "Good night, Christopher."

She climbed out of the car and started toward the house, followed by her mother's vow that they would be discussing this tomorrow. "Oh yes," Mrs. Gray said. "We will definitely be discussing this."

Aisha

I'll tell you what's scary: snakes. I mean, I know it's a real
common thing to be afraid of, but still, snakes can be bad
news. You can show me Nightmare on Elm Street one through
seventeen and I don't care. But don't get me around snakes.
You can't trust an animal that has no legs. I mean a land animal, of course. Dolphins have no legs and I'm sure they're fine,
but a thing on land with no legs is not to be trusted. Snakes,
worms, slugs: I have nothing good to say about any of them.

The other thing that's always kind of scared me is insanity. You know? Like the possibility that one day you'd be
going along fine, minding your own business, and then, all of
a sudden, your brain just loses it? You start hearing voices in
your head, seeing things that aren't there? You start gibber-
ing like an idiot and talking about conspiracies? It happens.
And it's usually during the teen years that insanity starts
showing up. That's true. They say it's all the hormones associated with going through puberty, and the fact is that the
closest I ever came to going crazy was mostly because of
hormone-related things. It was like all my life growing up I'd
been this perfectly normal girl. Some might even say boring.
I mean, I was still in Girl Scouts when I was fourteen, which

tells you I wasn't exactly running with the wild and crazy crowd.

But then, when I was fourteen, I did sort of go crazy. Dangerously, stupidly crazy. Only for a while, but enough to know I didn't want to stay that way.

What made me go crazy? Duh. A guy of course. What else would it be?

FOUR

ZOEY GOT UP UNUSUALLY EARLY. It wasn't something she'd planned, but despite having fallen asleep very late the night before, she woke up on her usual school-day schedule.

She woke fully alert and with the feeling that she had to be somewhere. A quick mental check showed that she didn't have anything at all to do this morning. Her friends were unavailable on Sunday mornings. Aisha went to church, and Nina had long since made clear that she would kill anyone who bugged her on a Sunday before noon. Lucas also went to church, so she wouldn't be able to see him till later.

Suddenly she remembered.

She wouldn't be seeing Lucas at all, if she could help it.

She showered and got dressed and put on casual clothes, a pair of gray sweatpants and her red fleece jacket.

She went outside and jogged for several blocks, not through any great desire for exercise but just to burn off the wired, over-alert feeling.

She jogged as far as the circle and dropped to a walk as she began to encounter the groups heading on foot toward early mass. The island's only church had to handle both Catholics and Protestants. Catholics got the earlier hours.

Zoey told herself she was surprised to see people already filing by on their way to the church. She told herself she was *worried* about the possibility that she might accidentally run into Lucas and his mother on their way to the services. And when she scanned the faces in the cluster of worshipers and didn't see Lucas's, she told herself she was relieved.

She walked on through the circle, feeling disgruntled and confused. She couldn't think of a good reason why she had come out this early, and now she couldn't think of anything to do. Maybe she should brave Nina's wrath and wake her up. There was no good reason why Nina had to sleep until noon. Or even eight.

Claire poured coffee into her covered mug and walked back upstairs from the kitchen, past Nina's second-floor room, to her own third-floor bedroom. She climbed up the ladder set in one wall of her bedroom. It led to a rectangular hatch in the ceiling. From long practice she had learned to hook one arm around the ladder, using that hand to hold her coffee mug and push the hatch open with her free hand.

She climbed up through the hole and out onto the widow's walk, a square platform atop the house with low railings all around and towering brick chimneys at each end.

It was her favorite place in the world.

Up here the breeze almost always blew. The view encompassed all the northern end of Chatham Island, all of the harbor that gave the tiny brick and shingle and cobblestone village of North Harbor its name.

To the north was the black-and-white-striped lighthouse on its tiny rocky islet. To the west the fishing boats rocked at anchor or were tied up alongside the pier. The ferry was just pulling in, appearing slowly and mysteriously from a fog bank like some magician's trick. Weymouth and the whole mainland were invisible behind the fog. To the south the piney ridge rose from the edge of the village and Claire could make out a glimpse of Gray House, Aisha's home, through the trees.

The breeze wasn't moving the fog, not yet. And there would be little sun to burn it off. Overcast blanketed the entire area, turning the small visible circle of the Atlantic the color of lead.

She looked down at the street below, at Lighthouse Road, which separated the row of old restored captains' homes like hers from the jagged rocks and tumbled granite boulders of the north shore.

Claire saw Zoey at the same instant that Zoey's eyes, looking up, met hers.

Claire sighed. Way too early for this, but it had to be done. It was the necessary last step in the process.

She made a slight wave. Then she held out her hand, making a sign for Zoey to wait. As she turned to descend the ladder it occurred to her that Zoey might not want to wait. Presumably Claire wasn't her favorite person in the world right now.

But no, of course Zoey would wait. Zoey would be hoping against hope that Claire would somehow tell her something to make everything all right.

Oddly enough, Claire realized, that's just exactly what she *was* going to do.

Jake woke to pounding on his bedroom door. The first thing he was aware of was a huge, all-encompassing pain in his head. It throbbed monstrously as he turned his head on his pillow.

With the pain came a terrible thirst. His mouth felt as if it had been stuffed full of cotton balls. He opened his eyes and almost cried out from the pain. Eyes swollen. Stomach sick and sour. Muscles cramped and bunched.

"Jake, get up now. You have to get ready for church."

His mother's voice through his door, seeming impossibly loud.

"Okay," he croaked.

"Are you awake?"

He had to fight down the urge to throw up. "Yes," he said tersely.

"Don't be late," his mother chirped in her relentlessly cheerful way.

He sat up and rolled his legs over the side of the bed. He was still wearing pants, though no shirt. At once he knew he would throw up. He jumped up and raced for his bathroom, almost crying from the pain in his head. He slipped and fell to his knees on the tile floor, clutching the toilet bowl with both arms, and heaved.

When he was done, he rolled onto his back on the tile. He was crying now but too dehydrated to form tears, just racking sobs of misery and pain.

At last he forced himself up and stripped off his pants. Damp sand was in the pockets and down his crotch. He staggered into the shower. He swallowed from the jet, gulping and gulping, then vomited it all back up again.

At last with at least some water working its way back through his system and three Advil, he made his way back to his bedroom, still throbbing with one large head-to-toe pain.

He looked around, befuddled. Obviously he had gotten drunk the night before. Either that or he had been poisoned.

Maybe they were pretty much the same thing. He had some memory of a party. He remembered music. A flash of people dancing. A flash of himself dancing with Zoey. A disturbing half-memory of Claire, in shadow, her eyes glittering, as dangerous as a snake's.

Then he remembered it all and wished he could have another drink.

Zoey met Claire in the Geigers' front yard. Claire was still carrying her mug of coffee and looking effortlessly elegant, as always. Zoey was acutely aware of her own relative frumpiness in sweatpants and the fleece jacket.

"Out jogging?" Claire asked pleasantly.

"Just walking. I woke up early and couldn't get back to sleep." Zoey waited for some sign of guilt on Claire's face, but there was nothing.

"Mmm. I wanted to see the fog," Claire said. "It's unusually dense. You can feel the moisture. You know, fog is really just a very low cloud. Warmer air moving in across the cold surface of the water and you get condensation that—"

"Claire, I don't want to talk to you about weather," Zoey snapped, surprising herself. Claire's eyebrows shot up.

"Sorry," Claire said.

"I just want you to know that I think you're a bitch," Zoey

said. "I mean, a *real* backstabbing bitch."

Claire colored slightly and stared with hard eyes. "What's your problem?"

"What do you mean, 'what's my problem'?"

"I mean, what's your problem," Claire repeated. "I thought we were having a friendly little chat here, and suddenly you go off." She waved her mug slightly for emphasis.

Zoey faltered. If Claire was just putting on an innocent act, it was a good one. "What do you think I'm going to do, Claire, just act like you and Lucas are no big deal?"

"What?"

"You and Lucas, Claire. You and Lucas."

"What about me and Lucas?" Now she sounded genuinely annoyed.

Zoey peered closely at her. Claire's big, almond-shaped dark eyes showed no evidence of guilt or even worry. "Jake told me all about it," Zoey said, but with less certainty.

"Jake? Now Jake's involved? Zoey, what the hell are you trying to say?"

"Jake told me at the party last night that you slept with Lucas," Zoey blurted.

Claire's rare, cool smile formed slowly. "Jake told you I slept with Lucas. Jake, who hates Lucas for taking you away from him; Jake, who still carries a major torch for you; Jake, who was so drunk he had to be carried home; *that* Jake told you I slept with Lucas."

"That's what he said," Zoey replied as staunchly as she could manage.

Claire sipped her coffee and gave Zoey a disappointed look. "I told Jake that Lucas and I went for a drive a few days ago. I was mad at Jake because I saw you and him hugging each other like you were back together. Lucas saw the same scene. That and other things made us both suspicious that you and Jake were thinking of getting back together. So we went for a drive to discuss it. That's what I told Jake."

Zoey tried to think of something to say, but now she was thoroughly confused. If what Claire was saying was true, then . . . then it had been Lucas who thought *she* was being unfaithful. And it was Lucas who had been wronged. And Jake was the bad guy, not Claire *or* Lucas. "Nothing happened between you and Lucas?"

"I did not have sex with Lucas," Claire said sharply. Then she batted her eyes in a parody of coquettishness. "Although he is cute, isn't he?"

"Oh, no," Zoey said, ignoring Claire's attempt to get a rise out of her.

"I can't believe Jake would tell you a story like that," Claire said. "I suppose it was a clumsy attempt to break you and Lucas up."

"But why would he want that?" Zoey asked.

"I told you," Claire said with just a hint of bitterness. "I think he's still in love with you. And"—she shrugged—"we're basically finished as a couple, so, frankly, you're welcome to him."

Lucas had gone to confession the day before, early Saturday morning. He had confessed to using bad language, to lying by omission, and to his normal array of sins associated with the vice of lust. The priest had given him the usual penances, seemingly unshocked by the fact that a teenage boy had lust in his heart.

He took Holy Communion with his mother. She was the main reason he attended mass. His father no longer did, and his mother seemed to appreciate or even need her son's company. He had even, somewhat absurdly, prayed for Zoey to come back to him. But he wasn't generally a big believer in prayer, since he'd spent the first year at Youth Authority praying they'd let him out early and that hadn't exactly worked. Neither had those last-minute prayers when he realized he was facing a pop quiz on some subject he hadn't studied. God had never stepped in and decided to give him a free *A*. Evidently, what with having to run the entire universe, God had better things to do with his time.

The fog that earlier had drifted across the circle was beginning to lift now as he and his mother stepped out of the church. Departing Catholics mingled cordially with the Protestants who were waiting around preparing to go in.

Lucas saw Jake and his mother standing some distance away. Jake was sitting on a bench, his head hanging practically down to his knees. Lucas grinned with the good-natured sadism sober people often feel toward drinkers. Jake was a classic, textbook picture of a guy with a brutal hangover.

He made his way down the steps as his mother was peeled off into a discussion having to do with potluck dinners and the need to avoid having duplicate bowls of Jell-O salad. He waved good-bye to her and headed around to the right. He wanted to check out the beach, see if there was any hope of surf. He had a lot to think through, and surfing always helped.

Just as he cleared the crowd, though, he came face-to-face with Zoey.

He stopped dead in his tracks. She was dressed sloppily, for her, but looked painfully beautiful to his eyes.

He tried to find something to say, but where should he start? What should he say? *Hi, Zoey, look, I didn't have sex with Claire, we just made out?*

Zoey came closer, and to Lucas's utter amazement, she put her arms around him, tilted back her head, closed her blue eyes, and drew his face down to her. She kissed him in a way that sent something very much like an electric shock through his system and immediately added to the list of sins he would have to confess next week.

"What?" he said when she drew back at last. "I mean—"

"I have to go see my dad now because I told him I would," Zoey said, "but if we could get together this evening, I would really like a chance to apologize to you."

"Apologize?"

"Claire told me what Jake said was a lie," Zoey said. "I am desperately sorry I suspected you, Lucas. And later I would like to show you just how sorry I am."

She kissed him again, despite the dirty looks of various parishioners, both Catholic and Protestant. Then she took off, leaving Lucas feeling foolish and giddy and aware that he was smiling stupidly and not caring.

The question was: Now that he had the prayer thing working, would it also work on tests?

FIVE

CLAIRE SAT AT HER COMPUTER and entered her login information for the weather site chat room.

	[17] Teen Only
Spanky	AAAARRRRGGGGHHHH
<DooMeeeNow>	never thought that always said STP sucked.
!WhattaMAN!	spanky get a grip dude
Spanky	EEEEYYYYAAAA!!!!!!!
:)martha	hi everyone
Beck	you used to love STP don't lie doomeee. hi martha.
Spanky	hi martha. i have to scream some more. NNNNOOOO!!! AAAAIIIIYYYEEEE!!!
:)martha	forget your prozac again spanky?

Claire read along for a while, seeing nothing that interested her. Then she accessed the "who's here" file and scanned down the list of names. Her heart beat a little faster when she saw the handle "Flyer." So he was there, just not saying anything. Was he there hoping she would show up?

She pulled down the Talk option and punched in Flyer's name. A private box opened up on the screen. This conversation would be just between the two of them. No one else could monitor it in any way.

Weather Girl

Hi, Flyer. I was wondering if you'd be here.

Flyer

WG, I was hoping you'd show up. I'm not usually on the system on Sunday afternoon.

Weather Girl

Me neither, but I had nothing else to do.

Flyer

Last I heard you were going to a party. How did it go?

Weather Girl

Not great.

Flyer

Problems?

Flyer

Still there, WG?

Weather Girl

I was trying to decide if I should tell you. I did something fairly rotten. I manipulated some things so it looked like . . . well, the details are too complicated to go into. But basically I used some people to get back at my boyfriend. Ex-boyfriend, I guess.

Flyer

Back at him for what?

Flyer

Hello, hello. Still with me, WG?

Weather Girl

It sounds too pathetic.

Flyer

Don't have to worry about being embarrassed with me, WG. I'm just a guy you've never seen, who's never seen you. You won't have to face me at school tomorrow.

Weather Girl

OK. He didn't love me.

Flyer

Oh.

Weather Girl

He was still in love with his old girlfriend.

Flyer

That must have hurt.

Weather Girl

I don't get hurt, Flyer.

Flyer

Everyone gets hurt.

Weather Girl

And now he's the one who's hurt. His former girlfriend now
thinks he's a liar.

Flyer

But that doesn't change the fact that he doesn't love you.

Weather Girl

No, it doesn't. Apparently I'm not the type of person that guys
fall in love with.

Flyer

I doubt that. You're smart and witty. You have goals and
ideas. What's not to love?

Weather Girl

Manipulative, self-centered.

Flyer

And honest about yourself. But I don't know if I should be
sad or glad about your boyfriend. Maybe he just wasn't
capable of appreciating you. Maybe he just looked at what's
superficial. Girls are that way with me, usually. I keep telling
them that deep down inside I'm sweet and nice and really
interesting.

Weather Girl

If I told people I was sweet, they'd just fall down laughing.

Flyer

Well, I like you, WG. Or should I say Claire?

Weather Girl

WG. That's safer somehow, Flyer.

Flyer

Yes. Friends unseen, unnamed, but friends anyway. Right, WG?

Weather Girl

Right, Flyer. Friends. Bye for now.

Flyer

Bye, Weather Girl.

Aisha was on her way into church behind her mother, father, and Kalif when she saw Zoey putting what looked like very major lip-lock on Lucas. She grinned and figured whatever argument they were having, they'd gotten over it.

After church she thought of stopping by Zoey's house on her way home, but her mother liked to make a big Sunday brunch after church, which was always great. What was not so great was that her mother was clearly waiting for the right moment to talk to her about what had happened the night before.

She would find a time when Aisha's father wasn't around.

Because as Aisha knew perfectly well, her mother wanted to bring up matters that her father knew nothing about.

The opportunity came as they headed toward the family's island car, parked across the circle.

"I think I'll walk home," Mrs. Gray told her husband.

"Up that hill?" Mr. Gray asked skeptically. "In Sunday shoes?"

"It will firm up my butt."

Mr. Gray grinned wolfishly and started to say something, then caught himself. "We'll meet you there. I'll start cutting the fruit."

Mrs. Gray shot Aisha an unmistakable look.

"I'll walk with Mom," Aisha said grimly. She watched her father and brother drive off, feeling like the one last refugee who couldn't get on the flight to freedom.

"About last night," Mrs. Gray began without preliminary as they set off.

"Uh-huh."

"You know I think the world of Christopher."

"But?"

"But I don't approve of you sneaking out of the house after dark to have an assignation," her mother said. She waved to a friend down the street.

"I wasn't sneaking, Mother, and I'm not even sure I know what an assignation is."

"Well, an approximate definition would be 'meeting a boy in his car at nearly four in the morning.' When your mother thinks you're sleeping safe in your bed."

"Oh," Aisha said.

Her mother took her arm and stopped her at the corner of South Street. "Have you had sex with Christopher?"

"Mother, of course not!"

Her mother's face relaxed. They started climbing the hill. It was slow going in heels. Very slow going. Aisha would have just taken off her shoes, but the ground was very cold and very damp. Barely above freezing.

"I just don't want another situation like with Jeff," her mother said. From something in her tone of voice it was clear to Aisha that her mother knew about Jeff's call.

"Speaking of Jeff, he called," Aisha said. *Ha. You probably thought I wouldn't tell you.*

"Oh, did he? And what did he want?"

Now who's b.s.'ing who? Aisha thought. She wisely didn't say it out loud. "I guess his group is doing pretty well. They're opening for Afrojack and Tiësto. They're playing on Halloween in Boston."

Mrs. Gray nodded, as if confirming that of course this was just what her husband had reported to her. "I have to admit, I'm surprised. I never expected much from that boy."

"I always told you he was talented," Aisha said defensively.

For a while they walked on in silence. Then her mother said, "So?"

"So what?"

"So are you going to ask me whether you can go down to Boston and hear him?"

Aisha shrugged. "I figured you'd say no."

"You are right about that," Mrs. Gray said firmly.

Silence again as they climbed the steepest part of the hill. The peak of the inn's roof was just coming into view.

"I'm with Christopher now," Aisha said. "I don't have anything going on with Jeff. Besides, he undoubtedly has a new girlfriend. Probably several."

"Maybe at least one will be his own age this time," Mrs. Gray said darkly.

"Mother, I think I would like to see him play, though. I mean, he's an old friend who's having his first big success. He wants to have all his old friends around to see him do well. It would be impolite to say no." Immediately Aisha winced. Wrong choice of words.

"Yes, you always did have a hard time saying *no* to Jeff Pullings, didn't you?"

"You know what I mean," Aisha said.

"And you know what *I* mean," her mother shot back.

"It's not like I would be staying with him or anything. I probably wouldn't even get a chance to talk to him. We'd all go down on Friday evening and drive back that same night."

"Who is 'we'?"

Aisha shrugged. "I was going to ask everyone. You know, the usual."

"And Christopher?" her mother asked pointedly.

Panting slightly from the exertion, they had reached the front gate.

"Yes, of course, Christopher too," Aisha said, trying to sound much calmer than she felt. "Why wouldn't I ask Christopher to go with me?"

"Does Christopher know about you and Jeff?"

Aisha looked down. "No one knows about all that. Except you and me. I don't think my friends would even believe it."

For a while they stood silently, remembering. Finally her mother said, "I guess if you went down there with a bunch of your current friends, you might be able to stay out of trouble."

"You mean I can go?"

Her mother nodded slowly. "Yes. It would be wrong of me to go on punishing you for something that happened three years ago."

SIX

"HELLO, IS JEFF PULLINGS THERE?" In the background a loud, steady drumbeat. The person who had answered the phone was a girl. She asked Aisha to speak louder.

"I'm calling for Jeff Pullings!" Aisha yelled.

"You mean T-Bone?"

Aisha rolled her eyes. "Yes."

"He's busy."

"Tell him it's Aisha Gray."

"Okay," the girl said, telegraphing her reluctance.

Aisha waited with the phone to her ear. Did she really even want to do this? Too late to back out, of course, since she'd given the girl her name. But did she want to accept Jeff's invitation, really? Or—

Suddenly the noise stopped. There was a scuffling sound and someone yelled, "You guys shut the —— up; I have a call.

"Eesh? Is that really you?"

"Yes," Aisha said, suddenly breathless. "I'm calling back

because my dad said you left a message."

"It's good to hear your voice," he said.

"It's good to hear yours, too," Aisha said. What else could she say? It wasn't like it was any big deal to say it was good to hear someone's voice.

"How are things in Maine?"

"Oh, you know. Same old stuff. School mostly. How are things in Boston?"

"Lonely," he said.

"Lonely?" the word came out in a quiver.

"I'm all alone here in the big city."

"Yeah, Boston is so much bigger than Chatham Island," Aisha said. She rolled her eyes. Could she have thought of anything dumber to say?

"So, are you going to able to come down? I'd like you to be there. It's a big deal, babe. Major stuff."

"I know; I couldn't believe it when my dad told me," Aisha said with genuine enthusiasm. "You know what he said? He said you were opening for Applejack."

Jeff laughed at that. "It's a benefit for ALS. Tiësto and Afrojack together, and they wanted to include a local act. Which is me."

"I'm really happy for you."

"Yeah, me too. They actually *pay*. Not a lot, but it's a start.

Plus, I get picked up in a limo, which beats catching the yellow line." Then, in a more serious voice, "By the way, Aisha, does your father know about me and you? He sounded like he wasn't too happy I was calling."

"No. He can never remember my friends' names," Aisha said. "And my mom never told him the other stuff. He gets upset by things like that."

"Yeah," Jeff said.

For a moment silence fell between them. Aisha felt the edge of sadness. Memories hovered at the boundaries of conscious awareness, threatening to take shape. Memories very good, and very bad.

"Anyway," she said at last.

"Anyway," he repeated.

"So, I'll definitely try to come," Aisha said.

"Don't say you'll *try*," Jeff said. "Say you'll be there."

"Can I bring some friends?"

"Hey, the more people come, the better I like it," he said. "How many tickets you want? Not too many, I hope. We are just the opening act. Most of the freebies go to Tijs. If you have too many friends, they'll have to be on their own."

"Tijs, huh?" Aisha laughed. "Now you're on a first-name basis with him?"

Jeff echoed her laughter. "Oh, I'm down with all the big stars now."

"Uh-huh."

"Okay, maybe we haven't actually met, and he has no idea who I am exactly, but I have talked to some guy who works for him. And he said, 'Look, kid, just make sure you do a quick set, no encore, and get your equipment the hell off the stage.' So you can see I have a huge amount of respect in the industry."

"Yeah, but it's a major, major step up from playing in the T station."

"Definitely."

"I'm proud of you, Jeff," Aisha said sincerely.

"Will you be there?"

"I'll be there."

"And your friends?"

"Whoever wants to come, I guess," Aisha said.

"Are these just friend friends? Or is there a *friend*?"

Aisha gulped. "Just friends," she said automatically.

"That's what I wanted to hear," Jeff said, sounding relieved. "I better go. Everyone's standing around here giving me the eye, like what am I doing when we should be rehearsing. See you there, babe."

"Wait, Jeff—" But the line had gone dead. Before Aisha

could tell him that . . . That what? That one of those friends was named Christopher and yes, he was much more than just a friend?

Yes, that's what she was getting ready to tell Jeff. Only there hadn't been time.

Nina lay on her back on the rug with two pillows behind her head. Her legs were propped on the side of Benjamin's bed. Benjamin sat on the bed, leaning back against the wall. Nina held a large paperback book over her head and read aloud: "*Round she went: the squared main and mizen yards lay parallel with the wind, the topsails shaking. Farther, farther; and now the wind was abaft her beam, and by rights her sternway should have stopped; but it did not; she was still traveling with remarkable speed in the opposite direction. He filled the topsails, gave her weather helm, and*—Good grief, Benjamin, this book is full of this kind of sailing stuff!" Nina cried. "*Abaft her beam*? What does that even mean?"

"Abaft her beam," Benjamin said placidly.

"Do I have to read all these dumb sailing parts? I mean, what's with this writer anyway? The romantic parts he just skims over, but he has to give you absolutely every single detail of what sail you should use to sail a boat that doesn't even exist anymore!"

"A *frigate*, not a boat, which you would know if you were

272

paying attention to what you're reading," Benjamin pointed out.

"This is like 'boy' book to the maximum amount possible. Sailboats and cannons and all the women back on shore while the guys go off and have fun."

"Well, I *am* a boy," Benjamin said reasonably. "Girls read books about relationships and female things like feelings and emotions, while boys read books about cool stuff involving ships and cannons."

Nina sat up. "I can't believe you'd say anything so sexist. Girls don't just care about relationships. We like other stuff, too. You sexist hound. You *male*, you."

"Really?" Benjamin looked thoughtful. "I hadn't realized that." He grinned. "Then I guess you'll enjoy reading me the rest of the chapter."

"You think you're so cute, don't you?" Nina demanded. And he was. He was so cute. Even when he was smiling that annoying, superior smile, he was so cute. It was funny, because when she'd first started going out with Benjamin, she'd thought the cool thing about a boyfriend who couldn't see would be that she could dress however she wanted, not wear makeup and so on.

But the most excellent thing about Benjamin was that she could look at *him* as long as she wanted, anytime she wanted, without him knowing it. She enjoyed watching his mouth when he smiled his ironic smile; and often, lying around his house, he'd wear a pair of old sweatpants that had been shrunk in the wash to the point where they would sometimes be tight as a second layer of skin, and that wasn't bad to look at, either.

"Are you going to go on reading, or are you daydreaming?" Benjamin asked.

"Daydreaming," Nina admitted.

"About what?"

"Let's get back to reading," she said. She finished reading the rest of the chapter, outrageously overemphasizing every mention of sails, and looking up each time to the reward of his smile.

"That's the chapter," Nina announced, closing the book. "Now it's my turn."

"Your turn for what?" Benjamin asked suspiciously.

Nina fumbled in her purse and produced her cell phone. "I just downloaded this excellent album . . ."

"Oh, no," Benjamin groaned.

"And since your speakers are so much better than mine . . ." Nina went on.

"Just tell me it's not rap, or Justin Timberlake or anything."

"It's Jack White. Even *you* will like it."

"Want to bet?" he grumbled.

Nina sat down on the bed beside him. She kissed his lips,

feeling amazingly bold, even after all the many times she'd kissed him.

"Okay," he said. "You can play it, but only if you put on rubber gloves and a surgical mask before touching the holy stereo. Also, no touching any buttons except play, *including* the volume. It's perfect right where it is."

"Absolutely, cross my heart," Nina vowed as she twisted the volume knob up and cranked the bass. Just as she hit play she heard the phone ringing in the kitchen. "You want me to get that?"

"Sure," Benjamin said. "If you don't mind. And bring a soda when you come back."

Nina had reached the kitchen by the time the first blast came from the stereo, rattling the windows and vibrating the floor. Nina grinned happily and caught the phone on the third ring, just before the answering machine could engage.

"Yo, Passmore residence."

"Who is this? Nina?" Aisha's voice.

"Yeah, you got a problem with that?" Nina said, putting on a belligerent voice.

"Jeez, Nina, what are you doing over there, having a party? I can practically hear the music without using the phone."

"Wherever I go, it's a party," Nina said. She searched the

pantry shelf distractedly. Low-fat cookies. What was the point? "What's up, Eesh?"

The music suddenly dropped precipitously in volume. "Now you're in trouble!" Benjamin yelled.

"I was calling to see if you guys wanted to go to a concert on Halloween, down in Boston," Aisha said.

"Sure," Nina agreed instantly. "Who's playing?"

"Tiësto and Afrojack. It's a benefit."

Nina held out the receiver and stared at it. "Excuse me? You say you're Aisha? Aisha Gray? Aisha 'hey, I don't think elevator music is so bad' Gray?" Nina banged the receiver several times on the countertop.

"I listen to music," Aisha said defensively.

"Aisha, you are the living, breathing proof that not all black people have rhythm. You couldn't keep the beat in time with Barney singing the 'I love you, you love me' song. You're worse than Benjamin. At least he really loves music. Not always the *right* music, but music. Whereas you own what, three CDs? And two of them are of that computer-music crap." She carried the receiver over to the refrigerator.

"Are you about done abusing me?" Aisha asked patiently.

"Mmm, I guess so. Hey, toaster strudel! Damn, it's cherry. Who on earth buys cherry toaster strudel? In Pop-Tarts and toaster strudel it's blueberry, maybe raspberry. Not cherry."

"Can we focus here a little? I have this friend whose group is opening for Tiësto and Afrojack at the Orpheum. I have free tickets. Are you in or out?"

"In, duh. Like I would say no?" Nina said. "Benjamin, too."

"Benjamin? At a rap concert? How are you going to get him there—use handcuffs?"

"Hey, we'll be there," Nina said. "I can't believe you have a friend who's in a band. I thought all you knew were math dweebs and techno-dorks."

"I know some just plain dweebs and dorks, too," Aisha pointed out. "After all, I know *you*."

"If I didn't have toaster strudel to soothe me, that would have hurt," Nina said. "I'll tell Zoey when she comes back, too, okay?"

"Sure. Like I wouldn't ask her? The more people the better. Oh, by the way, since it's on Halloween they're telling people to come in costume."

"Okay, now we're getting somewhere," Nina said. "Costumes, a concert, a trip down to Boston. Life has regained its meaning."

SEVEN

DURING HIS SEVENTEEN YEARS OF life Lucas Cabral had been tripped up repeatedly by one type of lie or another, and one type of secret or another. The problem was, he had never been tripped up consistently in either one direction or the other. Sometimes he had told lies and it worked out fine. Other times lies had gotten him in trouble. Sometimes keeping secrets had been a good idea, other times not so good. Sometimes, even when he did all the right things, when he was absolutely honest and open, he'd still gotten racked up.

What made it worse was that by some twist of fate he always seemed to be stumbling across other people's secrets. At any given moment he knew something about someone that he wasn't supposed to tell. It wasn't his fault; in fact, he tried hard never, ever to learn anyone's secrets, but it didn't help.

He thought all this through as he stood on the wooden deck behind his house. The deck was a few dozen feet up the side of the ridge, where Climbing Way made its first big loop. The deck was almost directly above the backyard of Zoey's house and gave him a view straight down to her kitchen, breakfast nook, and family room.

When it was dark, as it was now, and when the Passmores had their lights on, as they did now, he could see inside: seldom heads, which were cut off by the angle, but bodies sitting around the table, or, like now, Benjamin searching the refrigerator. It was probably wrong to look, Lucas reflected, but it was fascinating. Benjamin moved his hand slowly over each item, tentative and sensitive, recognizing milk, soda cans, poking into the plastic wrap that covered a bowl.

Zoey came into the room. Lucas could see from her body language that she was watching her brother, torn between helping, which would likely earn a sarcastic rebuke from Benjamin, and staying out of the way.

Benjamin's fingers touched a Rubbermaid container. He pulled it out and opened it triumphantly.

For her part, Zoey grabbed a soda and walked over to the window. Instinctively Lucas stepped back into the shadows. Zoey was peering, neck craned, up toward him. Could she see him? Probably not, as dark as it was. But her face looked questioning. She checked her watch.

Waiting for me to come down, Lucas realized with great satisfaction. From back in the shadows he looked at her face, framed by somewhat disarranged blond hair. There was no part of her face that was unfamiliar to him, yet he wasn't in the least way tired of looking at it. He fell asleep every night recalling that familiar face. True, sometimes there were other things about Zoey, not actually familiar but imagined, that also played a part.

She stepped away from the window and he moved forward. He hopped the deck railing, hanging out over empty space for a moment. Then he dropped to a sitting position, twisted to catch the edge of the deck platform with his fingers, and lowered himself down. With his boots just three feet from the Passmores' lawn he dropped, rolled, and stood up.

He walked around the circumference of the house to the front door and knocked.

The door opened on Benjamin, munching a piece of fried chicken. "Hey, babe," Benjamin leered. He advanced on Lucas with greasy lips puckered up. "Give me a big wet one."

"Very funny, Benjamin," Lucas said, not at all convinced.

Benjamin grinned. "Oh, it's you, Lucas. Imagine my embarrassment."

"How do you do that?" Lucas demanded, sliding past Benjamin.

"I hear a loud dropping noise in the backyard," Benjamin

said. "Soon thereafter there's a loud, *male* knock at the door. Also, Zoey's been all skittish like she's waiting for someone."

"Where is Zoey?" Lucas asked.

"How would I know?" Benjamin cried in sudden anguish. "She could be anywhere! I can't see her! She could be right . . . there!" He pointed suddenly at the coatrack.

Lucas rolled his eyes and waited patiently.

Benjamin took another bite of chicken, perfectly calm. "You're no fun, Lucas," he said. "You never fall for anything. Zoey's at the top of the stairs, eavesdropping on us."

"I am not," Zoey's voice floated down the stairs. Followed by her laughter.

Lucas ran up the stairs and caught her in his arms. He kissed her and at the same time lifted her feet off the floor and carried her toward her bedroom.

They closed the door behind them.

Lucas kissed her again, but then she held him off, giving him a serious look. "I really am sorry I doubted you. It's just that Jake sounded like he was sure, and besides, you know, Claire is . . ."

"What?"

Zoey shrugged. "She is slightly beautiful."

"No, *you* are beautiful."

"And she's kind of sexy, I guess."

"No." Lucas shook his head solemnly. "You're the one who's sexy."

"Anyway, I guess I could see where if she wanted to do it, you'd probably have a hard time saying no."

Now was the time if he was ever going to tell the truth. All he had to say was "look, Zoey, to be honest, while Claire and I did not have sex, we *did* make out. It was meaningless to both of us and it will never happen again."

That's what he should say if he was ever going to tell the truth. But truth hadn't always worked out all that well for him, and this was a case where a small lie of omission was probably the best policy.

Besides, he would be telling the absolute, undiminished truth when he said, "Zoey, I love you with all my heart."

Next confession he would have to remember the sin of lying by omission. And the other, very familiar sin of lust as he kissed Zoey again, and again, and again until at long last, and much later, she once again, gently but firmly, stopped him from committing the next sin.

Lucas

What am I afraid of? Hmmm. I kind of don't like small spaces, I guess. Fortunately when I was in the Youth Authority it was all barracks style, not little cells. Barracks are okay as long as you don't have a fear of snoring—or of being knifed in your sleep.

My other big fear is of myself. I have an amazing ability to screw up my life. I got myself thrown in jail for something I didn't even do; that was one example. A fairly major example. And I seem to be doing my best to mess up my relationship with Zoey, which is the most important thing in my life, for another example. So basically if I can stop screwing up and stay out of confined spaces, I'll be fine. But to be honest, I don't put much faith in my ability to deal with stuff successfully.

I guess I always figured I'd end up a loser of one type or another. When I got back to Chatham Island after jail and everyone made it pretty obvious that they wanted me to go away, I figured, well, that's it, you're marked forever as a loser. But then I was cleared. And more important, I fell in love with Zoey, and for some amazing reason she fell in love with me. I started thinking maybe I'm not such a loser, you know? Maybe in spite of myself things will work out okay.

Except that my relationship with Zoey hangs by a thread, and if she finds out the truth and leaves me for good . . . well, that's what I'm afraid of. To have something wonderful and perfect and incredible in my life and then to screw it up.

EIGHT

S (M) T W T F S

On Monday Aisha got definite commitments from Christopher, Zoey, and Lucas that they would like to attend the concert in Boston. Claire seemed unenthusiastic about the idea but didn't give a definite no. Jake gave a definite no. It was a curt, almost rude no, like he didn't even want to be talking to Aisha or, for that matter, anyone. He had stuck to himself on the ferry ride over to school that morning.

Benjamin also gave a definite no, but Nina said that he *meant* yes.

S M (T) W T F S

On Tuesday Aisha went to the mall after school with Nina and Zoey, supposedly to shop for possible Halloween costumes. But everything she considered seemed either dorky or like she was trying too hard, or not trying hard enough. She ended up buying a new purse that she didn't really like, just because it was on sale, normally seventy-two dollars, marked down to nineteen ninety-five. Zoey bought an earring for Lucas. Nina bought a set of drawing pens and a long black wig and a size 36 double-D bra to be part of a costume whose details she wouldn't reveal.

Nina claimed Benjamin had agreed to attend the concert.

S   M   T   (W)   T   F   S

On Wednesday Aisha awoke with memories of a very disturbing dream. In the dream Jeff and Christopher were fighting over her and she was fourteen again. At school that day she aced a calculus test and got a *C* plus on a French quiz. Coming home from school on the ferry, she asked Benjamin if he was coming to the concert, and Benjamin said he would rather be boiled in oil than be trapped in a rap concert. Nina explained that he *meant* yes.

S   M   T   W   (T)   F   S

On Thursday Aisha realized she still hadn't decided what costume to wear, if any. She wanted to look good for Jeff, and at the same time, she didn't. For the first time in talking to Christopher she used the words "old boyfriend" instead of "old friend" in mentioning Jeff. It took an hour and many, many reassurances to convince Christopher that it had all been nothing but a little freshman crush on an older guy who seemed cool. She didn't like lying, but at the same time she couldn't really tell Christopher the whole truth.

Benjamin called to say that no matter what Nina said, he would cut off his legs with a chain saw before he would go to a rap concert.

S   M   T   W   T   (F)   S

On Friday Aisha began to panic. She didn't want to see Jeff again. What was she thinking of? It was insane. She was totally in love with Christopher, and totally committed. And what she'd had with Jeff was history now. Ancient history. What she was feeling was just stupid nostalgia, mostly over a younger, maybe wilder Aisha. An Aisha who no longer existed.

She had to call Jeff and tell him how many tickets she needed. He was out, so she talked to his sister, relieved not to have to deal with Jeff while she was feeling confused. She ordered seven tickets. Herself, Christopher, Zoey, Lucas, Claire, even though she still wasn't sure, Nina, and Benjamin.

That night she had another dream. In this one she remembered the day her mother had taken her out of school and gone with her to the doctor. She woke up in a cold sweat and waited up until Christopher came by with the papers. She made out with him through the window and drove the dream and Jeff from her mind.

Saturday evening Claire logged on to the chat room, as she had done every night for two weeks now. And as had happened each night for two weeks, Flyer was there waiting. It had become a ritual between them. It had become the "place" Claire went in the evenings when she was done with homework.

Sometimes they talked for a long time, hours even. Other nights Claire kept it short. Two days earlier she had cut him off to climb up to the widow's walk and watch a wicked squall blow through. But an hour later, when the wind and lightning had rolled off out of sight over the Atlantic, she had gone rushing back to tell him all about it. And he had listened. Not laughing at her fascination, or writing her off as strange for sitting out in the middle of a storm. And she had told him how it felt to be up there, the storm all around her. In telling him she had explained it to herself: the feeling of powerlessness and awe; the sense of clean starts and change.

She typed in "Hello, Flyer."

Flyer

Hi, Weather Girl. Any more storms tonight?

Weather Girl

No. Clear and cold with lots of stars. Beautiful, I suppose, but boring.

Flyer

Same here. It's good weather for flying, though. I took the
plane up after school today and did some

There was a knock at the bedroom door. "What?" Claire
said in a loud voice.

The door opened and Nina poked her head in. "Hey, Eesh
is down in my room. She says are you coming to the concert
or not?"

"Didn't she already get me a ticket?"

"What are you doing?" Nina asked, inviting herself in.

Claire quickly punched the Escape key, clearing the screen.
"Nothing."

Nina gave her an amused look. "Sitting home on a Saturday
night talking to computer dweebs? I can't believe it's come to
this, Claire."

"I notice you're home tonight, too," Claire replied. But she
had been thrown by Nina's nosiness. She'd told no one about Flyer.

"We're all putting off the usual Saturday night date because
we're going to the concert on Halloween," Nina said.

Claire raised an eyebrow. "Benjamin is going, too?"

"Sure. He's excited about it," Nina said. "So, are you in or
out?"

Claire sighed. "Look, Nina, Aisha has already ordered me a

ticket, right? So I'm in. And if I decide not to go, *you* can have my ticket and sell it to someone at the door."

"Isn't scalping tickets illegal?" Nina asked suspiciously.

"I'm not sure, but you know, Nina, sooner or later you'll end up in jail, so why not get some experience early?"

"Very funny. Tell that to your compu-dorks."

"Go away now, Nina."

Weather Girl

Sorry I bailed, Flyer, but my little sister barged in.

Flyer

And you don't want her to know about me?

Weather Girl

No, I guess not.

Flyer

Why not? I'm just some guy you talk to on the net.

Weather Girl

You're a lot more than that, Flyer.

Flyer

Am I?

Weather Girl

Yes. To me you are. In some ways right now you're the closest friend I have.

Flyer

I am incredibly happy you said that.

Claire took her fingers from the keyboard and stared at her own words there on the screen. Had she just said that? Was it true? God, was her best friend really some guy she only knew via computer? She typed:

Weather Girl

It hadn't occurred to me until just this moment. But I guess it's true. I tell you things I don't tell anyone else. I suppose that makes you a friend.

Flyer

I guess I've felt right from the start that there was something special between us. Maybe it is strange, but I feel like I know you better than I know anyone. I sit here typing in my room and feel closer to you than to anyone.

Weather Girl

I suppose I should sign off now.

Flyer

I haven't upset you, have I?

Weather Girl

No, Flyer. It is strange, though, isn't it?

Flyer

Caring about someone you've never seen face-to-face? Whose voice you've never heard. Yes, it is strange, WG. And yet I do care about you. If it wasn't so improbable, I suppose I might even say that I love you. As much as it's possible to love someone under these circumstances.

Claire stared at the words scrolling up on the screen. Now he was going too far. This was ludicrous. She had never even seen Flyer. She knew his real name was Sean, just as he knew her real name. But what else did she know about him? That he was smart, kind, understanding? Yes. That he always made her feel better about life and especially herself when she spoke to him? Yes. But was that enough?

Weather Girl

I care about you, too, Flyer.

Flyer

That's better. Now you can sign off. You leave me very happy.

Weather Girl

Good night, Sean.

Flyer

Good night, Claire.

"Look, I said he was a *boy*friend," Aisha said. "I admitted he was a boyfriend. You two think I never had a boyfriend in my life before I came here?"

Nina and Zoey exchanged a look.

"Frankly, no, we don't think you ever had a boyfriend before you came here," Zoey said.

They were in Nina's room. An old U2 song played on the computer, at reasonable volume for once. The three of them were sitting cross-legged on Nina's bed around a bag of chips.

"I had a life before you two even knew me," Aisha said.

"You came here when you were fourteen," Nina pointed out. "No one has a life by the time they're fourteen. I'm sixteen and I just barely have one. Claire's seventeen and look at *her*. She's up there talking to fellow devil worshipers on her computer."

"I'm just saying he was my boyfriend, that's all I'm saying. It's no big deal, but don't act like I'm making it all up."

Nina took the unlit cigarette out of her mouth and pointed it at Aisha. "You were a freshman. And no offense, but I'll bet ten dollars you were a member of the chess club and the honor society. You didn't loosen up at all till you started going with Christopher."

"For your information," Aisha said hotly, "I was more loosened up *before* I ever moved here. I was in Boston, after all."

"Oooh, Boston," Nina said, cracking herself up.

"Stop picking on Aisha," Zoey said mildly.

"I can defend myself," Aisha said haughtily. "I'm just saying that while you two were probably still secretly playing with Barbie dolls, I was going with a senior."

"Going with," Nina echoed in a stage whisper. "That means she said hello to him in the hallway on her way to class."

"I could tell you something that would make you take that back," Aisha threatened. Instantly she knew she had gone too far. Nina and Zoey were exchanging interested, wary looks.

"She wants to tell us something," Nina said.

"It sure sounds that way," Zoey agreed.

"Hmm, Aisha has a secret."

"No fair," Zoey said, taking up the bantering tone. "*We* don't have any secrets."

"Forget it," Aisha muttered.

"Yeah, right," Nina said with a derisive laugh.

"Look, it's private, all right?"

"Private having to do with this alleged boyfriend?" Nina pursued, using her cigarette to stab the air. "I don't think so."

Zoey was looking at her thoughtfully. "Is it something dumb like—"

"I slept with him," Aisha blurted suddenly. The second the words were out of her mouth, she wished she could call them back. Zoey and Nina had frozen, mouths open. "Well, you dragged it out of me," she said defensively.

"You mean you *slept* or you had sex?" Zoey asked for clarification.

"We did it," Aisha said. "Okay? Are you happy now?"

Again Nina and Zoey exchanged looks.

Nina said, "I don't know about happy, but you certainly do have our attention, Eesh. Is this for real, or are you yanking us around?"

"Why didn't you ever tell us? I've been your friend for three years!" Zoey said.

Aisha shrugged and looked down at the chips. Telling them the truth was seeming less and less like a good idea. But the secret had begun to preoccupy her, now that she was going to see Jeff again. She'd almost put it out of her mind, it seemed, until his call had reawakened all the old memories.

"Wait a minute, are you doing it with Christopher, too?" Nina asked.

"No," Aisha said. "I don't do that anymore. At least not yet anymore, if you know what I mean."

"Wow," Nina said, awestruck. "So it was like really bad, huh?"

Aisha sighed. "That's not it," she admitted. "That part was nice, mostly."

"You didn't catch something, did you?" Zoey asked intensely. "I mean, it would be okay if you had . . ."

"Okay, look, stop pestering me," Aisha said. "I'll tell you, all right? We did it a few times. And then I missed my period and I was like a week late. So I had to tell my mom."

"Didn't you use anything?" Nina demanded.

"We used condoms except for one time when Jeff didn't have any. He told me one time wouldn't be a problem. You know, like what were the odds that I was going to get pregnant or anything?"

"Wow. So what happened?"

"My mom took me to her gynecologist and I wasn't pregnant or anything, but naturally my mom went off. I mean *way* off. She drove me down to the welfare office and parked outside and was pointing to all these teenage girls with babies going in and yelling is that the way I wanted to end up and so on and on and on."

"Wow," Nina repeated.

"Yeah," Aisha agreed. "Scared the hell out of me, the whole thing. I mean, seriously. I thought I was either going to have to get an abortion or end up living on welfare in some project."

"I can't picture you with a baby," Zoey said. "I mean, you're not stupid, obviously."

"Not stupid?" Nina echoed incredulously. "She's already

been accepted to Harvard. As a teacher. Next to you, Zoey, Aisha's the biggest suck-up, goody-goody, get-all-my-homework-done-on-time, study-every-night, wave-your-hand-and-go-ooh-ooh-I-know-the-answer, teacher's pet I know."

"Thanks, Nina," Aisha said dubiously.

"Who would have guessed you were hiding a deep, dark past?" Nina said.

No one, if I'd kept my big mouth shut, Aisha realized. "You both have to swear you'll never, ever tell anyone. I mean, absolutely no one."

"No problem," Nina said.

"Of course not," Zoey said.

"And Nina, when you tell Benjamin, make sure he knows not to tell anyone, too," Aisha added.

NINE

ON HALLOWEEN, ZOEY SKIPPED CLASS for only about the second time in her life. Aisha was anxious to get down to Boston as early as possible and avoid the dreaded Boston rush hour. It was extremely odd for Aisha to want to dump a class, especially her sixth-period calculus, but she was determined, so Zoey decided to go along. Lucas, of course, could be convinced quite easily to dump the afternoon classes.

Benjamin was the holdout. There was plenty of time for him to get through last-period physics and still get down to Boston in time for the concert. No one wanted to argue since Benjamin was at a severe disadvantage in physics, a class that depended too heavily on blackboard equations he couldn't see, and in which he was struggling to maintain a good grade.

Besides, even as he made plans to go, he was still denying he was going at all.

With Benjamin staying till the end, naturally Nina did, too.

Claire, likewise, wanted to wait until the end of the day.

She had been quite mysterious about why she was even going along. No one believed she suddenly liked rap, but at the last minute she had accepted the invitation, surprising everyone.

Only Jake had steadfastly refused.

A little after noon, under threatening gray skies, Aisha, Christopher, Zoey, and Lucas piled into the Grays' Ford Taurus and headed south. Their Halloween costumes were in the trunk.

It was three twenty when Claire drove off after them, alone in her father's Mercedes, turning on the wipers to deal with a chilly drizzle. She had no costume, despite Nina's repeated suggestion that she go as Morticia.

It was three thirty-five when Nina and Benjamin followed in the Passmores' van, with Nina driving through puddles and squinting at what had become a driving rain.

At four, Jake drank the three bottles of beer he found in his refrigerator. He no longer worried what his father would say about his beer disappearing. He only worried where and how he could find more.

TEN

INTERSTATE 95 HAD BEEN A nice, easy drive all the way, despite occasional showers that slowed traffic coming through New Hampshire. Aisha drove the whole way, her mind far from the conversation that floated back and forth between Christopher, Zoey, and Lucas. At first she tried to keep up a regular contribution, but as they passed by Portland, and through New Hampshire, and reached the big "Welcome to Massachusetts" sign, she barely managed the occasional "yeah" or "uh-huh."

She turned up the music on the radio, hoping to discourage further conversation. She didn't want to pay attention. She wanted to remember.

It was her first return to Boston since the family had moved to Maine. She watched the way the interstate grew from two lanes in either direction to three, to four. The number of overpasses multiplied steadily. The speed and aggressiveness of the drivers around her rose sharply.

A closed-in, almost claustrophobic feeling also grew. It was as if walls were growing higher around her, shutting out more of the sky. All the trees were behind her now; only gas stations and restaurants and grim, tall apartment buildings could be seen.

Boston. It reminded her of how small Weymouth really was, and how infinitesimal Chatham Island was. The entire population of Chatham Island could be housed in any one of these fortresslike condo buildings that sprouted on either side and looked down at the racing freeway traffic below.

Cars rushing in from the left and right. The road peeling away to off-ramps. Iggy Azalea's "Fancy" on the radio, adding to a sensation in Aisha that she was hunkering down, feeling the old urban paranoia return.

The other three seemed unaffected. They still chatted away, pointing at this or that. But then, they weren't going home after three years' absence.

Home to see a guy who had been her first great love.

She glanced at Christopher. This was her true love now, she reminded herself, and the thought comforted her. She could see Jeff and not feel about him the way she once had. She could talk to Jeff and leave all of that in the past.

She signaled for a lane change but was cut off by a Lexus. She gave the unseeing driver the finger and yelled an obscenity.

"Whoa, Aisha!" It was Lucas, grinning in surprise. "I didn't think you even knew words like that."

"Sorry," she said sheepishly. "Getting back into that urban mentality."

"Why is it that Massachusetts drivers are such jerks?" Christopher asked conversationally.

"It's *Boston* drivers, not everyone from Mass. I think it's the city that drives them insane. It's all narrow little one-way streets going whichever way you *aren't* going."

She cut right and just barely squeezed onto the off-ramp. "Look, um, I was thinking maybe I'd go look around the old neighborhood," Aisha said, as casually as she could. "I thought maybe I'd drop you guys off at Faneuil Hall; you know, you could shop or check out the aquarium."

"She's dumping us," Zoey said to Lucas.

"Oh, yeah, we're being dumped," Lucas agreed good-naturedly.

Christopher looked less inclined to be accepting. Aisha could see resentment clouding his eyes. He gave her a troubled look.

"I just want to look at old places where I grew up," Aisha explained. "You know, a trip down memory lane."

"I guess I would get in your way?" he said.

Aisha reached over and put her hand on his. "Christopher, it's just that this is about my not-very-wonderful past, all right? And you are a big part of my much-more-wonderful present and future, and I guess I feel like I don't want to mix the two up."

"Aw, isn't that sweet?" Lucas said sarcastically from the backseat. He made a gagging noise and Zoey punched him in the arm.

"Okay, babe," Christopher said. "But don't stay too long, okay?"

"I thought what I'd do is park down here by the marketplace. Then I could just take the T around town. I'll meet you guys outside the Orpheum an hour before the show starts." Aisha glanced at her watch. "We meet at the Orpheum at, say, seven? That gives us all a few hours."

She spotted a multistory parking garage and cut across traffic in best Bostonian style.

"What about the costumes?" Zoey asked. "I'm not walking around for the next four hours dressed like a zombie cheerleader."

"Okay, look, I'll leave you guys the keys to the car. I'll go ahead and change into my costume now, and you guys can come back later when you're done shopping."

303

"Zombie cheerleader?" Lucas asked curiously.

"Like a regular cheerleader but with really bad makeup," Zoey said.

"Well, the cheerleader part has potential," Lucas said with a grin.

"And what are you?" Christopher asked Aisha.

Aisha shrugged. "I kind of forgot about the costume thing until the last minute, so I just grabbed my old Girl Scout uniform."

"When was the last time you wore it?" Zoey wondered skeptically.

"When I was fourteen."

"And you still fit into it?"

"It's a little short," Aisha admitted.

"Girl Scout." Christopher shook his head. "You had a very different experience from me growing up. You could not have walked around my old 'hood dressed that way."

Aisha smiled. "People around my old neighborhood will think they're having a flashback. It will be just like three years ago, Aisha Gray walking around in her Girl Scout uniform with her merit badges, selling cookies."

"This is insane," Claire muttered to herself. "Insane, and now it's annoying, too."

The rain was coming down hard by the time Claire hit the outskirts of Boston. The rain was falling and the rush-hour traffic had brought everything to a dead stop. At the moment, she was staring out past her windshield wipers at a sea of wet cars, all sitting motionless. Occasionally there would be a frustration explosion and horns would start going off. Then they would all move ahead fifty feet and stop again.

She checked the dashboard clock. Still plenty of time to make it to the airport, but she had wanted to get there early—early enough to be there before "Flyer," who would undoubtedly also show up early for their strange blind date.

In some ways the rain was a godsend. If she decided to bail out of the meeting, she could say that the rain had delayed her. Too bad it wasn't snowing.

Claire looked at the small sheaf of papers on the seat beside her. This was probably an insane thing to do. Why would she want to meet a person she knew only from a computer chat room?

She knew the answer, of course. In a strange way Flyer—*Sean*—had become a big part of her life, filling a hole that had become ever more obvious as she found herself more and more isolated, more and more alone.

"Pathetic," she told herself roughly. "Nina would laugh herself into a coma if she knew."

She picked up the top few sheets of paper. They were print-outs of her last conversation with Flyer.

Flyer

I meant what I said yesterday. I know I can only judge you by what you've written me over the short time we've communicated, WG. But I like you a lot.

Weather Girl

You don't even know me.

Flyer

I think I do, in a way. For one thing, I know you without being distracted by how you look.

Weather Girl

What do you think I look like?

Flyer

I guess I don't really care that much. I suppose that's the point.

Weather Girl

What if I'm extremely unattractive?

A horn sounded right behind her, and Claire looked up from the paper to see that the traffic had moved twenty feet. She took her foot off the brake and crept up to fill in the gap.

Flyer

Again, I don't care. It's you the person I like. Unless you've just been lying the whole time, I see you as a very smart, private, reflective person. I also think you're lonely, and maybe that feeling of loneliness causes you to be hard with people sometimes.

Claire smiled faintly. That wasn't an image of Claire that any of her friends, let alone her sister, would agree with. Everyone else thought she was just an ice princess, given to manipulation, selfishness, and even ruthlessness.

Frankly, Claire thought, the truth lay somewhere between Flyer's rosy vision and Nina's less flattering version. Was she lonely? Maybe that wasn't far from being true. Especially lately. It had been driven home by the way she had managed to lose Jake.

She glanced at the conversation again.

Flyer

What if it turns out that I'm the unattractive one?

Weather Girl

I've never cared much about looks either.

Flyer

I have a proposition, WG. If you don't want to do it, then just say so. No pressure. You know I just got my pilot's license, and I thought I might fly over there to Maine to see you, or else maybe we could meet at some neutral spot somewhere.

Weather Girl

I'm not so sure that's a good idea. Maybe in person we wouldn't get along as well as we do here.

Flyer

Maybe we'd get along even better. Aren't you curious?

Weather Girl

I'll admit I am curious. I've talked more with you than I have with anyone in a long time.

More than anyone since she'd broken up with Benjamin, Claire realized. Jake had never been one for long conversations.

Flyer

Okay, how about this: Halloween is tomorrow. The perfect day for people who may not fit the standard definition of beauty. Meet me on Halloween.

Weather Girl

Halloween? Where?

Flyer

Somewhere public, so you can feel safe. Somewhere we can both get to that's a neutral spot. And then, if we meet and don't like each other, fine. We go our separate ways.

Weather Girl

I'm supposed to go to a concert in Boston on Halloween.
Maybe if I left here early, we could spend a little time
together.

They had decided on the airport as the logical place to get
together. Flyer—Sean—would be flying in, Claire would be
driving past. It was perfect. Logan Airport was a big, well-lit,
safe place on neutral turf. A place where, if she decided to, she
could bail at the last minute and melt into the crowds. And with
the concert, Claire had the perfect excuse to run for it early if
things went bad between her and Sean.

Nina

Halloween, the season of fear! Boo! Ha ha ha ha. Okay, you want to know what scares me? How about the possibility that I may wake up someday and find I actually like a Katy Perry song? Okay, no, my real fear is that I may someday see Rush Limbaugh at the beach! In a thong! No! The horror! Wait, worse: I'm kidnapped by a cult that forces me to buy all my clothes at Pappagallo's! Someone hold my hand, please. I'm frightened.

Seriously, though, what am I afraid of? I'll tell you, though even speaking about it gives me the willies. It's . . . it's the creature who lives upstairs from my room. Oh, I know you're laughing. I know you're thinking 'Nina, there is no creature living above your room; grow up.' But I assure you there is: a cold, ruthless monster! A destroyer of souls! Dare I speak the monster's name aloud? Yes, its name is Claire, which in Transylvanian means "ice princess with overly large breasts and no heart."

Those Transylvanians know how to load a single word up with meaning, don't they?

ELEVEN

"WHY AM I FEELING BUMPS?" Benjamin demanded.

"Okay, I'll play along," Nina said. "Why are you feeling bumps?"

"My butt tells me this is not the highway. That last pothole was not an interstate highway type of bump. That was a crappy little back road kind of bump."

Nina looked around at the fields on either side of the road. Plowed-up dirt turning to mud as the rain saturated the ground. Deep ditches on either side of the definitely crappy little back road were turning into streams.

"It's a shortcut," Nina explained as the van hit another shockingly deep pothole.

"Wait a minute. Doesn't the highway run almost straight from Weymouth to Boston?"

"Yeah, but how about rush hour? This will take us past all the traffic."

Nina turned on the radio, but the storm clouds overhead

had fuzzed out all but a mournful country music station. She should have thought to bring the cord that connected her phone to the car stereo. The only CDs available were from Benjamin and Zoey's mom. Simon and Garfunkel.

"Let me ask you something, Nina," Benjamin said. "What state are we in?"

"What state?" Nina looked around, trying to peer through the gloom. "Mmm, New Hampshire?"

"Oh, man, we're lost, aren't we?"

"Lost?" Nina shrugged. "How could we be lost? We're right here on this road."

"Which road?"

"You mean like a number?"

Benjamin shook his head. "Great. Well, at least there's a chance we'll miss the concert now. There's always that silver lining."

"We are not going to miss anything," Nina said. "Every road goes somewhere."

"Yeah. *The road goes ever on and on, down from the door where it began. Now far ahead the road has gone, and I must follow if I can . . .*"

"Cool. What's that, poetry?"

"It's from *The Lord of the Rings*."

"Well, see, like you said, the road goes on and on and it has to lead somewhere eventually."

"In *Lord of the Rings* it led to Mordor," Benjamin muttered darkly.

"What's Mordor?" Nina wondered distractedly.

"It's kind of like parts of New York City, from what I understand," Benjamin said dryly.

"Okay," Nina said cheerfully, "so we'll go to New York." It was a good thing Benjamin couldn't see, because the road had grown narrower and now, instead of plowed fields on either side, there were more and more trees, towering pines that crowded out what little light had penetrated the clouds. Soon, Nina realized, true night would fall, and without streetlights or moonlight this road would be invisible beyond the small circle of the headlights.

Maybe after she looked around the next curve in the road she should just admit she was lost and turn the van around and go back. Although there would be no way to hide that fact from Benjamin. He would certainly know they were turning around.

Nina flipped on the lights.

"Is it dark?" Benjamin asked.

Nina sighed. "You heard the switch?"

"Of course."

Nina sighed again.

"Okay, Nina, how lost are we?"

"Well, Benjamin, we're surrounded by trees, it's getting

dark, I haven't seen a house or a mailbox in a long, long time, and this road is looking more and more like it might be dirt real soon."

Benjamin took this news calmly. "Why don't we turn around?"

"We can try, but the road is so narrow and all. And there's ditches on either side. Oh, wait, we're at a field. I think I see a spot to turn around up ahead."

Nina hunkered over the wheel, peering ahead. Yes, the trees had opened up on one side, revealing a field. And there was a tiny dirt track leading away from the main road. That would be the place to turn around and race back to civilization.

She applied brakes and turned onto the dirt road. She stopped, put the gearshift in reverse, turned around and looked back over her shoulder, and stepped lightly on the gas.

There was a wild spinning sound. The van rocked and didn't move.

"Uh-oh."

She stepped on the gas again. More spinning, and she could just make out a plume of mud being thrown forward by the wheels.

The rain had caught up with Aisha soon after she exited the T station. But her coat had a nice hood that kept her hair dry and her upper body warm. It also hid the Girl Scout costume, which looked a little ridiculous for just walking around town in the evening.

She had lived in the south end back in those days. It wasn't one of Boston's more famous neighborhoods. It wasn't Back Bay or Beacon Hill or Southie. The south end was an area of close-packed bow-front Victorian town homes. Working class for the most part, people who drove cabs or worked as nurses or secretaries. There were bad streets, streets you didn't walk down at night, where cars had no hubcaps and sometimes no wheels and the bars over the windows were starkly functional. And other streets where the buildings had been occupied by invading yuppies who stripped the chipped green paint from their massive front doors and polished the oak beneath. People who hung stained-glass windows and parked Lexuses out front.

She passed the reflecting pool, a long rectangle where in summer she and other kids from the neighborhood had waded to beat the heat.

She walked along West Newton, fighting the wet wind that lifted the tail of her coat and tried to pull off her hood. On a nicer day people would have been out on their stoops, watching the passing show. But the rain had emptied the streets of everyone but the few commuters heading home early.

She had two goals in mind. First was to see her old home, a

narrow, drafty Victorian virtually identical to dozens on either side. The second goal was to see Jeff's house.

She didn't know why she wanted to see his home. She didn't even know if he still lived there with his mother and his odd collection of aunts. Perhaps nowadays Jeff was making enough money to be able to buy or rent a better place. The Pullings' home had always been one of the shabbier ones, a stark contrast to the Grays' restored bow front, where Aisha's mother had first discovered her fascination with decorating.

Aisha found her own home easily, of course. It was dark and silent. The new owners had added a piece of stained glass that Aisha was pretty certain her mother would hate. It was odd and even disturbing somehow to stand there in the rain, wearing her fourteen-year-old's Girl Scout uniform and experiencing this imperfect mix of the familiar and the strange. Somehow she'd expected a more cosmic experience.

But as she stared thoughtfully at the house some memories did surface, happy for the most part. Some melancholy. In the gray drizzle it was hard somehow to hold on to the happy ones. She remembered the names of her friends in those days. Lachandra, a hopelessly giddy girl who had been boy-crazy since she was eleven. Anna Maria, who at the age of fourteen had begun to see things and hear things that no one else did and had ended up being packed off to a mental hospital, from which she sent strange, self-pitying letters. And Kinya, Aisha's best friend until Jeff had come between them.

Aisha walked on, head bowed. Her feet directed her without conscious thought, down the street to the corner and right. She looked up at one point, surprised to see that she was halfway to Jeff's house. She even remembered the shortcut, down the alley.

What would she say to Jeff if he was at his old house? To know *that* she'd have to figure out how she felt about him, which was something she wasn't sure of, even now. She knew she loved Christopher. But did that necessarily mean she no longer cared at all for Jeff?

"Hey, sister."

Aisha looked up, breaking from her reverie. She was in the alley, surrounded by blank brick walls. Ahead of her two men. At least she assumed they were men. They both wore rubber Halloween masks. One was a gorilla, the other the Joker. For a moment she wondered if the guy in the Joker mask was Christopher. It was the same mask, but this person was younger and smaller.

Aisha clutched her purse instinctively. On Chatham Island or even for the most part in Weymouth there would have been nothing to be concerned about. But this was the big city. In Boston chance encounters with strangers in alleyways were not to be encouraged.

"Hey, sister," the gorilla called again, drawing nearer.

Aisha glanced over her shoulder. A long way back to the main street.

"You can't talk?" the Joker asked.

Aisha felt her stomach muscles clenching tight. She forced a smile. "Hi."

They were coming closer with each step. Aisha felt the hairs on the back of her neck standing on end. Somewhere she could hear music playing. Beyoncé, of all things. A song she had liked when she'd lived in this very neighborhood.

The guys in the masks were just ahead. Level with her. Now behind her.

Aisha breathed a sigh of relief.

Suddenly she was spun around by the force of someone yanking hard on her purse. She held on and yelled, "No!"

A mistake, she knew. She should have let them take the purse. There was no chance of her being saved by anyone, and the smart thing to do was let them have it.

The gorilla yanked again at her purse. The man in the Joker mask slapped her hard with the back of his hand. In shock Aisha released the purse. And now Gorilla pushed her viciously.

She slipped and fell backward. Her head struck hard against the brick wall. She fell to the ground. She heard laughter and saw a band of dark gray sky.

Then she lost consciousness.

TWELVE

IT WAS FULL NIGHT AS Claire pulled into short-term parking at the airport. She glanced at her watch. By the time she made her way from the parking lot to the terminal building, she'd barely be on time for the meeting, let alone early enough to spy the situation out safely.

She was beginning to bitterly regret having agreed to the meeting. What on earth had possessed her to say yes? For that matter, what on earth had possessed her to begin this weird computer friendship with some guy?

It wasn't like there was a shortage of guys at school. There were guys who would have sold their parents into slavery for the opportunity to go out with Claire Geiger.

Yes, she had been feeling resentful and hurt. Had felt unloved and even disliked. Cut off from everyone she knew. Lonely. Deserted. Yes, yes, all that, but that was no reason to start forming relationships with people who were nothing more than words on a screen.

"I'll take a look," she told herself. "Anything looks wrong, I'm out of there, and I just stay off that website in the future."

Claire checked herself in the rearview mirror and pulled a brush from her purse. She brushed her glossy, long black hair while checking her minimal makeup. Still fine.

She ran through the scattered raindrops to the terminal building. Inside she bought a *USA Today* at a newsstand. It would help her to fit in, to look unobtrusive. She found the restaurant easily, following the signs, and quickly scanned the dozen or so occupied tables. No one who stood out obviously as Flyer. The only person of the right age was a hugely fat guy sitting with another person whose back was turned to her.

Claire nodded in satisfaction. Now she would just grab a bench across the breezeway and watch who came and went in the restaurant. With a little luck she would be able to spot Flyer. After all, how many unaccompanied seventeen-year-old guys were likely to be at this airport, on this concourse, at this restaurant, at the right time?

Yes, she would surely be able to spot him. And then . . . and then she'd decide what to do.

She unfolded the newspaper, holding it up to conceal her face. She was deciphering a bar graph on the number of Americans who ate particular types of cheese when she became aware of someone standing nearby.

Reluctantly, and fearing the worst, she lowered the paper and raised her eyes.

He was six feet tall, broad shouldered, wearing a worn brown leather jacket and nicely fitted Levi's. He had shoulder-length blond hair, a perfect nose, a lopsided smile that revealed perfect white teeth. His eyes were a pale, slightly vacant blue, his only minor flaw.

Claire reminded herself that she didn't care what Flyer looked like. Didn't care at all.

"Weather Girl?" he said.

"Flyer?" she asked, standing up.

"Well, well," he said. "I mean, um . . . obviously you are one of those rare people whose inner beauty is fully reflected in their outer appearance."

Claire realized to her amazement that she was blushing. All the guys she had gone out with were good looking, but this guy was male-model good looking. Not that she cared. Flyer pushed the hair back out of his eyes, and Claire caught sight of something on his right ear. He acknowledged the direction of her gaze with a smile.

"A hearing aid," he said. "The result of a regrettable carelessness with firecrackers when I was even younger and dumber than I am today. It's why I've been a little nervous about meeting you face-to-face. I wasn't sure what you'd think."

Like I would run screaming from the room because you have a hearing aid? Claire asked silently. Aloud she said, "I couldn't care less. I'm just glad to meet you."

A guy this beautiful *and* this smart and he'd just been waiting around to be picked up in a computer chat room? Something told Claire the odds were way, way against it.

He smiled with his perfect teeth. "I feel like I already know you so well," he said.

Jake had pulled the quick cut, as islanders called it.

The outbound ferry went from Weymouth to Chatham Island, then on to the outer islands of Allworthy and Penobscot. On the return it stopped again at Chatham Island on its way back to the mainland.

There were forty-five minutes between the outward-bound ferry and the inbound ferry. Jake had caught the regular four o'clock home from school, arriving at Chatham Island at four twenty-five. Then he had gone from the ferry to his home, drunk his father's last three beers, picked up what he needed, and caught the five ten going back across to the mainland.

It was raining on the return leg, so he sat below on the covered deck. In a corner by himself he pulled the license out of his pocket and looked at it. It was something he'd kept these last two years since his brother Wade's death—Wade's driver's license. He had never consciously admitted why he was hanging on to it, but a part of his mind had known that the day would come when it would be useful.

He peered closely at the date of birth. How Wade had gotten it done, he didn't know, but the alteration was just about perfect. Someone would have to look very closely to see that the year of birth had been changed, making a five into a three. Of course, if Wade had lived, he'd actually be twenty-one soon.

Someone sat beside him and he started guiltily, covering the license with his hand.

A girl. She looked vaguely familiar, as if he'd seen her somewhere quite recently. Then it came to him. She had been on the outbound ferry just like him, and done the same quick cut. He narrowed his eyes suspiciously. He knew everyone on Chatham Island, and it was no longer tourist season. Besides, this girl wasn't dressed like a tourist. She had on a painfully short skirt over fishnet stockings and high, black leather boots. Her hair was brown and she wore it big. Underneath a cheap black leather jacket with too many zippers she had on an incongruous tube top.

She was looking at him as suspiciously as he watched her.

"Can I help you?" Jake said at last.

"I was just wondering," she said.

"Okay," he said guardedly.

"I went to see if I could find someone on the island. But there are more houses there than I thought. I thought it would just be like a few houses and I wouldn't have any problem."

"Who were you looking for?"

"This guy." She stared at him, as if anticipating a reaction. "This *blind* guy."

"Benjamin?"

She nodded. "Yeah, that's his name. Funny you should know right off like that."

"There's only one blind person on the island," Jake said. "The whole population is only three hundred, so it's not like they could sneak a new blind guy on without me noticing it."

It had been a joke. A feeble joke, but the girl seemed alarmed. "They?"

"Never mind," Jake said. "So you're looking for Benjamin. He's out of town tonight. Him and his sister both, they went to Boston for a concert."

The girl leaned close. Jake could smell perfume, hair spray, and cigarette smoke. "*I'm* his sister," she said.

"Excuse me?"

"I'm the blind boy's sister," she said. "His other sister."

"Okay," Jake said, humoring her.

"You don't believe me?" the girl asked craftily. "Well, I am. I found out last week."

It finally clicked in Jake's mind. Of course. What a relief; he had been starting to wonder if the girl was crazy, which would be a shame, because underneath the sleazy clothes and overly thick makeup she wasn't at all bad looking. "I get it now," he said. "You're the famous half-sister."

"Famous?" she demanded.

"Well, not exactly famous," Jake backpedaled. "We all know each other on the island, so naturally I know that Benjamin and Zoey have . . . have you."

"Who's Zoey?"

"Benjamin's sister. Or, I guess she's also your half-sister," he said. "Your name is Lara, right?"

She smiled suddenly, unexpectedly. "Lara McAvoy."

He stuck out his hand. "Jake. Jake McRoyan. We both have 'Mc' names. You, me, and McDonald's."

His earlier joke might have fallen flat, but this one caused a sudden, loud outburst of wild laughter. Lara laughed so hard that Jake couldn't help but join in.

She stopped at last and looked at him with her oddly direct gaze. "What are you doing tonight, Jake?"

Jake shrugged. He'd been planning on using Wade's old driver's license to buy a case of beer, then find a nice, comfortable place to drink it. Halloween night there would be parties going on in Portside Weymouth, and carrying a case of beer he'd be welcome almost anywhere a party was under way.

"I was just trying to decide what to do," he said. Then in a burst of frankness, "I was thinking seriously about getting drunk."

Lara nodded solemnly. "That's good. That's good. I like to get drunk, too. My boyfriend and I usually get drunk together, but he's in jail tonight."

"Jail?"

Lara shrugged. "He can't get his bail reduced until Thursday."

"What did he do?" Jake asked, not sure he wanted to know.

"I'm not supposed to tell," Lara said, putting a finger to her lips. "Can you get anything to drink?" she asked him.

Jake held out the license sheepishly. "I think I can."

Lara stared at it, her eyes wide. "That's a dead person," she said.

Jake felt a thrill go up his spine. "How do you know that?" he demanded.

But Lara only smiled dreamily. "Come and get drunk with me. Then you can tell me about my blind brother."

Jake

Wow. What am I afraid of? I'm not afraid of physical pain or anything like that. You play football, you get used to physical pain. The only thing I'm afraid of is that I might be weak sometime. You know? Like I'm starting to think maybe I'm an alcoholic or something, and I'm afraid of anything like that where it would be about me being weak. I don't like being out of control.

Of course you'd say, well, Jake, when you drink too much you are out of control, right? Only it's not like that. Getting drunk makes me feel like I _am_ in control. When you're drunk, you're not afraid of anything.

At least that's the way it seems.

THIRTEEN

FANEUIL HALL MARKETPLACE WAS A gigantic affair. Three long, narrow buildings, each almost two football fields in length, lay parallel to one another, separated by open plazas lined with outdoor cafés and pushcart vendors selling everything from T-shirts to pepper-gas spray.

In the summer it was a madhouse. Even now, on a rainy autumn evening with a chilly breeze blowing from the bay, it was packed inside, though the only outdoor cafés in operation were those with plastic enclosures.

Zoey, Lucas, and Christopher sat in one of these, chilly but determined to eat alfresco. Night was falling fast, but the rain had let up. Overhead there were even occasional glimpses of dark sky through the clouds. Zoey was halfway through a crab salad that cost eleven ninety-five, about twice what was charged at her parents' restaurant. Lucas had finished his burger and Christopher had consumed a pair of sautéed soft shells, offering expert criticism on their freshness and preparation to the point where both Zoey and Lucas were getting sick of him.

Before dinner they had changed into their Halloween costumes, and Zoey was disguised with death-blue makeup on her face, bare legs, and hands. A fairly realistic plastic ax was half-buried in her head, completing the zombie cheerleader costume. For the two guys "costume" meant nothing more than masks, which lay on the table.

Lucas was looking at her and shaking his head in amusement. "I always figured you more for a Snow White, princess kind of thing," he said. "But I like this. The combination of that whole cheerleader sexiness thing with the zombie thing counterbalancing it."

Zoey gave him a steely look. "You think cheerleaders are sexy?"

"Did I say that?" Lucas looked alarmed.

"You just said 'that whole cheerleader sexiness thing,'" Zoey said.

"You're in it now, man," Christopher said in an aside.

"I just meant that on you the cheerleader thing was sexy," Lucas said.

"Uh-huh. What exactly is it you guys like about cheerleaders?"

"I don't care about cheerleaders one way or the other," Christopher said. "All I care about is Aisha. And I'm not just saying that because I know you'll report that back to her when we see her later."

"Well, at least I managed to have a full costume, unlike you two," Zoey said.

"We have masks," Lucas said defensively.

"Big deal, masks. I had to put blue makeup all the way up my legs. You guys just pull on your monkey masks or whatever and that's it."

"*All* the way up your legs?" Lucas asked.

"I guess you won't find that out unless I do a somersault," Zoey said, batting her eyes. "And I'm not sure that zombie cheerleaders actually do the more acrobatic cheers. My point is, I put some effort into it, unlike you two slackers."

"I offered to help with the makeup," Lucas said wolfishly.

"Girls are into dress-up, unlike us manly men," Christopher said. "Although actually, as soon as I said that I realized Aisha didn't exactly go to much trouble. Just her old Girl Scout costume. What's Nina doing for a costume?"

Zoey grinned at the memory. "She got ahold of a long black wig and swiped some of Claire's clothes. Then she's going to stuff her bra with like eight pairs of socks."

"She's going as Claire?" Lucas asked. "Cute."

"Who is going to know that she's supposed to be Claire?" Christopher asked.

"Well, she says she's going to hand out cards that say 'for a good time call Claire,' with their phone number on it." Zoey made a back-and-forth gesture with her hand. "I don't know if she'll really go through with that part, though. Benjamin is going to be the devil. Nina says they'll be a natural couple: Mr. and Mrs. Satan."

Lucas glanced at his watch. "Have to get going soon."

"Yeah," Christopher agreed. "Besides, it's no fun being the single guy hanging around with you two. I need my little Girl Scout. Even if she *did* ditch me."

"Oh, Christopher, you know how it is. She probably wanted to hook up with her old girlfriends from when she lived here and tell them all about you. How could she do that if you were there?" Zoey said.

Christopher brightened amazingly. "Yeah, that must be it."

Zoey looked down at the check to conceal her grin. Guys. Appeal to their ego and they would believe anything.

Aisha groaned and opened her eyes. Her head throbbed painfully, and she reached to touch it. Only then did she realize that she was lying on her side. The cold, wet ground had numbed her left arm and leg. Her coat was soaked and sodden where it touched the ground, but a slight overhang of the eaves above her had kept her out of the direct rainfall.

She struggled to sit up. Pins and needles burned extravagantly as blood rushed back into her left arm and leg. She tried to stand, but with no feeling in one leg it was impossible. She leaned back against the brick wall. When her head touched the wall, she realized instantly that a large lump had risen. It was concealed by her hair, but her fingers found it and confirmed a bump practically the size of a golf ball.

She looked curiously at her surroundings. Where was she, and how had she ended up here?

It looked like the alleyway she usually took to get to Jeff's house. But how had she gotten this bump on the head? And what was she doing lying on the wet ground?

She opened her coat and saw that she was wearing her uniform. The hem of the skirt was soaked.

With feeling returning to her leg and arm, she made a second attempt to stand up. This was successful, although her head still felt as if it might explode.

She looked down at her skirt. For some reason it seemed amazingly short. Certainly it hadn't always been that short, had it? Or had it shrunk somehow? Maybe from getting wet? That didn't make any sense, but what other explanation was there?

She wrung the water out of the skirt's hem and out of the coat. She was very cold. Cold and stiff and strangely confused, unable to recall why she had been going down the alley.

Perhaps, she reasoned, the bump on her head had dis-combobulated her a little. Maybe she should see a doctor or something. Then she remembered: Jeff's mother was a nurse. She'd obviously been on her way there anyway. But what would Mrs. Pullings say about this uniform? And the way she was all wet?

"Okay, Aisha," she told herself. "Get a grip, girl. You were on your way to Jeff's house and you slipped and banged into the wall."

The sound of her voice, though strangely low, comforted her. Obviously her brain was working, and now that the numb-ness was gone she could move all her limbs, so no big deal. Everything was cool.

She certainly didn't want to go running home to her par-ents and tell them. Her mother would ask what she was doing in that alleyway when she'd told her daughter a million times to stay out of alleys. Her mother would know she was on her way to be with Jeff, and that whole fight would start up all over again. Then her mother would start in about leaving Boston and finding some nice, peaceful place where bad things never happened and there were no older guys chasing her daughter.

She began trudging down the alley. *See*, she told herself self-righteously, this *is what happens when Mother treats me like a child.* Now she couldn't even tell her mother that she'd hurt herself for fear of how her mother would overreact.

It was ridiculous. After all, she was fourteen years old and plenty mature enough to decide who she would go out with and even what she would do with Jeff, the guy she loved with all her heart.

"Okay, punch it!" Benjamin yelled. He leaned all his weight against the front of the van, digging his shoes into the soft, wet earth.

Nina pressed down on the gas. The front wheels spun backward, making a futile sound and spraying mud forward. After a few seconds she stopped and peered over the wheel. In the brilliant glare of the headlights Benjamin looked almost frightening. His jeans, his jacket, and one side of his face were plastered with mud. He stood there calmly, removed his shades, and squeegeed the mud off with a finger.

Nina rolled down the window and stuck out her head. "I suppose you blame me for all this?"

"No, no," Benjamin said, shaking mud off his sleeve. "There were two of us in the van when we were getting lost. Of course, one of us can't see, but still and all, I accept my part of the blame for getting lost out somewhere . . ." He shrugged helplessly. "Somewhere in the woods of either Maine, New Hampshire, or Massachusetts."

"I'm almost positive it isn't Vermont," Nina said helpfully. "So, we've narrowed it down to just three states."

Benjamin reached out to touch the front of the van. He felt his way around to the window. "Give me a kiss, and make it good," he demanded with mock severity.

Nina wiped mud from his lips and kissed him.

"Sorry we're slightly lost," Nina said.

"And stuck in the mud," Benjamin added.

"That too."

He found his way around to the passenger door and climbed in. "Well."

"You know," Nina said, "this dirt road must lead somewhere."

"This *mud* road," Benjamin corrected.

"Whatever. But someone put it here for a reason. There's probably a farm down there. Somewhere. We can go to the farm and call a tow truck."

"Yeah, we'll just tell him we're somewhere in one of three possible states."

"At least it's not raining right now," Nina pointed out.

"Oh, right, that is a huge blessing. Thank God there's no rain or I might be able to wash off some of this mud."

"If we're going to go find the farmhouse, we might as well go now while it's not raining," Nina said. "A ten-minute walk, we call a tow truck, and we still make the concert on time."

"On what planet?" Benjamin said darkly.

Nina crawled into the back of the van. "Let me see if your folks keep a flashlight in here."

"Is it dark?" Benjamin asked.

"Between the clouds and the fact that it's like getting kind of late, and the sun goes down at five this time of year, yes, it's dark out."

"Well, don't be scared," Benjamin said, softening. "The dark is nothing."

Easy for you to say, Nina thought. Frankly, to her the dark— the starless, moonless dark, the rural, backwoods, no city lights, no car headlights, no reflected TV glow kind of total dark— was utterly unnerving.

But she couldn't start acting scared. Once you started acting scared, you just got more scared. Like when you'd walk faster past a graveyard or something, and the faster you walked the more you became convinced that something . . . something hideous and terrible was following you, chasing you with evil eyes glowing, sharp teeth—

"Here!" Nina said loudly. "A flashlight." She snapped it on. To her utter relief the light came on strong, casting sharp, dancing shadows around the inside of the van.

"Okay, let's go. Now at least one of us can see," she

announced, trying to sound confident.

"I'll have to hold on to your arm," Benjamin said apologetically.

"I can live with that," Nina said. "But you have to carry the bag."

"What bag?"

"My backpack. I have my purse and our costumes in there."

"Costumes? You figure we'll have to trick-or-treat out here?"

"It's cold; we might appreciate any extra clothes we can get," Nina pointed out.

Outside on the road she let his hand close around her right arm. In her left hand she held the flashlight, playing it down the path, down what she fervently *hoped* was a long driveway. The beam illuminated the first few dozen yards of gravel, just to the point where the track veered left, away from the open field and into the trees.

They set off together, feet crunching on wet gravel. In ten steps the van was invisible. Darkness closed around them, hemming them in, blanking out everything but the unworldly bluish light from the flash.

"I hope it's got those bunny batteries," Nina muttered.

"What?"

"Nothing. Quiet, isn't it?"

"Very," Benjamin agreed. "That's good," he added. "I'd hear if there was something dangerous."

"Like what?" Nina demanded sharply.

"Nothing. Bears. I don't know."

"Bears? Try insane serial killers," Nina said. They had reached the line of the trees. She stopped. "We're at the trees. I think maybe the farmhouse will be right around the corner."

"Okay."

Nina tried to shine the light through the trees, but the undergrowth and the tightly ranked tree trunks swallowed the beam. Now there was the sound of dripping. Rainwater dripping from a thousand tree limbs. Then a shockingly loud hoot.

"Damn!" Nina cried.

"What?"

"Didn't you hear it?"

"What, the bird?" Benjamin said.

"Bird?"

"Yeah, it was an owl, Nina." Benjamin laughed. "*You* just worry about what can be seen. I'll let you know if there's anything that can be heard."

"Deal," Nina said shakily.

They advanced again, taking small steps, close together, Nina playing the beam back and forth from the woods on one side to the woods on the other side.

Benjamin suddenly tightened his grip on her arm and pulled her to a stop.

"What?"

"Shh," he said. "Listen."

"If you are playing games with me, Benjamin, I swear—"

"Quiet!"

She shone the light on his face. His head was tilted sideways, listening intently.

"Violin," he said at last. "I thought it might be a viola, but I'm sure it's a violin."

"A violin? *What's* a violin?"

"That music. Can't you hear it? Someone's playing Bach."

"I don't care if they're playing Monopoly," Nina said, breathing a sigh of relief. She listened herself now and could just make out the thin, distant sound. Her cell hadn't had service since they entered the woods. "Anyone with a violin must have a phone."

FOURTEEN

"**DO YOU WANT TO GO** into the restaurant?" Claire asked.

Tables were emptying out now as more flights were called. The fat guy was still there, although his companion was gone. For some reason this seemed significant to some corner of Claire's mind.

"No, it's pretty crappy, really," Flyer said.

Claire smiled at him. "Crappy?"

"I mean it's . . ." He paused. "Okay, let's go in and have a seat. I think that would be great."

They were given a table by the windows. Night had fallen. Colored runway lights cast long red lines across the wet tarmac. Just outside, a Delta 727 waited to take on passengers. Farther out a United jet roared down the runway and disappeared beyond the range of Claire's vision.

"What can I get you?" Flyer asked.

"Coffee, I suppose."

"So." Flyer smiled gorgeously. "Shall we go on calling each

other Weather Girl and Flyer, or may I use your real name?"

"I guess real names would make more sense."

"Claire," he said, savoring the word. "I remember that you told me it might not be your real name, that perhaps you had just made it up, but I knew instantly that it was real. It fit perfectly. As soon as I saw it show up on my screen I felt a chill of recognition. Like, yes, of course it's *Claire*."

Claire gulped and was glad for the arrival of the coffee as a distraction. Flyer was so much more than she had expected. It was almost overwhelming. The guys she'd gone out with in the past were people she'd grown up with. Handsome, yes, but familiar. This guy, this guy whose mind she knew well before she'd ever had the first sight of him, was like some vision of perfection. So smart, so charming, *and* so good looking?

And he liked her. Even after she had confessed so much to him.

"I'd like it if you called me Claire," she said. "'Weather Girl' seems a little strange for two people sharing a cup of coffee. And can I call you Sean?"

He grinned again, and again Claire felt an answering glow.

"You remember? I'm flattered."

"Of course I remember . . . Sean," Claire said.

"So," he said.

"So," she said.

"I guess this is our first awkward pause," Sean said.

"Mmm-hmm."

"We never had these when we were typing to each other," he said.

"No. I guess that's because we . . ." She shrugged. "Well, it's different face-to-face."

"I suppose it is," he agreed. "Although you always said that appearances didn't matter."

Claire grinned wryly. "I did say that, didn't I?"

"I mean, it's really your mind and what you believe and think that has meaning for me," Sean said. He raised an eyebrow as if he disapproved of what he had just said.

"Well, I feel the same," Claire said. "I mean, really. I guess we're friends, in a way. I don't know; it's confusing, isn't it?"

"Is it?"

"I mean, I think of you as someone I know. We've had what, maybe a dozen or so conversations, and in some ways I've been more honest with you than I am with people I really know." She shook her head. "But see? I say *people I really know*, and by that I just mean people I've seen in person."

"This is something of an undiscovered country, isn't it?" Sean said, looking thoughtful. "Friendships that are formed between people who have only met through a computer screen."

"Like pen pals in the old days," Claire suggested.

"Exactly. That's right; I'd forgotten that people used to have pen pals. So all we've done is update things. We can interact more. Instead of me sending a letter one week and you writing back the next week and so on, we can write back and forth. Still . . . there is the same big moment when the pen pals or computer friends meet in person."

"In the flesh," Claire said. She instantly regretted the choice of words, especially when, as if on cue, Sean's eyes dipped to the green silk stretched over her breasts. That was definitely new, she told herself. "Flyer" couldn't give her looks like the one Sean had just given her.

Not that she resented it. It was just different.

"I have to, uh, run to the little boys' room," Sean said.

"I'll wait," Claire said.

He stood up, and with a last smile that had the same dazzling effect as his earlier smiles, he turned and walked away.

Claire sipped her coffee. With as much casual disinterest as she could manage, she eyed his form threading his way through the tables. Nice form. Very nice form. Yes, despite her best intentions, things were different when bodies were involved as well as minds.

She followed him till he disappeared, aware that she was smiling slightly, and not caring. Her gaze drifted away, and for a moment she caught the eye of the fat kid, still sitting, hunched over a book. Probably waiting for a delayed flight. Claire let her usual curtain of disdain settle over her face, feeling embarrassed to be caught leering openly at a guy's tightly jeaned butt.

Now, while Sean was away, was the perfect opportunity for her to bail out if she wanted to.

Only, she definitely didn't want to.

Jake wiped his palms on his jeans and ran his hand through his hair. He glanced over at Lara. She was standing by the pay phone outside the convenience store, smoking a cigarette and looking tough and nonchalant.

He shrugged and went inside. He blinked like a mole in the fluorescent glare, then took a quick look at the clerk. A middle-aged guy, thin, ridiculous in a too-small, stained blazer.

He passed down the candy aisle, going straight for the cooler. There was no point in pretending he was really there for chewing gum and the beer was some kind of an afterthought. That was stupid. He was there for beer, and the sooner he tried to buy it, the sooner he would know if the man in the blazer would accept his fake ID.

But just to show that he was cool and calm and it was all no big deal, he did bend down and pick up a bag of Doritos. Then he went to the beer cases at the back of the store.

He pulled out two twelve-packs of Bud, balancing the chips

on top, and made his way back to the counter. A woman in front of him was buying lottery tickets and taking her time.

The rain had made his jacket damp, and now he found he was both cold and sweaty simultaneously. He adopted a blank, slightly impatient expression and stared at the *National Enquirer* and the *Weekly World News*. Apparently a chemical plant explosion in Louisiana had released a cloud of smoke that showed Elvis in mortal combat with the devil.

He reached the counter at last and hefted the beer up onto the high counter.

"Sorry, but I have to see some ID."

Jake smiled. "Sure. No problem." He dug out his wallet and slid out the license.

The man looked closely at the license. Then at Jake. "Wade McRoyan, huh?"

"Yes," Jake said. "That's me."

"Name sounds familiar."

Jake tried not to show any sign of panic. This guy remembered his brother? It wasn't impossible. Wade had been a big high school football star, and high school football was one of the few sports in the area. And then, too, his death, the accident, had made the news.

"Lots of guys named Wade," Jake said lamely.

A smile flickered on the man's thin lips. He handed the

license back to Jake and rang up the purchase.

Jake breathed a huge sigh of relief as he passed through the doors to the outside. Lara came sidling over, tossing her cigarette on the ground. She didn't offer to help carry the beer but sauntered off, past a carload of partygoers dressed in costume and playing Metallica at ground-pounding intensity.

She led him to the four-story brick building on Independence, two blocks away. He followed her up the stairs, to the fourth floor, where she extracted her keys and unlocked the door.

It was dark inside.

"This is it," she said.

"Looks great so far," Jake said dryly.

She turned on the light. It was a single large room, with low windows overlooking the street and a high ceiling that sloped up sharply. A small kitchen in one corner. An unmade bed in the opposite corner. Only the bathroom was closed off separately.

The walls were bare brick. The floor was bare wood. Several unframed paintings lay stacked against the walls. Lara went to the stereo, raised on plank-and-cinder-block shelves. She pushed the power button and stared at Jake, almost apprehensively.

The music was unlike anything he'd ever heard. In fact,

there was no music, at least not in the sense of instruments. Just male voices singing in an austere choir.

"What is that?" Jake asked, cracking open the first beer and taking a grateful swallow.

"Gregorian chant," Lara said. "It's very old."

Jake nodded. *Okay,* he told himself, *so the girl has strange taste in music.* "Sounds like something Benjamin would like," he said.

Lara's eyes widened. "Really?" she asked eagerly.

Jake shrugged. "I guess. I mean, he listens to everything, but mostly he's into classical music."

"I knew he would be," Lara said mysteriously.

For lack of anything better to say, Jake offered her a beer. She took it and opened it with practiced ease, drinking off the first third in one swallow.

Lara took Jake's hand and walked him to the bed. She sat down, cross-legged despite the fact that she was wearing a skirt, and pulled Jake down beside her. She leaned forward, fixing him with her moist, intense eyes. "Tell me about the blind boy."

"Benjamin," Jake said.

"Yes. He says he's my half-brother."

"Well, if Benjamin says it, I imagine it's true," Jake said. He finished the first beer and got up to get them each a second.

"Maybe he only *believes* it's true," Lara said, smirking knowingly.

"I guess maybe it caught you by surprise, huh?" Jake said. "I mean, did you already know that you had this other father out there somewhere?"

"I knew the man who *pretended* to be my father wasn't," she said. "I asked my mother, and she told me it had been someone else. Only, she didn't tell me who."

"So I guess Benjamin was the one who spilled the beans."

"I knew before that. Benjamin doesn't know. He thinks he knows. But my real father isn't a *person* at all."

That stopped Jake in mid-swallow as alarm bells started going off in his head. He finished the second beer quickly and wondered whether he might not be able to find a better person to get drunk with on Halloween night. There must be parties going on all over the place.

On the other hand, this apartment was dry and warm, and he'd already carried the beer up four flights of stairs. And Lara might be a little loopy, but she was also quite pretty when you got beneath the bad makeup. The truth was, from certain angles she struck chords of memory in Jake, powerful, evocative memories of Zoey. When Lara smiled, especially, there was a clear flash of Zoey.

They were half-sisters, after all, Jake reminded himself.

He cracked a third beer and handed one to Lara, who was keeping pace drink for drink. "So," Jake asked, knowing he really shouldn't, "who was your father?"

"Not who," Lara said. *"What."*

Aisha reached the end of the alley and stepped out into the street. It was still rain slick, though the rain itself had stopped. Her head was feeling a little better. The throbbing was still there, but reduced to more supportable levels. The numbness on her side was almost all gone, just a hint of residual weakness remaining.

"I must look like a total mess," Aisha said to herself. "Jeff will think I'm a skank."

Her hair had suffered somewhat from being pressed down onto the ground. It was flatter on one side, with bits of grit stuck in it. Somehow, maybe because it was wet, it seemed slightly longer than should be right, too. First her uniform got all short and tight and now her hair had gone the other way, growing too long.

And where was her purse? Surely she wouldn't have left the house without her purse, with her brush and makeup. Had she left it back in the alley? No, she would have noticed it lying on the ground.

She started down the dark street, feeling a strange sort of anticipation, or was it nervousness? Not that she had anything to be nervous about. She was going to see Jeff. They would go up to his room and listen to music, and then his mother would go off to her night shift at the hospital. Jeff's mother left at eight, and Aisha had to be home by ten, her curfew, but that would still give them two hours of privacy together. At least it would if Jeff's aunts went out, too.

She thought of how much she enjoyed kissing Jeff. He was the only boy she had ever kissed, but just the same she was sure he was about the best kisser in the world. It was impossible to imagine anyone being sweeter, or more gentle, or more passionate.

He always told her how beautiful and sexy she was. And Aisha didn't need anyone to tell her how lucky *she* was that he liked her. He was older, after all, already seventeen years old, which was practically grown up.

Of course, him being older, he expected her to act more grown up than just some dumb fourteen-year-old.

Aisha thought about that as she turned onto Jeff's block. She wasn't stupid or anything; she knew what Jeff wanted her to do. Lots of girls at school were already doing it, and lots of them were doing it with dorky guys their own age. At least Jeff was older and more experienced. Not to mention so much more handsome.

And someday Jeff was going to be a big success with his

music. He had already started performing on weekends in the T station downtown.

Aisha looked up, her attention drawn by a very unusual sight in this part of town: a limousine. It was black and glistened with raindrops and was coming toward her, slowly crawling along the street.

Aisha stopped to watch it go by. Possibly some major star was inside and she might be able to get a glimpse, although the windows were opaque.

The limousine stopped, and suddenly the door opened. To her complete and utter amazement, Jeff jumped out. He ran to her, crying out her name. He put his arms around her and twirled her around.

Aisha giggled. "Stop, you'll make me dizzy."

"Aisha," Jeff said happily. He held her out at arm's length, looking her over as if it had been a long time since he had seen her last, instead of just yesterday. "Damn, you look good, girl."

"I'm a mess," Aisha protested. "I think I tripped back in the alley. My uniform is soaked."

"Uniform?"

Aisha opened her coat. "See, it's wet all up one side."

"That your same old Girl Scout uniform?" Jeff asked, grinning delightedly. "Oh, I get it. Halloween. Well, this is my whole costume." He stepped back and spun around. He was dressed in hugely baggy jeans and a jean jacket with no shirt on underneath.

"Halloween?" Aisha asked, repeating the word uncomprehendingly.

"Not really," Jeff said with a self-deprecating look. "Just my stage rags. Now that I'm a big star I have to dress down."

"How come you're riding in that car?" Aisha asked, pointing at the limousine, as long as two normal cars.

"They sent it over for me from the Orpheum, baby. Like I say, now that I'm a big star I guess I rate a limo."

Aisha looked closely at him. He was acting very strange, and in fact he looked a little strange. Almost as if he was older. But that might have just been because she'd never seen him looking quite this happy. He couldn't stop smiling.

"So, me being an old friend and all, is it like cool if I give you a kiss?" he asked, smiling roguishly.

"You never asked before," Aisha pointed out.

Jeff took her in his arms and held her close. At first he gave her a light little kiss, just brushing her lips. Then he started to release her. Then he looked at her and must have seen her half-closed eyes and parted lips, because he came back again for a more normal kiss. They had been french-kissing for a few months already, and Aisha liked it a lot. It made her feel totally incredible.

Though as he kissed her, a strange thought crossed her mind. It was like a picture of some faraway place, a dark yard, and she herself in a bathrobe and a big green parka. Then the picture was gone and she was back, reveling in the way Jeff made her feel.

"Come on, baby," he said in a husky voice, pulling away at last. "I don't want to be late."

"Where are you going?" Aisha asked.

"Where are *we* going, you mean. Baby, we're on our way to the big time. The Orpheum."

"Why are we going there? What's going on?"

Jeff looked at her queerly for a moment. Then he laughed. "I see you picked up that dry Maine sense of humor."

"I did?"

"Okay, I get it," Jeff said. He laughed again. "Come on, hop in. This is it, babe. The first great gig. Opening for Tiësto and Afrojack at the Orpheum."

"No way!" Aisha exclaimed. Then, more doubtful, "What is Tiësto?"

Jeff sighed. "You never were big on music, I know, but come on. Even *you* must know who they are."

Aisha felt embarrassed. Obviously she was revealing her ignorance again, something she did frequently on the subject of music. "Of course I do," she said quickly. "I was just teasing."

She got in, shocked by the feel of the cold leather seats on her bare legs. She had to lean way out to close the door, but the driver had gotten out to close it for her. "Wow," Aisha said.

"You got that right," Jeff said. "Wow."

BENJAMIN

Well, I guess this is obvious, but my great fear is that somehow I'll lose my hearing. I'm already blind. I think being blind and deaf would be a little too much. No music. No conversation. No talking books. That would definitely be unpleasant. I might have to check out permanently at that point. I mean, what's left then? Taste? Smell? Touch?

I'll admit the sense of touch has some interesting possibilities. And with taste I could become a wine connoisseur and a serious gourmet. Which means a really hot Saturday night would be a delicious dinner, accompanied by an excellent wine while I enjoy the subtle hints of my girlfriend's perfume, and after dinner we give the sense of touch a workout . . .

Okay, so I guess I'm not afraid of anything. Unless you want to get into the whole "I'm-blind-so-any-passing-pinhead-can-beat-me-up" thing. Yeah. Well, all right, there is still this little bit of fear that someday someone, or several someones, will realize how defenseless I am. It's a world that still wants guys to be tough and able to protect themselves. And I'm not tough, not in that way at least. And I can't do much to defend myself. And yes, that does still scare me.

But I can put stuff like that out of my mind most of the time. The bigger fear, on a day-to-day basis, is just that I'll make some incredible fool of myself. It's taken a lot of work to earn people's respect, and boy, when you can't see, it is so easy to make an ass of yourself.

FIFTEEN

BENJAMIN MOVED FORWARD CAUTIOUSLY BECAUSE Nina was moving forward cautiously and because this was as far from familiar territory as he had been in a long time. Here there were no points of reference. Here he hadn't measured out distances, counting the number of steps, memorizing them. *Here* he was truly blind. Absolutely blind. If Nina decided for some reason to abandon him and walk away, he could wander for days or weeks or forever out here and never find his way to anything.

The only touchstone he had, aside from the reassuring contact with Nina, was the sweet sound of the violin. He could fix its direction: ahead and to the right. To some extent he could make an educated guess at the distance—perhaps a hundred yards now.

The other many things he heard, smelled, and felt added no clarity. His footsteps crunched on gravel and sandy soil and scattered pine needles. The air smelled of pine and mildew, decaying leaves and faint wood smoke. He heard water dripping down from branch to branch in the trees all around, plopping onto the forest floor. He heard the sound of Nina's breathing and his own. Both she and he, excited, breathing a little too fast. He knew his own heart was pounding and imagined that Nina's was as well.

"I see a light," Nina whispered. She stopped. Benjamin felt the muscle in her arm tighten.

"What kind of light?"

"I can't tell. It's yellowish. Looks like it's square, but I can only see it through the trees."

"Like a window?" Benjamin asked.

"Exactly like a window," Nina confirmed.

"That's good," Benjamin said, trying to exude confidence. "Where you have a window, you have a house. Where you have a house, you have a phone."

They started forward again, and in a few seconds Nina said, "Definitely a house. Wait! I see someone inside. He's . . . he's doing something, like swaying back and forth and moving his arms—"

"You mean like playing a violin?"

"Oh. Yeah. That's it. Duh."

"Duh," Benjamin agreed. "What's the house look like?"

"I can't see much, but I think it has a porch and it's wood."

"Okay. Forward."

They had gone a dozen steps when loud barking erupted.

"A dog!" Nina yelled.

The violin music stopped instantly. Benjamin heard the barking coming at them. At any moment the dog would be on them, springing for his throat. The squeak of a door opening, then a rattling slam. A loud snarl, shockingly close.

"Hold, Moloch! Hold."

The voice was definitely not Nina's. It was harsh and male. Old, Benjamin decided, and then congratulated himself on being so analytical at a point when he was afraid his knees might buckle.

"What in hell are you doing on my land?"

"Um, we're like lost?" Nina said, falling into squeaky uptalk.

"Our van broke down," Benjamin added. "We were wondering if we could use your phone to call Triple A."

Silence. The dog still growled, only inches away, Benjamin was sure. Yes, within easy biting range.

"We heard your violin," Benjamin said helpfully.

"I wasn't playing it for you," the old man said.

Again silence. And now the rain began to fall again. Just a steady drizzle, not a downpour, but enough to quickly wet Benjamin's hair.

"Got no phone," the man said at last.

Benjamin could feel Nina's disappointment, transmitted through her arm.

"Better step inside," the man said, sounding doubtful and reluctant. Although no more reluctant than Benjamin. Still, the rain was falling harder now. There was a snarling dog at his feet. It was cold. They were lost. There weren't a lot of other options.

"That would be very kind of you," Benjamin said. *And if you don't murder us and feed us to your dog, that would be very kind, too,* he added silently.

Nina led him to steps. "Three," she said.

He climbed them and gratefully felt the moment when he passed under the shelter of the porch and the rain stopped falling on his head.

The sound of a rickety screen door opening on rusty hinges.

Nina shifted his grip and sidled through. It was warm, and from both the smell of smoke and the crackling sound, Benjamin knew there was a wood fire going.

"Blind, huh?"

"Yes, sir."

"Not too damned smart going for a walk in these woods when you can't even see."

Hard to argue with that, Benjamin admitted.

"Sit down," the old man said.

"Sharp right," Nina directed. "Two steps."

Benjamin followed the directions and found the chair. He sat down wearily. The fire's warmth could be felt not far away. Creaking floorboards, the sound of someone walking away.

"He stepped out of the room," Nina whispered. "By the way, don't make him mad. He's about ten feet tall."

"Ten feet?"

"Okay, about six inches taller than you, and big. He's old, but he looks all leathery and tough, you know?"

"Yeah, how big is the dog?" Benjamin whispered back.

"The dog? Oh, let's see: if you were standing and he was to walk right up and bite you, you'd be screaming in a soprano voice. Does that draw you a picture?"

"Wonderful. I could have lived without that particular picture."

"Here he comes."

"I made you each a cup of coffee. It's all I have. I don't do a lot of socializing. Not since the wife departed."

"Departed? Where did she go?" Benjamin heard Nina ask. He winced. Bad question.

"Departed this earth." The old man laughed, a dry, rasping sound. "She's burning in the everlasting fires of hell."

About ten seconds of absolute silence.

"Oh," Nina said.

"She hated it here. Couldn't stand the silence and loneliness," the old man said. "She wanted more. She wanted people around her. Excitement." He laughed the same harsh laugh. "So she got her excitement. Ayuh. She was excited, all right."

Another ten seconds of absolute silence.

"Well," Nina said brightly. "Thanks for the coffee. If you don't have a phone, I guess we'll just head back to the van and wait for someone to drive by."

"You wouldn't like the sort of folks who might drive by on *this* night," the man said. "And you wouldn't half like the things you might see in these woods on a Halloween night."

Neither Nina nor Benjamin could think of a single thing to say in response to that.

"You'll sleep in the barn," the old man said with an air of absolute finality. "You'll keep warm and dry in there. Ol' Moloch will watch over you."

In the barn, Benjamin repeated. *Watched over by Moloch.* A dog named for an ancient god who was known to prefer human sacrifices.

Benjamin decided he probably should *not* mention that little fact to Nina.

"TV," Jeff said. "Check it out."

"Cool. I guess it can't get cable, though."

Jeff laughed. "Have to be a long cable."

He was showing her the features of the limo. The power window that went up, blocking off the driver. The refrigerator. The stereo.

They drove past the Granary Burying Ground in the limo and pulled up to the private back entrance to the Orpheum. It was beginning to dawn on Aisha that Jeff was telling the truth. She couldn't imagine how he had kept this from her, it was an awfully huge secret, but now it was starting to look as if it was true.

"I can't believe you didn't tell me about this. You sure can work a surprise."

"Now, Aisha, if I didn't tell you this was on, how is it you're here?" He looked at her with concern. "You didn't hurt yourself when you tripped in the alley, did you?"

Aisha didn't like his implication that she was being weird or something. He was the one being weird. But this certainly wasn't the time to start a fight.

They were shown to a dressing room with a ragged leather couch, and Aisha waited there while Jeff went off to hook up with his DJ and the other guys and check out the stage. He asked her to come with him, but Aisha felt amazingly weary and said she wanted to take a little nap. That way she could be totally up when the show started.

"Yeah, I understand, Aisha," he said. "After that drive down here and all."

Aisha decided Jeff was a little distracted by all the excitement. He seemed to be saying things that made no sense at all. But given this sudden, amazing break in his career, his barely begun career, it wasn't surprising that he might get a little strange.

She'd intended just to rest a little, but waves of sleepiness reached up to her from the couch and drew her irresistibly. She couldn't remember ever being more tired.

Her sleep was confused and chaotic. Dreams melted one into the next. Images of Jeff, but a Jeff who kept turning into someone else, a smiling, handsome guy Aisha felt she must know; of a Girl Scout uniform that was too short; of spinning and falling; of a large boat, a ferry, approaching a small, quaint village.

She was standing in the dark, outside in a bathrobe and big, puffy coat, in front of a large house. Someone was approaching her, coming nearer in slow motion, his face hidden. But she wasn't frightened. On the contrary, she wanted the person to come closer, much closer. His name was . . . It was right there, on the tip of her tongue.

And then he was there, kissing her lips. It felt profoundly, deeply wonderful.

Aisha opened her eyes. Jeff pulled away, looking sheepish.

"Sorry," he said. "I couldn't help myself."

"I didn't mind at all," Aisha said shyly. "I was just dreaming about you." But as soon as she said it Aisha felt strange. Had she been dreaming about *Jeff*?

He leaned over her and kissed her again, and she forgot about her doubts.

"Missed you, baby," he said in a hoarse whisper.

Aisha felt his hand moving in a way that she had only recently begun to allow. Her mother would kill her if she knew she was letting him touch her this way, but it felt so good. "There's never been anyone like you for me," Jeff said in a whisper.

"I love you, Jeff," Aisha said.

His eyes widened in surprise. "You do? Still?"

"Of course, silly," Aisha said. "I only tell you every day."

"It's been a while," Jeff said.

Aisha frowned sternly. "Just yesterday."

"You're right," Jeff said with a smile. "It is just like yesterday."

There was a knock at the door. He rolled his eyes and yelled, "I'll be right there, stay out!" Then, in an intimate whisper, "It's getting close," he told Aisha, his eyes shining. "I can't believe this day. My biggest gig ever, and my number-one babe, right back here in my arms."

Aisha kissed him again. It was so cool that he really, really loved her. And she really, really loved him, too. "Maybe after the show something else lucky will happen," she said.

His eyes were smoldering. "Don't tease me."

She nodded slowly. "It's what I want," Aisha said, feeling suddenly very grown up and mature. It was something she'd been thinking about for a long time. And what better night than this for it to happen? She was honored that he wanted her to be a part of all this.

"Are you sure?" Jeff asked. "Those are just the same words you used before. I don't know if you remember, but I do. Only this time, you know, I'll be totally careful." He made a cross-your-heart motion.

Again Aisha experienced that strange disconnection, the sense of confusion, of having not quite heard right or something. There was a second loud knock at the door. Someone yelled, "Five minutes, Mr. T-Bone!"

"Coming!" Jeff yelled. "Come on, baby," he said. "I want you out there with me. I don't want to take any chance that you'll suddenly disappear on me again."

"So where in the hell is she?" Christopher demanded for the thousandth time. They were standing in the crowd outside the Orpheum, a fairly unruly but not threatening bunch. The smell of pot smoke drifted by from time to time. Several competing speakers were blasting away just across the street in the

Commons. A lone protester was parading around carrying a homemade sandwich board that denounced abortion, godlessness, the Trilateral Commission, the U.S. Postal Service, and Howard Stern.

At least Zoey *believed* he was a protester. It was hard to tell in a crowd of people, at least two thirds of whom were in costume. Zoey's own zombie cheerleader was among the tamer zombies, ghouls, and beasts, all breathing steam in the cold air. "This is the place, right?" Christopher demanded. He stood up on his toes and scanned the crowd as well as he could. "I mean, they open the doors in a few minutes and once we're inside, how's she going to find us? Man, I knew this was screwed somehow or other. I didn't know how exactly, but from the start it felt like some kind of mess about to happen."

"Christopher, Aisha's not the only one missing," Zoey pointed out. "While we're at it, where are Nina and Benjamin? Where's Claire? Okay, forget Claire, she did say she probably wouldn't come at all. But we are definitely missing three people."

"Iron Man and Batman," Lucas remarked, pointing at a couple wearing the easily recognizable masks. "Two Barneys. And about two hundred gangsta-looking types who may, or may not, be in costume. And an awful lot of gorillas." He sighed. "I guess gorillas are fairly common, huh?"

"Maybe that's it," Zoey said. "Maybe we can't see them because they're in costume."

"Aisha was just wearing her old Girl Scout outfit, right?" Christopher argued. "I'd recognize that."

"There! That's like the eighth gorilla," Lucas said, outraged. "They're everywhere!"

"What are you worried about?" Zoey demanded. "You've barely put on your mask. And I have yet to see Christopher do his Joker, while here I am, walking around Boston wearing a pleated skirt, blue body makeup, and this dumb plastic cleaver on my head."

"I can't put on my mask," Christopher said. "I want Aisha to be able to spot me easily. I just don't see what could be keeping her so late." He looked at his watch yet again. "Damn."

"Look, Christopher," Zoey said impatiently, "Aisha is the last person we have to worry about. She grew up here. She knows her way around, unlike Nina and Benjamin. Aisha has friends here. Maybe she hooked up with some of them. Or maybe her old boyfriend—I, uh, I mean this guy T-Bone, Jeff, the guy who's playing, maybe she hooked up with him."

Zoey waited, hoping against hope that Christopher hadn't heard the word *boyfriend*. But Christopher had frozen in place. And now he was turning his suspicious glare on Zoey. "Boyfriend? Old boyfriend? This guy, this rapper, used to be her boyfriend? See, Aisha let that slip once before and then she went off telling me no, he *wasn't* ever her boyfriend."

"I didn't mean boyfriend like that," Zoey said quickly. "I meant he was a friend, and a boy, as opposed to a friend who's a girl."

But Christopher wasn't buying a word of it. "Boyfriend. I knew there was something going on here. Now I see it all clearly. That's why she wanted to come down to do this. And that's why she ditched us." He was pacing around in a tight circle and throwing his arms out every few words. "She's off with this dude right now, I guess. Talking about old times, huh? Yeah, I'll just bet they're *talking*."

"It's all ancient history," Zoey said placatingly. "Aisha was fourteen at the time. She doesn't even like to talk about him because it all ended badly. You know she loves you."

"She doesn't want to talk about it," Christopher said, "but here we all are to watch him, right? And where is *she* while we're out here?"

"Look, she asked you to come, Christopher," Zoey argued. "That should tell you something."

"She's probably backstage with him right now, him telling her how he's going to take her to Hollywood with him. Let her be in his music video, dancing around wearing those little shorts," Christopher said darkly. "And I'm out here worrying."

"Why don't we go on in?" Zoey suggested. "Maybe she's inside waiting for you."

But Christopher's face was all suspicion. "Maybe it might be interesting if I was to see her *before* she sees me," he said craftily. He slipped the Joker mask on over his head. "Maybe I'll just go in and see what she's up to." He dug his ticket out of his pocket.

Lucas and Zoey exchanged a look. "Nina will take care of Benjamin," Zoey said with a shrug. "And vice versa. Whereas I think Christopher may be losing it."

"Hey, Joker," Lucas called after Christopher. "Wait up. The dead cheerleader and her gorilla are coming with you."

SIXTEEN

"I DON'T KNOW IF THE blind boy is my true brother or not," Lara said. "Many things are not what they seem." She nodded in profound agreement with her own statement while Jake popped his seventh beer.

"Yep," Jake said indifferently. "Can't argue with that."

The first twelve-pack was finished. The red-white-and-blue cans were stacked in a pyramid on a low, cigarette-burned coffee table. The second twelve-pack had been unwrapped, and Jake was gratified to see that he had begun to pull ahead of Lara. She had drunk him can for can until this seventh beer.

Not that she was acting drunk in any way. On the contrary, while Jake was getting more light-headed and beginning to think that Lara was, after all, quite a pretty girl, and one who flopped around without the slightest seeming concern for modesty, Lara was growing ever more intense.

She had started several times to tell him her theory of who

her father really was but had been interrupted by the need to fetch more beer from the refrigerator, the need to go to the bathroom, where she peed with the door open while singing along off-key with the chanting from the stereo. And once she had been interrupted by an apparent need to go to the window and shout obscenities at a car far below on the street that had blown its horn.

She was not an entirely normal girl.

Lara was sitting cross-legged now, halfway across the bed, leaning toward him with a serious expression. She pointed at him with her cigarette. The end glowed mesmerizingly, drawing unsteady circles in the dimly lit room. "No," she reiterated, "the blind boy may or may not be my brother. I don't know . . . *yet*. But what I do *know* is that the man he thinks is his father is not *my* father."

Jake stared at her stupidly for a few seconds. "How does that work out?"

She cocked her head sideways and looked at him appraisingly. She blew cigarette smoke toward him. He wondered what she would do if he tried to kiss her.

"I *know* who my real father was," Lara said, smiling mysteriously.

"Okay," Jake said patiently.

"I even know *what* he was."

"Yeah, you mentioned that before." Jake finished the seventh beer, upending the can.

"His name is Necrophage."

Jake nodded. "That sounds foreign."

Lara smiled mysteriously again, a smug, knowing expression that Jake realized vaguely would probably have annoyed him if he were sober. "Oh, it's foreign, all right."

"Greek? Sounds like it might be Greek. Is your real father Greek?" In about ten seconds he was going to make his move. What was the worst she could do? Slap him?

"He's a demon," Lara said.

"My dad's like that sometimes," Jake said.

"No!" Lara nearly shouted. Her eyes blazed angrily. She puffed several times dramatically on her cigarette. "Don't act like I'm crazy or something. He's a demon. I'm not saying he's Satan *himself* or anything. *That* would be crazy."

Jake had been within seconds of reaching for her exposed, accessible leg. He looked sharply at her. "Huh?"

"My father is the demon Necrophage," Lara said, managing to sound almost proud.

"A demon. As in from hell?"

"He can be in hell any time he wants," Lara said, "but he

374

walks the earth. Only in bed does he reveal himself as a demon. The only thing I can't figure out is the blind boy."

Jake was sobering up slightly. "That's *all* you can't figure out?" he asked cautiously. Maybe she was just drunk and free-associating and a little unusual. Or maybe she was insane. Really, truly insane.

"I don't know if the blind boy is a son of Necrophage or not," Lara said. "The blindness may be a sign."

Jake actually smiled. The image of Benjamin hearing that he was the son of a demon named Necrophage was definitely amusing. "I guess I could ask him, next time I see him," Jake offered.

"We can find out right now," Lara said.

"Oh, really?"

She jumped up suddenly and ran to one of the plank-and-cinder-block shelves. She came back with a rectangular brown board and a heart-shaped piece of plastic. "Have you ever consulted a Ouija board before?" Lara asked. She set the board reverently between them on the bed, carefully positioning the plastic shuttle.

"I, uh . . . no." More beer would be needed for this.

"Just place your fingers very lightly, like this," Lara instructed.

"You know, Lara, it's getting kind of late," Jake said.

She looked at him appraisingly for a minute, staring straight into his eyes in a way that made him want to flinch. "I'll call on my spirit," she said at last. "And after I learn about the blind boy I'll ask her whether I should give you my body." She grinned slyly, knowingly. "You do think I'm that other girl's half-sister, don't you? That's why you look at me like that."

Jake fought to keep his expression calm. It was the second time that night that Lara had seemed to reach into his mind and extract information she shouldn't have known. How had Lara guessed that when he looked into her burning, intense blue eyes he was looking for echoes of Zoey?

The same way she had known that Wade's license picture was of a dead person?

Without a word Jake put his fingers on the shuttle. The song reached its last few notes and died away, leaving silence behind. The atmosphere seemed to have grown thick and stifling. Just the cigarette smoke, Jake reassured himself. And this sense of strangeness, of things creeping around him unseen, that was just the beer. He made a mental note: in future, don't drink with lunatics.

"Look into my eyes and concentrate," Lara ordered.

Jake did. Their eyes met, and it was as if an electric connection had been made. Her eyes captivated him, held him. Like

Zoey's? Yes. The same blue. The same shape. But what was behind them was different. Very different.

"Are you with us, O spirit?" Lara asked the smoke-laced air.

For a long while they waited, barely breathing. Fingers trembling on the edge of the shuttle.

"Are you with us, O spirit?" Lara asked again.

Suddenly, to Jake's amazement, the shuttle moved. It slid in a shallow arc across the board and came to rest pointing at the word *Yes*.

Drunk or not, Jake was beginning to feel very nervous. He glanced over his shoulder toward the dark corner of the room. They were alone, he reassured himself. Lara might be crazy, but he was twice her size. There was nothing for him to fear.

"It feels different," Lara said, creasing her brow. "Is this Amber?" In an aside she explained, "Amber is my spirit guide. Amber Shores. She was killed by Indians in 1649."

Despite himself Jake felt a crawling sensation on his skin. Sweat was trickling down his back. His fingers were twitching from the effort it took to hold them still.

"Is this Amber?" Lara repeated the question.

The shuttle moved quite strongly to *No*.

Lara's eyes opened wide in surprise. "Then please tell us your name, O spirit."

The shuttle moved slowly, uncertainly around the board,

wandering, as if it was learning its way around. It stopped, pointing at *W.*

"Go on," Lara urged. "We wish to speak to you, O spirit from beyond the grave."

The shuttle moved to the *A.*

Jake stopped breathing. He could swear *he* wasn't moving the shuttle.

"*W* and *A*," Lara whispered. "Remember that."

The shuttle moved, strongly this time. *D.*

Jake felt his heart miss several beats. The hairs on the back of his neck were on end. He wasn't going to let the shuttle move. He wasn't going to let it show the next letter. He wasn't going to let it move to *E.*

"You're fighting it," Lara said accusingly.

"No," Jake said. The shuttle moved. Despite his every effort to hold his hands still, the shuttle moved. Inch by inch across the board.

"Spell out your name, O spirit from beyond the grave!" Lara cried in a transport of enthusiasm.

Jake stared in horror as the pointer moved vindictively, irresistibly to the *E.*

"W-A-D-E," Lara said. "I wonder if there's more?"

Jake stood up and backed away. He tripped over his feet and fell down but was up in a flash.

"Don't be scared, Jake," Lara said. "It's just a spirit. The dead can't hurt us."

But Jake was past hearing.

"Are you hungry?" Sean asked.

"No," Claire said. "I don't seem to be interested in food."

He smiled. "I'll take that as a sign that you aren't bored with me just yet."

No, she wasn't bored. Very far from it. She was interested in everything about him.

They had talked and talked for what seemed like hours. In the time that Claire and Sean had been sitting in the airport restaurant, drinking cup after cup of coffee, they had talked more than they had in all their computer conversations.

She had gotten used to his odd, slight hesitancy every time he spoke. The way he seemed to be searching for the right thing to say, and inevitably finding it.

She sat now with her chin resting on her hand, feeling like she had never felt before. Feeling like some great power of the universe had given her exactly what she had been looking for. Looking for, without ever consciously knowing it.

Sean was brilliant, and witty, and had flashing perfect teeth. He was sexy, without being pushy or crude. Funny, but not condescending. Handsome, but modest. He laughed at her jokes.

He remembered everything she had ever told him about herself.

He had thought about her, considered her as a person. Yes, he knew her weaknesses, but he also knew her strengths. He was forgiving and kind, and still had flashing perfect teeth.

She had liked him as an abstraction when he had just been a line of type on the computer screen. She had thought even then that he was uncommonly smart and thoughtful. But in person the effect was overwhelming. And Claire wasn't a person who had ever been overwhelmed by anyone or anything.

He was in every way perfect. And he had no girlfriend. And he liked her very much. And Claire's usual cool reserve was being swamped by her growing desire to touch him, to kiss him.

"I know it's a cliché about flying that it makes you feel free, but I can't help the facts: it *does* make you feel free. It is exhilarating."

"So, how long before you can fly a passenger jet like your dad?"

The hesitation. The flash of teeth. "A very long time. Right now I can only fly myself and whatever fool will volunteer to fly with me."

"I'll fly with you," Claire said, sounding ridiculously sultry to her own ears.

Sean's eyes flew open in alarm. Beyond him Claire saw the fat guy, still reading his book, smile wickedly. Then the smile evaporated, and he looked back down at his book, mumbling the words to himself.

"That's awfully nice of you to show such confidence in my flying," Sean said, "however misplaced." He grinned self-deprecatingly. He reached across the table and for the first time took her hand in his. "But on a rainy night like this, I wouldn't want to endanger a person I care a great deal about."

Claire was aware—very aware—of a physical response to his touch. Of a warmth that made her squirm a little in her chair. She blushed again, practically making a habit of it. "Too bad we have to hang around here," she said.

"Who says we have to?" Sean said in a low voice. He flushed and put his hand to his hearing aid. Then he said, "You know those Z-iosks? They have them all around the airport, and it's like this little room, you know? With a chair and table and like this bed? I guess people like sleep in them while they're stuck waiting."

"I've seen them," Claire admitted. The word *bed* had brought her up short. Apparently it had disturbed Sean as well. He was stammering and flushing and not sounding at all like himself. Still, Claire reflected, some privacy would be nice. She badly wanted Sean to kiss her. Probably more than once. Probably in a way that he couldn't do out here in a restaurant.

"All you need is a credit card," Sean said. "Do you have one?"

"Sure," Claire said.

"Then let's go, okay?"

She considered for a moment. Saying yes would make it so obvious that she wanted to kiss him. It would mean surrendering all her power over the situation.

Saying no would be worse.

"I've never seen inside a Z-iosk," she said.

Sean got up quickly, threw some money down on the table, and took Claire's arm. He hustled her away with surprising force, almost enough to make her resentful. He led the way to the Z-iosk. It looked from the outside like a cross between a tiny trailer and an oversize, old-fashioned phone booth.

Claire extracted her Visa card and stuck it in the slot. The door opened, and inside she saw a narrow, built-in cot on one side, a chair, a TV set high on the wall, and a table.

"Perfect," Sean said, rubbing his hands together.

Claire wasn't so sure. With the door closed behind them and the blinds on the door drawn shut, it was completely private. Completely. She wanted to kiss him, yes. But it would be awkward if he thought she was ready for more.

Quite suddenly Sean took her in his arms and kissed her lips. It was a surprise, but oh, not a bad one. After a moment's hesitation Claire returned the kiss. And after a moment's more hesitation she let Sean draw her down onto the bed.

Claire

What am I frightened of? Severe, third-degree burns. Paralysis from the neck down. I could live without either of those. I'm not fond of pain and helplessness.

Also, I guess I'd rather not end up completely alone. Mostly alone would be great, but not completely. I suppose I would be happy if I had just one good friend. And one real boyfriend, a guy who loved me for what I am. Or despite what I am. And yet it's all too easy for me to envision a future where I don't manage even that much. I don't worry about school, or money, or success. Those things are all easy for me. It's just the little human things I have problems with: trust, love. Those things.

I can see me ten or twenty years from now. A success, of course. Respected. Admired. Desired.

Alone.

I guess it sounds pathetic and maudlin, but I'm afraid that there is just something about me that will never let me be truly loved. But I'm not going to change just to make people love me. I make people take me as I am. Or they can forget it.

What I'm afraid of is that they might just decide, given those options, to forget it.

SEVENTEEN

THE OLD MAN AND THE dog together led Nina and Benjamin to the barn. He pointed to fresh straw they could sleep on. He pointed to the cow and advised them to stay away from her. He showed them the water pump. Then he left them.

"He's gone," Nina whispered.

"How about the dog?" Benjamin whispered back.

"Him too."

The two of them breathed a sigh of relief.

Nina looked around at their surroundings. A single light-bulb, swinging lazily from the roof on a long cord, provided light. "It seems we have a cow," Nina said. "She's in a stall. There are like three other stalls, but they're all empty. There's an upstairs."

"A loft?"

"Okay," Nina said, "sure, I guess that's a loft. I've never seen a loft before. It's like half an upstairs, you know what I mean?"

"Yeah, it's called a loft," Benjamin said.

The cow stuck its head over the railing of its stall and glared at them with a single, huge brown eye. Then it mooed, an amazingly loud sound.

"Damn!" Benjamin said.

"That was the cow," Nina said quickly, putting a hand over her fluttering heart.

"Really?" Benjamin grinned. "You're telling me the cow goes moo?"

"You know, you're getting sarcastic, Benjamin," Nina warned.

"I have mud *inside* my pants," Benjamin said. "If all I get is sarcastic, it will be a miracle."

"There's water over there," Nina said. "You could wash off. You could change into your costume while your regular clothes dry. See, I told you it was a good idea to bring the costumes. Ha!"

Benjamin considered for a moment. "I know this is a silly question, but you don't really think Farmer Joe here is a mad killer who will reappear in a few minutes wearing a hockey mask and swinging a machete, do you?"

"What makes you think that?" Nina asked, trying unsuccessfully to sound nonchalant.

"Oh, maybe it was the remark about his wife burning in hell. Maybe that's what set off my suspicions."

"There's that sarcasm again."

"Or it could have been all that stuff about not liking what we'd see in these woods on a Halloween night. You have to admit, that sounds an awful lot like something a guy in a horror movie would say, right before he gets ready to hack everyone up with a machete."

"I was telling myself maybe he's just a lonely old guy whose wife died."

"Died? You don't think he killed her?"

"I was thinking like she ran off with someone exciting, like some kind of rock star or TV executive or something," Nina said thoughtfully. "Ran off and left the old man here all alone and bitter. Then it turned out that she died in an earthquake out in Los Angeles, and even though the old guy hated her for leaving, he was still destroyed over her death and it drove him nuts."

Benjamin waited. "Are you done?"

"Yeah, that's it," Nina said.

"My question is: Should we try to get back to the van or stay here?"

"If he's a mad slasher, he can get us here or there, and here it's nice and warm and we have light. Also," she pointed out, seizing on the idea, "here we have a pitchfork for self-defense."

"We do?"

"Yep." Nina went and lifted the pitchfork from where it

was leaning against the wall. She handed it to Benjamin, who ran his hands over it thoughtfully.

"Okay, point me to the water. I'll wash off this mud. If I'm going to be hacked up by a madman, I'd like to be clean."

Nina led him across the barn to an old-fashioned-looking water pump in one corner. It spilled into a long wooden trough that was half-filled with water. A greenish scum had formed over the surface. Nina worked the handle a few times, using all her strength, and after several pumps the water splashed out clear and clean.

"Just use the water from the pump and stay out of the trough," Nina advised. "The backpack is right here." She dropped it beside him.

"Okay," Benjamin said. "Um, where are you going to be?"

"Oh." Nina looked around. "I'll go up to the loft and lay out our beds of nice, clean straw. Maybe later the Wise Men will come by with some frankincense."

"Okay," Benjamin said uncomfortably. "You're not going to be immature and look, are you?"

"I'm not that tacky," Nina said haughtily. "Your secrets are safe with me. Like I'd even be interested."

She turned her back and began climbing up the ladder to the loft. Up there, with the rafters just over her head and clean hay stacked in neat bales, it was a more pleasant, reassuring place. Armed with a pitchfork they'd be fine.

"It's nice up here!" Nina yelled down. There was no answer. Nina went to the edge of the loft and looked down. What she saw made her catch her breath. Benjamin was bent over, rinsing his clothing under the stream of water, his bare flesh lit by the single overhead light.

Nina pulled back and drew several deep breaths. Tacky. Tacky and sleazy and dishonest and not very nice, she told herself. Not that she had looked on purpose.

Of course, when she crept silently back to the edge of the loft and looked again, it *was* on purpose. Benjamin was pulling on his costume, muttering to himself as he got his foot stuck in an armhole.

"I'm putting on a red satin tuxedo, dressing up as Satan, in a barn in the middle of nowhere, with no one around but a nutty old man and a dog named Moloch," he said, pitching his voice loud so she could hear. "I'm telling you, there are elements of a Stephen King story here. And I don't like it."

Suddenly, from an indeterminate distance, a shriek broke the silence. It rose, a desperate, horrible wail, and fell, and rose again, louder than ever.

The dog started barking ferociously somewhere outside, howling and baying as if in answer to the terrifying wail.

"Nina!"

"Benjamin!"

"What was that?"

It came again. It was fairly far off, Nina decided, but not far enough. Not nearly far enough.

Nina began clambering down from the loft, shaking so badly that she missed several rungs in the ladder. She fell and rolled over, then bounded to her feet. Benjamin felt for the pitchfork, frantically pulling on the rest of his costume.

"What was that?" Nina cried.

"I don't want to know!" Benjamin yelled.

"Let's get out of here before he comes after us!"

"I'll stab this pitchfork right into that damned dog if he comes after us!" Benjamin threatened.

Nina grabbed his free hand and raced for the big, swinging door. To her relief it opened. Ha! The farmer had forgotten to lock them into his little trap.

"Let's run for it!" Nina yelled. Benjamin grabbed her arm and together they raced across the yard in front of the house, running in blind terror, followed by the frenzied howls of Moloch.

Aisha stood off to the side of the stage, feeling silly and conspicuous and far too young to be cool, especially in her dorky Girl Scout uniform. It was really time to quit Scouts, she told herself. Now she was actually glad the uniform had mysteriously shrunk. It at least made her look slightly sexy, and it was Halloween after all, so maybe people would just think it was a costume or something.

Halloween? How had it come to be Halloween?

The backstage area was filled with people, all of whom looked terribly busy and kept jostling her aside to run off on one last-minute errand or another. Jeff was onstage with his group, checking the amps and making last-minute changes in the program. The curtain was still down, but Aisha had heard an old man with a microphone headpiece yell to Jeff, "One minute to curtain!"

From beyond the curtain came a huge, restless noise. More than a thousand rowdy, yelling, singing, impatient voices. Most were chanting rhythmically now for the show to begin.

Jeff checked his mike for the hundredth time and wiped his palms several times on his pants. He rolled his head around on his shoulders, trying to ease the tension. Then he looked over at her and smiled. A smile that said, Wow, can you believe this?

Aisha smiled back.

The curtain parted. Brilliant lights hit the stage, turning Jeff's familiar face blue. The crowd exploded in sustained applause and shouts. They would make more noise later for the well-known acts, Aisha knew, but she could see the way Jeff soaked up the waves of approval that washed over the stage.

He took a deep breath.

"About time," Christopher grumbled from beneath his Joker mask. "They're five minutes late. Okay, do you guys see Aisha anywhere?"

"I don't see Aisha, or Nina, or Benjamin!" Zoey said in frustration, yelling to be heard over the music. She was hemmed on every side by weirdly costumed, heaving, hand-waving, dancing bodies.

"They could be ten feet away in here and we wouldn't see them!" Lucas yelled. "Should have stayed back in our seats, not come down here to the mosh pit."

"If Aisha's here at all, she'll be down here, kissing up to her famous *former, ex, used-to-be* boyfriend!" Christopher said, yelling twice as loud to be heard through the rubber mask and still convey the heavy sarcasm. "She'll be down here dancing around where he'd notice her, no doubt. So *that's* the guy, huh?"

Zoey saw he was pointing at the lead rapper, a handsome guy with quite an excellent build. She remembered him from a picture Aisha had shown her, after she'd blurted the truth to her and Nina. He didn't look as if he'd changed much, if at all. "I don't know if that's him," she lied.

"I'll bet it is," Christopher said. "What, is he like hotter looking than me or something?"

Lucas put his hand on Christopher's shoulder. "Christopher, you know I've always thought you were the hottest looking."

The joke didn't mollify Christopher. He continued peering through the eye slits of the mask, trying to see past the blinding spotlights into the gloom of the backstage. "I wonder if I could get back there."

"They have bouncers, man, get a grip," Lucas said. "You'll get your ass kicked."

The first rap ended in a flurry of verbal agility and the room erupted in applause.

Up on the stage, Jeff knew. He could feel the quality of the applause. This was no longer polite applause. It was no longer "Hey, brother, we'll listen to your rap and give you a chance" applause. This was different. They had *loved* it. He had killed. They were smiling up at him now, those who weren't wearing masks. Smiling up at him and waiting for his next number.

Ah, so sweet. He raised his arms to take in the applause. Not too much, didn't want to look like he was getting too into it, but damn! The applause!

He caught sight of a figure out of the corner of his eye. Aisha standing in the wings and applauding wildly. Standing there in her silly Scout uniform, she looked so much like the girl he had loved three years before. Unchanged, almost, except that now she was taller, and her hair had grown out a little more. Still beautiful. Still so sexy. And after the performance here, he would give her another performance back in the dressing room. They would do the wild thing together, just like the good old days. And after that, pack her back off to Maine and, well . . . he looked down and saw an especially pretty girl, with an exceptionally nice body, who was most definitely giving him the eye . . . well, now that he was a success, the opportunities were so plentiful.

Aisha applauded till her hands hurt. Jeff launched into the opening riff of his next rap, bounding around the stage with a degree of confidence she'd never seen before. It was amazing. It was like he had acquired years of experience overnight. Maybe that's what having a huge audience did for a performer. And these raps, she'd never heard either of them before and both were so much more sophisticated.

Not that she knew much about music, she reminded herself. She wasn't like Nina or Benjamin, obsessed by it.

Aisha froze. *Nina? Benjamin?* Where had those names come from? She didn't know anyone named Nina or Benjamin.

Did she?

She searched her mind, but her head had started spinning.

Images flashed before her eyes. An alleyway. Two figures coming toward her, a gorilla. Yes, one was a gorilla. No, a man in a gorilla mask. And the other? A man with a painted face. Something familiar about the man. Like she knew him from somewhere. Unconsciously Aisha put her hand to her head. She could feel the lump where her head had struck when she'd tripped in the alley.

Tripped? Had she tripped, or—

Applause again, louder than before as Jeff finished his second number. And now he was suddenly emerging from the brilliant spotlights, coming toward her, smiling hugely and catching her up around the waist.

He kissed her at the edge of the spotlight. Kissed her in sheer joy and exuberance. "I'm so glad you're here, baby," he said in her ear.

"SON OF A BITCH!" Christopher cried from beneath his mask.

"Oh, my God," Zoey said a little more quietly.

"Whoa, Aisha," Lucas said, an astonished gorilla.

"Look!" Christopher cried, pointing unnecessarily.

"I saw," Zoey said. She nodded, and the plastic cleaver slipped off her head.

"I think everybody saw," Lucas pointed out mildly.

"He kissed her!"

"Well . . . "

"He kissed her on the mouth. And there was tongue!"

"You can't be sure there was tongue!" Zoey said, shouting again over the renewed music as Jeff started his third and final number.

"There was tongue!" Christopher howled.

"Look, they're old friends," Zoey said. "They used to go together. Maybe she was just caught up in the excitement of the moment."

"Excitement of the moment?" Christopher bayed. He pulled Zoey close, yelling in her ear. "That 'old friends, used to go together' bull may be okay for you, Zoey, but not for me. Just because you don't care if Lucas sticks his tongue down Claire's throat in the front seat of her daddy's Mercedes does *not* mean it's okay with me for Aisha to be frenching some sleazy *pimple* in front of a thousand people."

It took several long, slow seconds for what Christopher had said to begin to sink into Zoey's consciousness.

Christopher tore off through the crowd, making his way to the stage, an angry, determined Joker. A gorilla chased behind him, shouting that the bouncers would kill him.

EIGHTEEN

"MMM," CLAIRE SAID.

"Yes," Sean breathed. "Definitely, mmm."

It was a very good kiss, Claire decided. As was the next one, and the one after that. Sean was definitely an overwhelming physical presence. She felt hard, lean muscle beneath his shirt. Strong, corded arms wrapped around her. It was one of the sensual pleasures she had always appreciated in Jake. And Sean was like some perfect combination of Jake's powerful physique and Benjamin's intelligence and even Lucas's tough sweetness.

"I think we'd better do that again, sweet thing," Sean said.

She was lying half-atop him on the bed, her black silken hair falling down around his shoulders and neck. He put his hand behind her head and drew her lips down to his again. Yes, he could kiss.

Claire heard a strange tinny sound, like a tiny radio far off. A voice yelling.

"What's that?" she asked.

Sean looked startled. Then his eyes narrowed craftily. "Oh, *that*. Just my hearing aid. Sometimes it picks up radio, believe it or not." He removed the device and fumbled at a minuscule switch. Claire heard the voice more clearly now, though not enough to make out the words. Then it went silent. Sean laid it on the table and pulled what must have been the battery pack or something, a rectangular object as small as the smallest tape player, out of an inner pocket. He tossed all this on the table.

"Now, babe, it's just you and me," he said, leering up at her. His hand went with practiced confidence to the buttons of her blouse. At the same time, with his other hand he pulled her down for another kiss.

It was still a wonderful kiss. But something had gone wrong. Claire felt it: a nagging feeling, deeply submerged in her consciousness. Deeply submerged but rising.

He was touching her now, expertly, wonderfully. "Damn, you are a hot bitch," he said.

Damn, you are a hot bitch? Claire reran the phrase in her mind. And the earlier *Now, babe, it's just you and me.*

His lips followed the line of her throat down, down. She shuddered and felt her body respond, even as her mind, her ever-cool, too-detached, too-reasonable mind worked at the problem. She had communicated with Sean via computer for many hours. She had now talked to him face-to-face for several more hours. There were few people with whom she had talked as much in one way or another. And she knew the way Sean talked. Knew his choice of words.

His lips drew an involuntary moan from her. "Oh, you like that, don't you?" Sean said in a whisper. "Just remember, babe, don't scream too much when we get to the good stuff. These walls are thin."

No, Claire told herself. *Don't. Don't let your suspicious mind do this. Don't spoil this wonderful moment with this perfect, transcendently wonderful guy, this guy who likes you . . . maybe even loves you . . . despite all he knows about you.*

I can put it out of my mind, Claire told herself firmly. *I can ignore the doubt. I can just enjoy . . . I can just let myself go . . . I can just—*

No. No, she realized ruefully, in the end she couldn't.

She pushed away, rolled off Sean, and stood up.

"What's the problem?" he asked. "Not getting cold feet, are you? Is it the rubber thing? Because I have condoms with me, sweet thing, never you worry."

Claire buttoned her blouse and looked down disgustedly at him. "Damn. I was almost going to buy it," she admitted. "I mean, I knew something was off, but I guess I didn't want to accept it."

"What are you talking about?" He flashed a quizzical smile.

A smile full of perfect teeth.

Claire sighed heavily. "What is your name, really?"

"Sean," he said. But doubt and worry were there in his eyes, too.

Claire laughed. "No. Afraid not, although I sure wanted you to be."

"What do you care who I am?" he asked. "You see something here you don't like?"

"Yeah. I see a lot of teeth and no brain. And by the way, whoever you are, I may be a bitch, but anyone who knows me could tell you: I'm not a *hot* one."

Aisha retreated from the edge of the spotlight, but even as she sidled gratefully back into obscurity, she saw a strange figure shoving his way through the crowd below the stage, a person in a mask—a mask that tugged at chords of memory. And then she could almost swear someone had yelled out her name, though in all the noise, that seemed unlikely. And yet the person in the mask was waving his arms at her. And now she was certain he was pointing at her, almost angrily. Suddenly another person emerged from the crowd. This person wore a gorilla mask.

Aisha reeled. An alleyway. Two people coming toward her. One was wearing a gorilla mask and the other . . . this same, unfamiliar mask of a painted face.

They had grabbed her purse and pushed her! Now she remembered. And she had fallen. She remembered the solid impact of her head against the brick wall.

The one in the Joker mask was trying to climb the stage now. . . .

Aisha shook her head, trying to clear away a deluge of strange flashes, familiar images, and other images that seemed familiar but couldn't possibly be.

Aisha turned away in panic and confusion and ran, stumbling back toward the dressing room. From behind her, applause erupted, loud and sustained. She found the dressing room and closed the door. She leaned against it, panting in the dark.

"Am I going nuts, or what?" she asked the empty room. Yes, maybe that *was* it. Maybe she *was* going crazy.

Something was in her head, twisting her thoughts, and suddenly Aisha realized that she was very afraid.

The security guards caught him halfway up the side of the stage.

"Let me go, man, I'm cool!" Christopher yelled. He got a hand free and tore off his mask. "I'm cool, I'm cool. I just wanted to talk to the lady."

"Let him go," one guard told the other. "Can't go onstage, man," he instructed Christopher.

"He knows that, he understands," Lucas said, removing his

own mask. "Jeez, Christopher, get a grip."

The zombie cheerleader finally made her way through the crowd and caught up with them. Zoey gave Lucas a cold, deadly look. Lucas had been holding on to a faint hope that somehow, in all the noise, Zoey hadn't heard Christopher stupidly blurting out what he should *not* have blurted. Her look put an end to that hope.

Amid all the noise Lucas felt a terrible, empty quiet settling around him, as if he had been cut off from all sensation. He should have known that sooner or later the truth would come out. Maybe he *had* known it.

"Oh, God," Lucas murmured. He looked pleadingly at Zoey, but she turned stonily away, focusing on Christopher.

"Are you okay, Christopher?" Zoey asked.

"I'm cool," he said. The first band had left the stage and now, waiting for the main acts, the audience had taken up a raucous chant.

Zoey nodded. "Lucas, I need to talk to you." She walked away several feet, finding what privacy there was in a relatively quiet corner, still hemmed in by bodies, but at least not crushed.

"Lucas, what did Christopher mean about you making out with Claire in the front seat of her dad's car?"

"Zoey, look . . ." Lucas tried desperately.

But Zoey had already seen the truth in his eyes. She shook

her head bitterly. "Aren't you clever?" she snapped. "So you didn't *sleep* with Claire. You just made out with her. And I spend all week apologizing like I was a jerk for believing Jake."

"We didn't do anything but kiss a little," Lucas said lamely.

"You bastard."

"Zoey," Lucas pleaded, "it was nothing. We were both mad. Claire was mad at Jake, and I was mad at you. I thought you were getting ready to dump me and go back to Jake."

"You and Claire," Zoey said bitterly. "My mother screwing Mr. McRoyan, you trying to screw Claire, and look, even Aisha now. God, it's sickening. Is everyone just that way? Is everyone on earth just ready to stab anyone in the back?"

"Zoey, look, sometimes people make mistakes. I made one with Claire. I'm sorry. I knew even then it was a mistake."

"Right after she said no, right?" Zoey demanded cynically. "Then you thought, 'gee, I guess this is a big mistake.'"

"Zoey, I love you," Lucas said. "I'm sorry!" He had to shout because Tiësto had come onstage to thunderous applause.

"Let me ask you something, Lucas," Zoey snapped furiously. "What button were you undoing at the moment you decided you were making a mistake? Or was it a bra hook? Or was it a zipper?"

Lucas was shocked at the force of her attack. But what could he say? Don't lump me in with what's going on between your mom and dad? Don't punish me for what you're feeling about them?

"I'm going home," Zoey said coldly. "I don't know if I can catch a train, or a bus, or maybe I'll rent a car; I don't give a damn as long as I'm not with you anymore."

He grabbed her arm. "Zoey," he pleaded, "you have to forgive me. You're . . . You're all I have."

For a moment it looked as if she might soften. But then her eyes went opaque, and she shook off his arm. "I guess you should have thought of that."

"Please, Lord, help me," Aisha begged, clasping her hands tightly together.

She had left the lights in the room off, an attempt to help soothe her headache. The headache had in fact lessened, but the confusion had not. Her brain was swimming with faces and places she half-knew, but knew she couldn't *really* know: a pretty girl with blond hair and blue eyes, a yellow and red and white ferry, a blind boy with an infectiously amused smirk, a big house with dozens of windows.

And mostly a guy who looked sort of like Jeff, only different.

She was losing her mind. Going insane, and this was the way it felt—all confusion and fear.

The door of the dressing room flew open. "Damn, we kicked out there!" Jeff said enthusiastically. He came running over to her and sat down, almost vibrating with excitement. "Did you hear the crowd? I mean, amazing. They were yelling out 'T-bone, T-bone' like it was some big thing, you know? Like . . . Like, I don't know."

"You were great," Aisha managed to say, trying to rise out of her mental confusion, feeling relieved just to have him near. She couldn't go insane as long as Jeff was there with her. He would keep her grounded.

"I mean, I thought it might be good," he said, "but I wouldn't let myself even start to think it would be this great. I'm on the way now. I'm on the road. People have to listen to us now, Eesh. I wouldn't be surprised if I'm talking record contract within like a week or two."

Aisha forced a smile and seized his arm tightly, holding on for dear life. "I am so proud of you," she said, chattering, talking to drive the voices of lunacy out of her mind. "I can't believe this all happened so suddenly. I didn't even know."

"It has been three years," he said. "I don't know if that's sudden."

"Three years?" Aisha said bleakly. "Don't do that, Jeff. I mean, it's only been a few weeks. Okay?"

"I guess it does *seem* like it hasn't been all that long to you, baby, but to me it feels like it's been a long time in coming." He turned more to face her. She clung to him. "Let's celebrate the whole night."

"I . . . I don't know if my mom will let me stay out all night," Aisha said. Her mother. Home in Maine. Maine? Boston? Where did she live?

Jeff laughed, as if she'd told a joke. "What she doesn't know won't hurt her," he said. Then, in a lower voice, "And what I'm going to do won't hurt you either."

Aisha felt a little sick, but whether it was from the terrible, swirling voices in her head or the thought of what Jeff wanted to do now, she wasn't sure. Both, maybe. She had told him she would, but now it was the last thing she was interested in. She was losing her mind! She could feel it.

Jeff kissed her, and that cleared some of the confusion away. His closeness helped her focus. She knew where she was. She was with Jeff. *This* was real. The feel of his lips as he kissed her again, more urgently, passionately. Yes, *this* was real.

His hands were moving over her body, faster, more confidently than he had ever done before. No hesitation. So direct! He was moving over her, laying her down on the couch before she had any time to think or object. And mostly she didn't *want* to object. She wanted to do this if only to hold on to the one stable image in her brain.

Yes, that was the answer. Just do it quickly. With her eyes closed and Jeff in her arms, the other images faded and the strange voices quieted.

But even now another voice reminded her. She smiled to herself. This voice at least wasn't part of the insanity. "Jeff, don't forget to use a thingy," she whispered in his ear.

"We don't need to worry about that," he said.

"Christopher," Aisha said, mustering more determination, "that's what you said last time."

"*Christopher?* What did you call me? Christopher?"

Last time? Aisha reran the phrase in her mind. *That's what you said last time?* What had she been thinking of? What last time? And who was Christopher?

Christopher was her boyfriend.

No, no, *Jeff* was her boyfriend. She didn't even know any Christopher.

Christopher! She saw the face clearly in her mind. No longer confused but clear and definite. Yes. Christopher was her boyfriend.

"The name is Jeff, baby," Jeff said. "Get it right." Then he shrugged. "Or hell, call me whatever you want." He slipped his hand beneath the hem of her strangely too-short uniform.

What in the world was she doing here?

"Oh, baby, yes," Jeff moaned.

Aisha shuddered. "What the *hell* do you think you're doing?" she demanded suddenly.

"Nothing yet," Jeff said in a low moan, "but hang on one second—"

The door of the dressing room flew open.

"Get out!" Jeff yelled angrily.

"You BASTARD!" Christopher cried.

"Christopher!" Aisha screamed.

"Christopher?" Jeff repeated, just before Christopher's swinging fist caught him in the jaw.

NINETEEN

CLAIRE STEPPED OUT OF THE Z-iosk back into the flow of airport pedestrians rushing to and from their planes. She straightened her clothes as best she could and scooped her hair back over one shoulder.

For a moment she considered just walking away. It would certainly be the easier thing to do. Easier by far. And yet, she told herself that whatever else she might be, she was no coward.

She walked back to the restaurant, past the harassed hostess to the table where the fat guy sat, no longer mumbling over his book but sitting, watching her come near with an expression of mixed triumph and sorrow.

Claire stopped at his table. She looked down at him. He was not in any way attractive. Probably a hundred pounds overweight. His complexion had a greasy, pallid look. His eyes, while bright and alert, were nearly swallowed by his cheeks and his heavy brow.

"Hello, Sean," Claire said.

"Hello, Claire," he said. "Would you like to have a seat?"

Claire pulled out a chair and sat down.

"How did you figure it out?" Sean asked.

Claire pursed her lips thoughtfully. "I guess it was the words. I know the way you express yourself. I know the way you use words."

Sean nodded, looking gratified, though that expression barely touched the more profound underlying unhappiness. "You understand how I did it, I suppose?"

"Yes. The hearing aid. It's a receiver."

"And a transmitter," Sean said. "I could hear everything you said and tell Dennis—that's his name, by the way—how to respond."

"I noticed the hesitation when he talked. And I saw you looking like you were moving your lips reading your book. I think I understand *how*. I don't understand *why*."

"You don't?" Sean smiled faintly and met her gaze. "You really don't?"

Claire looked away, embarrassed.

"I assumed all the time when we talked on the computer that you were . . . I suppose, plain. I had pictured you as a girl who might be as much a victim of her looks as I am of mine. It didn't matter to me what you looked like. I loved your intelligence, your sense of humor, your introspection. When you told me things that made me see you as ruthless, self-serving, Claire, I thought well, she's just an unattractive girl fighting back against a world that isn't prepared to look beneath the surface."

"I never lied to you about that," Claire said. "I never said I was . . . unattractive."

"No, you just said how little looks mattered to you." Sean laughed bitterly. "People who say that usually say it because they've been on the wrong end of the looks war. People like me say it."

"So, why Dennis?"

"It occurred to me, quite late really, that there was one other group of people who went around pretending looks didn't matter. People like you. This terrible fear grew . . . a fear that maybe you weren't at all what I thought you were. And so, it being Halloween—"

"You arranged to wear a mask," Claire said.

"A mask. Yes. A Halloween mask that would make me as handsome as any girl could want. I hoped, I even convinced myself that it was silly, that I had brought Dennis with me for no reason. I told myself I was being stupid. I told myself that no matter what you looked like, *you* would be able to see beneath . . . this." He held out his hands in a gesture that presented his vast bulk.

"Maybe I would have," Claire said. "You didn't give me the chance."

"No, I didn't," Sean admitted softly. "I saw you as you arrived. A girl of the right age, alone, not carrying luggage. I knew it was you. You stopped my heart, Claire. You were this vision of perfect beauty, of elegance, of confidence. Everything I could never be, and everything I could never have. All my courage evaporated. *I* couldn't talk to a girl like you. Not *me*. So I told Dennis he was on." Sean managed a ruined smile. "He wants to be an actor, I'm sorry he got a little carried away. *That* was never part of my plan."

"I might have surprised you, Sean," Claire said. "I'm really not superficial. I'm really not obsessed with looks. I'm really not one of those girls."

"Remember when Dennis got up to go to the men's room?" Sean asked. "Remember the way you followed him with your eyes? And then when your gaze drifted over to me?"

"Yes," Claire admitted. *Yes*, she remembered.

"I've seen that look before, Claire. The way the curtain comes down, the face goes blank, the eyes drift away indifferently. The way your lips curled with just the hint of a sneer. The look that says 'don't even bother to dream about it, fat boy.'"

Claire felt her face flush. Yes, this was the real Sean. The perceptive, intelligent Sean she had come to know. And yet had not known.

"Someday," he said gently, "a girl will come along, and I *really* don't care what she looks like, who will care more about what is in my mind, and my heart . . ." His voice tripped at the word *heart*. In a ragged whisper he went on. "A girl who will care more about what's in my heart than how I look."

"Sean . . . Sean . . ." Claire couldn't think of anything more to say.

His eyes were wet, but his gaze met hers, unflinching. "Are you that girl, Claire? Are you the girl who can love me for what I am inside? Not *like* a brother, or a pal. You know what I mean."

Am I? Claire wondered. *Am I, really? Or am I as cruel to people like Sean as everyone else in the world?*

"I, uh, have to go to the men's room," Sean said. He levered himself heavily up out of his chair. He tucked the tail of his shirt back in his pants. "Do me a favor, Claire. Be honest, okay? And if you are *not* the girl I'm talking about, then please, don't be here when I get back, all right?"

Jake ran from Lara's apartment like he was being chased. He ran along rain-glistening cobblestones painted with reflected neon.

He dodged slow-crawling cars squeezing their way through the narrow Portside Weymouth streets. He ran until he was gasping for breath among the gloomy, darkened warehouses of the waterfront. Ran away from the lights, and into the darkness.

The beer had taken a toll on his stamina that even the adrenaline of terror couldn't overcome. He sagged against a loading platform that smelled of the urine of earlier drunks, watched by the glittering eyes of a cat on the hunt.

Lara had done it deliberately, of that he was certain. Lara was insane or perhaps just evil. She had known about Wade and had made his name come up on the Ouija board. Lots of people still remembered Wade. Lots of people knew Jake's big brother had died. Why Lara had wanted to frighten him Jake couldn't guess, but he knew one thing: it had been a fake. Spirits didn't speak through Ouija boards. It was ridiculous. And anyway, Wade was in heaven. He wasn't some disconnected spirit wandering around waiting for Benjamin and Zoey's drunken, probably crazy half-sister to call him up.

Jake felt as if his skin was crawling. He scratched viciously at his arms and shoulders. Like ants on his skin. The damp, that's what it was. The clamminess of the rain that made his clothing stick to him.

He looked up and saw a bright light. Neon and fluorescence,

414

a block away. A lone beacon of brightness in this grubby neighborhood of abandoned buildings, parking lots, and warehouses.

He pushed away from the loading platform, trying as he walked to steady his breathing. He was an athlete, after all. He was in better shape than this. A few beers couldn't throw him this far off.

He walked fast, suddenly uncomfortable among the shadows, wishing he had stayed among the brighter lights of Portside. Nothing bad could happen over there, amid the expensive restaurants and overpriced tourist shops. But he was drawn not back to Portside but toward the rapidly growing light, now just a few hundred yards away. He could read the individual beer signs in the windows. Budweiser. Bass Ale. Miller.

Where had this liquor store come from? It had to be new. He'd never noticed it in this area before, certainly. And wouldn't he have noticed?

He knew he probably shouldn't drink any more. But his nerves were a wreck. The fault of that crazy bitch and her crazier ideas. Her father a devil! Good Lord. Had the girl thought about Prozac? She needed professional help.

Jake giggled, then laughed, loud and defiant. "Crazy damned bitch!" he yelled up at the night sky.

Yes, a drink would calm his nerves right down. Then he'd

head on back to the island. Just get calmed down, and then straight home.

He opened the glass door of the store. The brilliance of the light, reflected back by a thousand glass bottles, made him squint and cover his eyes. He was the only person in the store except for a redheaded, middle-aged woman chain-smoking behind the counter. She leered at him as he came in.

"Tough night, honey?" she asked.

"Yeah. It's raining," Jake said. He went to the tequila section, grabbing a fifth of Cuervo Gold. He carried it defiantly back to the woman.

"I'll need to see some ID," she said around her cigarette.

Jake felt a chill. Wade's driver's license.

He stared at the bottle. He looked at the woman. She grinned back. Cigarette smoke rose from her, for a moment giving Jake the eerie sense that she herself was smoldering.

Wade's license. He reached reluctantly back and pulled it from his pocket.

He slid it across the counter. The woman glanced down at it and gave him a grin. "That's it," she said. "That's it."

Jake threw damp, crumpled bills on the counter and grabbed the bottle. Outside it was dark and welcoming. He started away, plunging into the nearest shadow. There he twisted the cap off the bottle and raised it high, draining a quarter of the liquid fire down his throat.

"Oh, man, that's better. That is *so* much better."

He set off aimlessly, staying to dark streets, sidling away from the rare passing cars. Moving to avoid the chance of being intercepted by a cop who might take his bottle away.

He took a new drink every few minutes, and soon he was staggering in a way that struck him as amazingly funny. The more he drank the more he staggered and the more he laughed, roaring at lampposts and fire hydrants.

It surprised him when he looked down and saw that the pavement had become grass. He glared around him, laboring to focus his eyes. They focused on a cold, white angel.

"Ahh!" he cried. Then, focusing more carefully, he saw that the angel was just a marble figure. A statuette atop an elaborate tombstone.

He was in the graveyard.

He spun around. Everywhere, the moonlit markers. Everywhere, chiseled in marble, the names of the dead.

Jake wanted to run, tried to run, but his feet tangled and he fell, hands and knees in the wet grass. The bottle! It had rolled away and he felt around for it, nearly crying with relief when his hands touched it.

Jake snuggled the bottle close and sat back against a tombstone.

And then, without turning to look, he knew. With a dread that soaked through to his bones, he knew the name on the tombstone.

TWENTY

"THERE! LIGHTS!" NINA CRIED.

"Where?" Benjamin yelled.

"There are lights through the woods. Lots, like fire or something!" Nina cried. They had gotten away from the farmer's barn, but it was still all too close. Nina had wanted to run for the van, but Benjamin had pointed out that it was stuck, and it would be the first place the murderous, psychopathic farmer would look for them. So they had taken off across the muddy field, panic-stricken, babbling like idiots, racing at top speed without any idea where they were going.

Now, looking anxiously back, Nina could still see the single light of the farmhouse. And looking ahead, she saw flickering firelight just within the nearby woods.

"Hey, maybe it's a campground," Benjamin said excitedly. "You said fire."

"Yes. That must be it!" Nina cried. They were both talking in slightly hysterical whispers and panting heavily. Running through mud was exhausting. Benjamin still carried the pitch-fork in his free hand. It made a strange contrast with his mud-spattered, red silk tuxedo. But fashion statements were the last thing they needed to worry about.

"The old man said there were strange things in these woods on Halloween night," Benjamin cautioned.

"Yeah! Him and his damned dog," Nina said. "Come on."

She led the way as quickly as she could across the mud, mut-tering the whole time under her breath. "Campers. Campers are always nice people. Probably make us hot chocolate. Over there, roasting marshmallows and having sing-alongs." Nina paused to consider. They *were* having a sing-along.

"Yeah, I hear it," Benjamin said without being asked. "It sounds like religious singing of some kind. They're so off-key I can't be sure."

"Religious music?"

"Sure. Hey, they're probably like some church group on a campout."

"Exactly," Nina agreed. "Church groups are always camp-ing out and singing 'Kumbaya' around the fire." She felt at least the sharper edges of terror recede. They would reach the camp-ers in a few minutes. And so far, there was no sign that the psycho farmer or his psycho dog was following them.

They slogged along enthusiastically and reached the first

trees. "I can see them better now," Nina said. "Big bonfire and people dancing."

"I still don't get the music, though," Benjamin said. "It sounds kind of old. Like, I don't know, like out of the Middle Ages almost."

"Who cares what kind of music they like?" Nina said, exasperated now that safety was at hand. "Like we should go off and look for people with better taste in music?"

The fire was in a clearing. It wasn't until Nina and Benjamin emerged into that clearing that Nina noticed something odd. There were people dancing around the bonfire, all right. People wearing nothing but gauzy, flowing garments. Some had body parts painted with broad slashes of color. And on their heads, huge masks. Goats, from the look of them. Great, elaborate goat heads with exaggerated horns.

"Benjamin." Nina tried to flatten the terror that was urging her to scream. "Benjamin, there are half-naked people dancing around with these big goat masks on their heads."

"Huh?"

"Oh, my God," Nina said in an awed whisper.

"Oh, my God," Benjamin repeated. "It's like a . . . like a black mass or something!"

Suddenly from the woods behind them the tramp of heavy boots, crashing toward them. And then, a beastly growl.

"It's the farmer!" Nina screamed. "Run!"

She grabbed Benjamin's arm and ran, tearing through the last few bushes. Nina slipped and fell hard. Benjamin, not knowing where she had gone, ran on several steps.

He emerged into the circle of firelight, waving the pitchfork wildly and screaming, "Down, Moloch, down!"

The singing stopped dead.

Twenty half-naked figures, of both sexes, froze. Stock-still. Staring at him from beneath their elaborate goat masks.

And then one of them screamed. And then others screamed. In blind panic they ran, flinging aside their goat masks as they went, bare legs and painted arms flashing in the firelight.

"What the *hell*?" someone shouted. "What the hell is going on?"

"Nina!" Benjamin cried.

"Benjamin!" Nina ran to him, clutching his arm tightly.

"Kee-rist!" someone yelled in annoyance. "Cut. Cut. Don, go see if you can round them up again. Delia, you go with him. Tell those idiots . . . tell our guests it's just some kid in a costume."

From the far side of the fire Nina saw a man emerge. He was wearing a baseball cap and carrying a clipboard. He stopped in front of them, hands on hips. "I suppose you two think this is funny?"

"Nina, what's going on?" Benjamin asked.

"What's going on?" Nina asked the man in the cap.

"Like you don't know."

"Mister, I promise you, we have absolutely no idea. . . . Our van got stuck in the mud . . . and then this farmer and his dog and . . . We have no idea."

"None," Benjamin agreed.

"It was *supposed* to be an authentic recreation of a witches' coven, holding their Halloween ceremony," the man said. "You know, like the witches of Salem? Back around 1692? They teach you kids any history in school nowadays?"

"I may have heard something about them," Benjamin said.

"Well, it was quite a show. Until you pop up, dressed like the devil and waving a pitchfork."

"Oh," Nina said, feeling confused. Should she still be terrified? This guy didn't seem very frightening.

"You scared them half to death." The man allowed a wry smile. "These people are into doing historic re-creations. Most of them are university kids, so I doubt they believe in any of this nonsense, but then again, I don't think they expected to see someone all dressed in red and carrying a pitchfork show up."

Nina groaned and covered her face with her hands. "Um, did they start off with this like, bloodcurdling scream? Like maybe a couple of minutes ago?"

"Well, it sure wasn't me," the man said.

"Sorry if we screwed up your ceremony," Benjamin said, clearly fighting an urge to giggle hysterically.

"Not *my* ceremony. I'm just here to get some video on it," the man said. "For the show."

"The show?"

"*Dateline*. Should be on sometime next week. We're having some descendants of some of the original witches of Salem. And these folks . . . these folks you just scared half to death . . . were reenacting what they say was one of the ceremonies that got the witches in trouble."

"I warned you there were some strange things in these woods tonight." The farmer was standing behind them. Moloch panted contentedly.

Nina felt her body sag in relief. In a moment, she knew, the embarrassment would start to set in. But for now she was still enjoying the relief. "Um, let me guess," she said to the farmer. "You didn't murder your wife, right?"

"Murder her? What are you, crazy? She run off with some punk to New York. Electrocuted from a downed power line in 1968, may she rot in hell."

"Come by to bring me flowers, little brother?"

Jake's heart felt as if it was being squeezed by a giant, cold hand. His throat was tight. His hands were trembling so badly that he dropped the bottle. It rolled off his lap and onto the grass.

Jake knew it was just some drunken hallucination. Had to be. And yet . . . it *was* Wade's voice.

He fought the paralyzing terror to slowly raise his head. Yes. Standing there before him, only a few feet away. Just as he had always looked. The same Wade. Only . . . somehow not. Insubstantial. Jake realized he could see the outline of a gravestone behind Wade. Could see it *through* his brother.

"Not going to wet your pants, are you?" Wade sneered.

"You're not real," Jake whispered.

"Oh, I'm real enough."

"You're dead, Wade," Jake said. His voice was like gravel. His teeth were clenched tight.

"Well, yeah, I'm dead. But I don't think you should hold that against me," Wade said.

"This can't happen."

"Sure it can, little brother. It *is* happening."

"Why are you doing this to me?" Jake moaned.

"Me? Jeez, kid. I'm not the one with some explaining to do. Why don't you tell me what you're doing, sitting stinking drunk on my grave?"

Jake felt around on the grass for the bottle. A drink. He had never needed a drink more than right now.

"Yeah," Wade jeered, "reach for the bottle."

Jake found the bottle and put it to his lips. Wade shook his head slowly. "Don't do that, man."

"*You* did it," Jake said accusingly.

Wade nodded. "I know. But don't *you* do it. You're a drunk, Jake."

Jake managed a sneer. He was getting used to the hallucination now. This figment of his own imagination. "I have plenty of reason to want to get drunk."

Wade smiled sadly. "And there will always be plenty of reason, Jake. Every day you'll be able to find some good excuse. So, soon you'll be drinking every day."

"Maybe so," Jake said. He raised the bottle a second time.

Wade came closer. Without sound, without rustling the grass under his feet, he was closer. He knelt down now, squatting comfortably. "You know, I was a lousy big brother, Jake."

"You were the best," Jake argued gruffly.

"No. You told yourself that because you felt bad over me dying. But I was a creep to you." He smiled. "No point in b.s.'ing myself now that I'm dead. I was a dick."

Jake shrugged.

"So, I'm glad I have this one opportunity, little brother," Wade said. He reached out a hand to touch Jake's shoulder. Jake felt a cold shudder pass through him. "You have to stop it, man. You have to stop destroying yourself, Jake. Just stop. Because see, if you don't stop trying to kill yourself, little brother, you're going to succeed."

"What are you talking about?" Jake asked, his voice rattling with renewed fear.

"You're on a path, Jake," Wade said. "Stay on that path, man, and a year from now you'll be with me. Right here." Wade patted the grass in the empty space beside his own grave. "Live, Jake. Everyone dies eventually, little brother, but for now, live. Just live."

TWENTY-ONE

THE LAST TRAIN HAD LEFT. There were no more buses. Car rental companies wouldn't rent to a driver under age twenty-one. So Zoey had to wait for Aisha and the two boys to come back to the parking garage and Aisha's car. Zoey stayed inside the tiny, overheated office where the parking lot guard was watching *Night of the Living Dead* on a small TV.

She had hoped that she might find the van, her family's van, the one that Nina was supposed to have driven down with Benjamin. But no van. No Nina. No Benjamin.

Zoey worried a little over what might have happened to Nina and Benjamin, but decided they would most likely be fine. Nina could see, and Benjamin could think. Between them they made one fully responsible, capable person.

After a while Zoey spotted Aisha, Christopher, and Lucas coming down the street. Lucas. She looked at him with all the hatred she could summon.

She would never forgive him. Never.

Claire waited a full minute after Sean left the table. She wanted to wait for him to come back. She wanted to show him that she *was* the girl he had hoped she would be.

But that would be a lie. And giving him false hope would be too cruel, by far. She still believed in her heart that she wasn't a person who cared about looks. That she wasn't prejudiced, unable to see beneath the surface.

And yet, she would never be what Sean wanted. That was the truth. He hadn't realized it yet, but his image of her was of a person whose faults were understandable, acceptable, because she was fighting back against a world that mistreated her.

But Claire knew she was no victim. She had been given everything the world could give. She had no excuses. And when Sean understood that, the truth would be clear: it wasn't that *he* was somehow not good enough for her. She would be doing him a favor, leaving him now.

Or perhaps she was just rationalizing, Claire told herself. Yes, that was more likely, wasn't it?

So Claire got up and walked away, a beautiful, elegant girl, ignoring the tears that streamed down her face. And by the time she had reached her car, she was composed again.

She drove back toward home and with all her willpower, resisted the picture of Sean, sweet, smart, thoughtful Sean, coming back out to find her gone.

Gone as he had known in his heart that she would be.

"Okay," Nina said. "Anyone asks, we ran out of gas."

"Ran out of gas," Benjamin concurred. A guy from the *Dateline* crew had helped push the van out of the mud. Benjamin had retrieved his clothing from the farmer's barn. He had left the pitchfork where he had found it.

"Silly us, we never even thought to check the gas gauge."

"Exactly," Benjamin said. "We certainly did not get lost on a back road, decide that an old farmer was a mass-murdering Freddy Kreuger clone, and run in terror from a howling dog, with the result that I burst into the middle of a black mass, dressed as Satan, carrying a pitchfork, and screaming 'down, Moloch, down' at the top of my lungs."

"Nope. That certainly never happened. Because, see, if we told people that, then we'd look like idiots," Nina said.

"Ran out of gas."

"No gas."

"Not a drop."

"Temporary amnesia," Christopher said, savoring the phrase yet again, with the same vengeful malice. He was driving the car. Aisha was sitting sullenly in the back alongside an equally sullen

Zoey. Lucas was in the passenger seat, staring out into the black night. "Temporary amnesia. Oh, yes."

"It happens to be the truth," Aisha mumbled.

"Your purse is snatched and somehow, as a result of this, you end up in this guy's dressing room about two seconds away from doing with *him* what you flat refuse to do with me."

"I told you, Christopher, it's more complicated than that," Aisha said.

"Oh, yeah. Complications. Complications." He nodded grimly. "They better be some really great complications. Temporary amnesia! Thought she was fourteen again."

Aisha rolled her eyes. Okay, it *was* a little hard to believe. But Christopher should be more understanding. If the situation were reversed . . . bad example. If it were Christopher telling *her* this story, she'd have killed him by now.

Plus, Christopher hadn't walked away pouting when he'd seen her in an embarrassing position with Jeff. He'd come rushing in to save her. Which was really pretty sweet.

She leaned forward and put her arms around Christopher's neck. She nuzzled his neck and kissed his earlobe.

"Trying to make up, huh?" he grumbled.

"Yes," Aisha said. She kissed the side of his neck again and rested her head on his shoulder. "I love you, Christopher," she whispered.

He stared ahead stonily for about fifteen seconds. Then, "Okay, Lucas, your turn to drive. I can't drive and make up at the same time."

They arrived home in separate groups, spread across the night. Aisha, Christopher, Zoey, and Lucas made it back to Weymouth a little after midnight and caught the water taxi home, splitting the cost four ways. The trip across to the island was spent with Aisha and Christopher in quiet conversation as Aisha told Christopher more details. Not *all* the details, but at least the important ones.

Later that night Aisha went around with Christopher, helping him deliver the morning papers in his pathetically beat-up island car.

Zoey and Lucas didn't speak on the trip over. Simple geography required them to walk in the same direction from the ferry landing to their homes, but Zoey pointedly stayed ahead of him and didn't look back.

Benjamin and Nina arrived back at three in the morning, exhausted but in good spirits. They caught the water taxi and charged it to Nina's father on the grounds that after all, he was rich.

Claire drove for many hours after leaving Sean in the airport. She had driven down from Boston to Cape Cod, restless and too far gone in thought to feel sleepy. At last, she had turned back north. She arrived back in Weymouth and parked the Mercedes in the parking garage, just as the city was waking up to a gray dawn and the first day of November.

She had a light breakfast in a diner and decided against going home at all. It was a school day, after all. She didn't have her books, and she was overdressed for a day of high school, but she didn't much care if people wondered what she was doing in heels and a silk blouse. Claire had never worried much how she looked.

Jake woke up in the graveyard just before dawn. His head was splitting. He was half-frozen and stiff. His mouth felt like he'd been eating dirt. His throat was raw, his stomach ravaged. He saw the half-full bottle of tequila lying on the grass.

The hair of the dog, as the saying went. That's what he needed: a good, stiff drink to kill the pain of the hangover. Right.

He lifted the bottle and without hesitation emptied the contents out over his brother's grave. He staggered to school long before it was open. He had a key to the gym, let himself in, and slept for two hours in the locker room. Then he drank a quart of water and, fighting the agonizing pain in every fiber of his body, put himself through an hour of calisthenics, sweating the last of the alcohol out of his body.

"Oh, no," Zoey moaned. "No way."

The alarm had gone off way too early. She'd barely closed her eyes. As exhausted as she had been, she'd not been able to fall asleep. Instead she had tossed and turned, pursuing bitter, resentful thoughts. Wallowing in anger. Unable to turn off the images of Lucas with Claire. Unable to separate them in her mind from the devastating images of her mother with Mr. McRoyan. No more capable of forgiving Lucas than her father was capable of forgiving her mother. And not wanting to try.

She swiped angrily at the alarm and reluctantly threw back the covers. The Boston Bruins jersey she slept in was twisted around, and she twisted it back. Then she stubbed her toe on the corner of her dresser and let loose a string of violent curses. What a wonderful start to the day. Another stinking, rotten day.

Her gaze swept angrily around her room. She was tired of it. Sick of it. The walls felt like they were closing in. The ceiling, slanting low in the corners, made her feel claustrophobic. Not too many more months and she would be on her way to college, and good riddance to this house, and her parents, and this tiny, tiresome island and its tiresome people. When she got away from Chatham Island, she would stay gone. And when she was off at college, finally she would no longer give a damn about Lucas.

She was trembling with anger still. Anger and weariness and resentment at her parents, at her supposed friend Claire, even at Benjamin for not being there last night and for being so contemptibly happy when her entire life was falling apart.

She drew on a robe and went downstairs. Coffee. She needed coffee, even before she showered. She found Benjamin in the kitchen, drinking a cup. He smiled at her.

"Oh, here you are," Zoey sneered. "Where were you last night? Didn't it occur to you that I might be worried?"

"Sorry, *Mom*," Benjamin said complacently. "The van ran out of gas."

"Don't call me Mom," Zoey snapped. "I consider that an insult."

Benjamin tilted his head quizzically. "PMS? Or are you just being an unholy bitch for no reason?"

"Benjamin, you know something? I don't really like—" She stopped, listening. A noise from upstairs. A low voice. A man's voice. Zoey slammed her cup down on the table, making Benjamin jump. "Damn it, does she have that man here in our own house?"

"Zoey, jeez, get a grip," Benjamin said, annoyed now. "If you want to know—"

"Don't you condescend to me!" Zoey yelled. "I know what's going on, and I'm not going to put up with it." She spun on her heel and raced for the stairs.

"Zoey, don't—" Benjamin yelled after her.

But Zoey was beyond listening. If her mother thought she could have her *boyfriend* spend the night like it was perfectly normal, well, she was going to find out differently. Zoey ran up the stairs, bristling with all the rage that had built up in the last few weeks.

She reached her mother's door. Yes, a male voice, murmuring inside. Incredible! Zoey pounded with her fist on the door. She snatched at the handle and threw it open, already loading up the cry of outrage.

And there she was. Her mother, just hastily pulling on her robe. And the man—

The man. Her father.

"Daddy?"

Her father looked embarrassed. Fortunately he was dressed in his old flannel robe, having been quicker than Zoey's mother.

"Did you want something?" her mother asked pointedly.

"What are you doing here?" Zoey asked her father.

Mr. Passmore smiled sheepishly. "Well . . ."

"He lives here," Zoey's mother said quietly.

"After what . . . after all the things that happened?" Zoey asked, absolutely astonished.

Her father looked at her mother. Zoey saw the way their

eyes met. She saw that there were tears in her mother's eyes. Mr. Passmore shrugged, and shook his head slowly. "We've gotten past all that."

"Past it? How could you forgive her after what she did?"

"She forgave me," her father said. "And I forgave her." He shrugged again. "It's what you do when you love someone, Zoey."

Benjamin was looking wonderfully amused as Zoey reentered the kitchen. "I hope they were dressed, at least," he said. "Seeing your parents naked, that's worth like an extra year in therapy."

"They forgave each other," Zoey said blankly. "That's what Daddy told me. Just like that."

Benjamin nodded. "Yeah, I thought all along that's what would happen eventually."

"You thought so?"

"Sure. They're in love, Zoey. Man, I would have thought you of all people could have seen that. Don't you know that love conquers all?" he asked ironically. "Where have *you* been?"

Zoey retrieved her coffee and went to the kitchen window. She sensed eyes watching her and looked up, knowing what she would see. Lucas was standing at the railing of his deck, looking sadly down at her.

Zoey sighed. She went to the telephone and carried it back

to the window. She dialed and waited.

Lucas disappeared for a moment, then came back into view carrying a phone. He *was* awfully cute, and awfully sweet, and awfully sexy, even if sometimes he had the potential to be slightly a *pig*.

But she did love him, and she had it on good authority that when you loved someone, you forgave.

"You're a jerk, Lucas, and I hate your guts," she said into the phone, looking up at him. "Unfortunately, I also love you."

She cut the connection before he could answer. But she saw his lips form the three magic words. *I love you.*

"That was sweet," Benjamin said.

"Yeah. You happy now?" Zoey demanded.

"Are you?"

Her parents came down the stairs, looking sheepish. Lucas still watched her from above, smiling radiantly as the early sunlight hit his face. "Yes, I guess I am," Zoey said.